Badge of Dishonor

To John Hare - gone but not forgotten.
Thank you for challenging my point of view and
being a great big brother!

Badge of Dishonor

J. Patrick Hare

Library of Congress Control Number:		2022909087
ISBN:	Hardcover	978-1-6698-2189-2
	Softcover	978-1-6698-2188-5
	eBook	978-1-6698-2187-8

Print information available on the last page.

Rev. date: 05/12/2022

To order additional copies of this book, contact:
Xlibris
844-714-8691
www.Xlibris.com
Orders@Xlibris.com
842104

Preface

If science has proven that nurture and not nature largely determines mental health, social health, and strength, then the treatment of blacks and other minorities by white supremacists, the Ku Klux Klan (KKK), and similar groups are deliberate acts to improve the chances of whites.

For a white person to accept the advantages that come with the color of their skin is to not only harm Black people, but also, to harm themselves. This is true because they will never fully know their potential because they do not fully experience the challenges of life.

In order to fully realize achievement, that one can aspire to, one must endure the burden of many failed attempts before conquering any skill that is uniquely theirs.

Because whites are afforded such privilege, we are left to wonder what could they—and in fact, humanity—achieve if white privilege was removed from society, and we all achieved that of which we were capable through an equal amount of hard and thoughtful work?

Everyone brings unique thoughts and skills to every interaction; however, when we exist in a space where some are more valued than others, we lose the opportunity to work together to achieve the best we can. This is especially true when you consider the number of people on this finite space called Earth.

Racism hurts everyone. In an attempt to help a specific group, racists wind up weakening them. Conversely, in the attempt to hurt another group, racists wind up making them stronger, but the whole is still weaker. This may be defined as institutional racism, the process of making the dominant group weaker, the minority group stronger, and the whole group inferior as a whole.

Life cannot be about what we can do, it has to be about what we could do.

Racism stifles the could.

Badge of Dishonor

Chapter 1

Brown faces crowned with conservatively styled black hair atop mostly fit bodies all dressed in black. Beautifully manicured green grass almost as far as the eye could see. Picturesque, were it not for the absence of trees and the stones that sat atop graves of loved ones long gone. An honor guard detail stood in dignified reverence a few yards away to pay tribute to one of their own that had fallen.

Bobby wasn't sure why it had to be his father. He stood in the chill of fall, the orange, brown, and maroon leaves gathered at the feet of his grieving family. It should be just another day, a day in which he played in the streets of his Virginia city without a care in the world. A day filled with laughter and games, like so many he had enjoyed before.

He'd been born in Newport News, Virginia, nine years ago on a warm, July day, but he always loved the fall. The large Victorian home where he grew up, was too cold in the winter, too wet in the spring, too hot in the summer but perfect in the fall. It was then that he easily and comfortably fell asleep, nestled next to his brother. Fall was the time he looked forward to—or at least, used to. Now, fall meant only one thing—his father was gone, shot dead on a perfect October day, and he didn't understand why.

His father James, everyone called him Jimmy, was a tall, strong man with whom Bobby shared similar facial features. Bobby hoped that one day, he'd grow to be the imposing figure his father was. In fact, except for his father's mustache à la Magnum P.I. and his broad, muscular frame, Bobby was a chip off the old block. A slim boy, a bit small for a

9-year-old, he had thick black eyebrows, curly hair, and skin kissed by the sun to the color of milk chocolate. He was considered by many to be a cute kid.

Shy but not afraid, he smiled all the time. A necessity because people would often come up to him and talk to him or pinch his cheeks.

Whenever anyone pointed out how much young Bobby looked like his father, he smiled with pride. He was his father's son. When his dad got home from work, Bobby would rush to the door where he was greeted with a swift lift into the air. Of all the children, he felt he was the most special because he looked just like his dad, and that was something no one else could say.

Bobby loved his father in a way that he could not describe. Though not perfect and certainly a disciplinarian when needed, his father loved and cared for his family, showing the kind of tender emotional love that often-escaped fathers and sons.

As the leaves rustled, a cool breeze blew. The sounds of the birds grew more distant as they continued their migration south. He stood next to his father's casket, looking in disbelief at the man lying there, peacefully, thinking not about the arrival of fall but about his father, who was now gone. Despite his confusion, overwhelming sadness, and uncertainty surrounding the details of his father's death, he knew one thing for certain, fall would never be the same. His life would never be the same.

He looked up at his mother silently crying. Standing at 5'2," Thelma's petite stature did not accurately represent what was inside. A kind gentle mother that generously gave warm affectionate hugs to family and friends.

She was a firm disciplinarian, but never mean spirited. She acted with the purpose to either teach or protect. She was standing up straight, as she always did, determined even in sadness to exude poise and grace, taught to her by women who knew slavery and were determined to never go back.

She was educated but told since the day she entered school that she was doing well by never needing to do much. So, she happily got married and had children and became a nurse with no other ambition.

Her silent tears were a stark contrast to the past week full of the loud cries of grief which overwhelmed her. She kept in her bedroom most of the time unable to muster the strength to get out of bed. Her mother and father had come over to help with the kids, allowing her grief to run its course with their love around her.

Bobby had never seen his mother collapse the way she did when the officer standing at the door informed her that there had been an officer involved shooting and her husband was on his way to the hospital. There on her knees in front of the officer and Bobby remembered the tight hold she had on him and his siblings as tears poured from her eyes, she prayed for her husband's life before rushing the family out the door and to the hospital behind the police cars blaring siren which excited and scared Bobby at the same time.

Rushing into the hospital Bobby's little legs struggled to keep up with his mother who followed behind the officer whose ironic kindness and concern willed him to get this family to their father before he died. Their efforts in vain because Jimmy had died on the way to the hospital.

Now at the funeral with reality firmly set in, Thelma had to be strong for her children. This fact did not escape Bobby whose eyes were fixed on his mother's grieving face full of tears which flowed from her dark brown eyes and around her broad nose where she wiped them delicately with a handkerchief.

His grandmother who was an older almost carbon copy of his mother, did the same. Her grey hair in stark contrast to his mother's jet black Native American influenced locks. Even with her grey, she did not have the appearance of a 65-year-old woman. Her lines and wrinkles masked by dark brown skin stretched smooth by weight gained from years of unhealthy southern food but kept in check by the hard labor she did in the southern fields she worked until she could no longer and was forced to retire at 60.

His grandfather, Papa Martin as all the grandkids called him, looked strange, almost unrecognizable. The broad white smile formed by full lips and kind big brown eyes that always greet Bobby were not present today, in their place was a face Bobby hardly recognized.

Papa Martin, a retired Army Sargent who upon retiring left behind all the anger a life of oppression inspired, dedicated his life to helping the Black families in his community with his lifetime of experiences and wisdom. This created a light that emanated from him, but that light was present today. Towering over the shorter women around him, strong and stiff, Papa Martin's face was lifeless, tired, and angry.

It was the face of a man that had been through a long life and had weathered enough injustice to know that what had happened to his Jimmy was almost inevitable because he was Black. Bobby looked at Papa Martin's face, wondering if he would ever be the same, if he'd still be his secret ally in the world. Whether it was defending him to his parents for whatever shenanigans Bobby had been involved or allowing him to stay up late and watch TV when he slept at his grandparents' house, Papa Martin was always there when Bobby was in a pinch, to help him out.

Bobby hated collard greens, and Papa Martin always ate them for him. Papa Martin was also source of fun and candy, these yellow circles that Bobby loved. Papa Martin's candies were different from any other candy Bobby had eaten. They only served to make Papa Martin that much more special.

Now, Bobby looked at Papa Martin's face as another source of confusion. Bobby stood there, confused and unsure of what to do or feel. He looked at his family around him. Feeling powerless, he started to cry.

He looked around through tearful eyes at the hundreds of people at the grave site. Everyone dressed in black and everyone crying just like him. His mother had dressed him and his siblings in the early morning and told them to stay inside because there was a lot she had to do and didn't have time to chase them around or clean them up a 2nd time. Which meant Bobby just sat thinking about his missing father, the hugs and kisses that were gone forever, the spirited play and life lessons, all gone.

Why would someone kill his father? He thought it constantly since the day it happened. He was such a good Dad? Not knowing the details, but knowing it was not an accident, to Bobby was all unbelievable like some bad movie, but it wasn't.

His father was gone.

After the long funeral was over, Bobby watched as his father was slowly lowered into the ground. It was too hard to watch, Bobby looked away only to see the few that weren't crying before were now. Bobby's mother dropped to her knees and held her children tight as they all cried. Friends and family in close proximity rushed to her aid offering words of encouragement, "it will be alright" and "the Lord will give you strength" trying their best to be strong at such a difficult time.

Bobby watched as his mother slowly stood, leaving him and his siblings with friends and family, as she walked to the grave, which now housed his father, she stood for a moment then dropped a queen of the night tulip in on top of the casket. She returned and instructed her children to say their final goodbyes informing them that they could talk to him but that they needed to say goodbye because they wouldn't see him again. They all complied walking to the opening, Bobby stared at the beautiful tulip atop his father's casket and through heavy tears said goodbye to the hugs, the fun times, the games, and the kisses that were now gone. After a few moments their mother gently ushered them to the car to head back to the house for repass.

A delicate green tablecloth with embroidered trim covered a strong table only revealing its polished cherry legs completely free of dust, not because of the event but because that is how Thelma kept her house.

A glazed ham perfectly cooked with caramelized brown sugar glaze and purposefully charred whole pineapple slices. Collard greens with thick bacon pieces partly for visual appeal partly for flavor. Succotash rich with butter recently removed from the stove warned of its temperature with a steady flow of steam. Crisp fried chicken legs and thighs placed next to golden squares of cornbread placed next to pecan, apple, and sweet potato pie all on doilies crocheted by old delicate brown hands.

The southern feast sat undisturbed as sadness had long overtaken hunger and tired tear-filled eyes could only see despair. Bobby's mother soon made an appearance to fix him, Michael, and Nancy a plate—his, thankfully, without collard greens. As he sat there eating, he noticed the ladies gathering in the living room, talking, laughing, and crying, all at the same time. The men gathered outside.

His Papa Martin had told Bobby he was the man of the house now because he was the oldest son, so he felt like that was where he should be. After a few quick bites of chicken, he went out to join them. The man of the house at nine. His older sister, Nancy, was ten, but she was a girl. His younger brother, Michael, was too young, being only six.

"Go back inside," his cousin, Chris, ordered as Bobby appeared at the top of the porch stairs. Papa Martin immediately objected. "He needs to hear this," he said. "They all need to hear this! They need to know about the dangers of being brown, how it's a target for crooked cops."

Crooked cops? Bobby was completely confused. *Cops...as in police officers?*

He was always told that if he ever needed help, he should find a Black police officer. If he was lost, he should try to find a Black police officer. If someone tried to get into the house, he should call 911, and a police officer would come. Officer John, the police officer that worked at his school, was his friend, and he was always so nice to everyone. They talked every day. Even though Officer John was white, Bobby had developed a friendship with him.

What had Papa Martin meant by crooked cops?

Bobby listened more intently.

"They had no reason to pull him over," one man said.

"He didn't own a gun," another said.

"He did own a gun, and it was perfectly legal," another said.

He'd owned a gun? His father had a gun? How was it possible that there was a gun in the house, and Bobby didn't know?

His father always told him that if someone had a gun, he should leave right away because guns were dangerous and unpredictable in the wrong hands. Officer John had a gun, but when Bobby asked him about it, Officer John had smiled and said it was only to protect the kids at his school and not to worry.

Bobby was afraid and even more confused. Not knowing what else to do, he stood closer resting his head on Papa Martin's hip and he slowly wrapped his arm around his strong leg as he continued to listen.

"They'll pay for what they've done," one man said.

Then, Papa Martin said something Bobby hadn't expected, "Don't be too sure. They kill Black men all the time, and nothing happens."

Police killed black men? Why would they do something like that?

The more he listened, the more scared he became. The idea of being the man of the house brought tears to his eyes. He didn't want the other men to see, so he turned and headed back toward the house. Bobby felt small, weak, and dumb. He had no idea what was going on. In his house or at school—*what was going on?*

Bobby wanted his mother. He needed comfort. His mother was always there for him when he left for school, and when he got home. She was there to make him a snack or meal when he was hungry, or to help him up when he fell. She was there when he'd fallen at school and broken his arm. She took him to see Dr. Chien.

He liked Dr. Chien. She was kind and had a gentle touch. She was younger than all the other doctors at the hospital and prettier. He didn't see her often, but when he did, she always greeted him the same way, saying, "Hello, little man." She made him feel comfortable and safe, even when she had to give him a shot. He hadn't seen her in a long time because he wasn't a kid anymore, and he could take care of himself.

He walked around the house but couldn't find his mother. He went to his parents' room. The door was closed. He opened the door slowly, without knocking, even though he wasn't supposed to, but he'd heard voices inside and a noise he didn't recognize.

His grandmother came to the door and opened it for him. She knelt in front of him and said that he should go downstairs. She was blocking his view at first, but he saw his mother crying like he'd never seen before. There were women he didn't know, some of them sitting next to her while others stood. Some had Bibles while others looked at papers as they spoke to his mother. His mother wasn't listening. She was crying too hard.

His grandmother turned him around, slowly and gently, took his hand, and walked him away, closing the door behind her. Bobby was worried. Worried about his mother and what the women were talking about.

One said, "God always provides."

Another said, "He was a good man."

Several said, "Praise Jesus!"

His grandmother took him back downstairs, leaving him in a room with his sister, Nancy. Athletic and lanky not having the benefit yet of puberty, but more fit than most girls her age because she was more likely to be found playing sports than playing with dolls. Out of necessity, her mother styled her hair with two pig tails, one on either side of her head.

She'd noticed that he was outside with the men earlier and asked, "What were they saying?"

"What was who saying?" he replied, even though he knew exactly to whom she referred.

"The men and Papa Martin—what were they saying?" Nancy always wanted to know everything that was going on, partially because she was young and curious, partially because she loved her family and felt like she was her younger brother's protector. She saw Bobby hiding his tears as he left the men's conversation.

He was unsure of what it had all meant, but he didn't want his sister to know. "Nothing," he said.

She looked at him suspiciously. "Didn't look like nothing. What did they say?"

Bobby never kept secrets from his sister; they were like two peas in a pod. They spent a lot of time together, doing all kinds of things. They had similar interests in sports and playing cards, and they stayed up late at night, talking and sharing dreams about what their lives would be like when they were older. She was his best friend, and he was hers. They'd spent many a late-night sitting on her bed—especially during the summer—doing whatever they could to avoid going to sleep. When school was out, they'd spend even more time talking, joking, and playing cards. Rummy Five Thousand was their game; they could play for hours.

He decided to tell her what he remembered, which wasn't a lot. When he was done, they sat there, confused. What did it mean? Why had they said not to trust the police? Why did their father have a gun when he'd always told them how dangerous they were?

"You got it all wrong," Nancy finally blurted out, but she didn't seem to believe what she'd said. She seemed scared.

Bobby was frustrated. Not wanting to argue with his sister, he gave her his typical reply, "Whatever."

When the day finally ended. Bobby was happy to be put to bed by their mother and grandmother. He was exhausted, and he hoped the next day might bring his father back. He knew it wouldn't— he'd wished the same thing since his mother had told him that his father had gone to the angels, only a short week ago. She told the children that they could talk to him anytime they wanted and that he would always hear, but he couldn't respond. He spoke to his father often, believing what his mother told him. Talking to his father made him feel better and often softened the tears that overtook him daily.

He lay in his bed, asking his father questions about what the men had said. Questions about guns and crooked cops. Questions about what might happen to his mother, his brothers, and sister. Finally, he asked what might happen to him. He was afraid to be the man of the house. Afraid to walk around the house with all the lights off. Afraid he'd have to quit school and get a job. He didn't know how to get a job. He was just a kid. He didn't know how to do anything.

He started to cry, until eventually, he fell asleep.

Chapter 2

Bobby woke up to the same first thought he'd had many nights before—had he dreamed it? His mother came into his room to make sure he was awake; it was time for the kids to go back to school. Bobby looked forward to that because he hadn't seen his school friends in what seemed like forever, even though it had actually only been five days. His mother seemed to be acting normal again. She wasn't crying anymore.

The smell of oatmeal, the family in the kitchen, the loving good mornings and chatter not as loud as usual greeted Bobby. His father was the instigator of morning tickles and chases throughout the house as their mother got her children organized for the day ahead, today she was looking at some papers. Bobby wondered if they were the same ones from the day before, but he quickly turned his attention to his oatmeal, and the idea of going back to school.

Bobby stared in his oatmeal thinking about the day ahead as his mother demanded two bites before removing it and shuffling everyone out the door. Bobby's best friend, Brian, greeted him with the one question he didn't want to hear, "What happened to your dad?"

Bobby and Brian had no secrets from one another, he grabbed Brian's hand and took him to a quiet corner. "A crooked cop shot him! My Papa Martin told me that there are a lot of crooked cops, and they shoot black people. I didn't even know," Bobby's eyes began to tear, "Did you know?"

Brian stared at Bobby in disbelief. "What about Officer John?"

"I don't know," Bobby said wiping his eyes. "Don't tell anyone, and maybe we'll be okay," Bobby said but didn't fully believe.

Brian not knowing what to say or do nodded his head in agreement. "We better get to class" was how they left things.

Everyone in school seemed to know what had happened and wanted to know how the family was, how his mother was, if he needed anything, and if he was okay. Normally, Bobby loved attention, but this wasn't the attention he wanted. He wanted everything to go back to normal.

Bobby broke routine at lunch and found a quiet spot in the cafeteria in which to sit and enjoy his lunch, when his stomach twisted into knots. He didn't know what to do, should he run and hide? He was afraid, but he didn't know whether he should be or not; Officer John had entered the cafeteria.

What the men had said after the funeral entered Bobby's mind, was Officer John a crooked cop? Was Officer John going to kill him?

Bobby inspected Officer John as he never had before, his neat dark brown hair, dimpled square face, and welcoming smile were all familiar, but the gun attached to his belt was not. Bobby wondered if it was always there or new. He began to question everything he thought he knew about Officer John and with that uncertainty came the instinct to run.

Officer John had prepared for this interaction as he did for all of his kids who had to deal with tragedy. His kids, as Officer John referred to them, were ill equipped to deal with the challenges their racist town was forcing them to deal with. The first time a shooting happened to the parent of one of his kids, Officer John had to discuss the situation with his wife, the guidance counselors, and his supervisors at work on how to best deal with the situation. By now he was an unfortunate expert.

His face showed kindness without smiling as he approached Bobby, who still didn't know what to do. He couldn't move for some reason. Bobby decided he should run away, but he couldn't get his legs to move. That was when it happened. For the first time ever at school, Bobby started to cry.

Officer John knelt in front of Bobby. "It's ok, Bobby, I'm not going to hurt you, and I'm sorry those officers hurt your dad." He placed his hand on Bobby's shoulder. "Sometimes, bad things happen, and you don't know what to do or believe. I want you to know not all police officers are bad, but police officers are people. You know there are some good people and some bad people, right? If there was anything, I could have done to protect your dad, I would have done it." Officer John looked at Bobby's face to see if the fear and confusion was still there. "It's okay to cry because your dad is gone, but I want you to know that you're safe, and you don't have to worry because I'm here to protect you. Do you understand?"

Bobby was starting to feel better as his tears began to dry. "Why are some police good and some police bad?" It was a question that Officer John routinely got but did not know how to honestly answer to his kids so he lied to them and framed it in a way kids would understand, though he knew it was a false equivalence.

"You know how some little boys and girls are not nice? Well, sometimes they grow up to be adults that aren't nice. It's important that we forgive them because it's often that bad things happened to them, they get angry about it, and their anger never goes away. Remember what we teach about getting angry? It's ok to get angry, but we must forgive because if we don't, who do we hurt?"

"It only hurts me." Bobby knew the answer. It was taught to all the children, especially the Black children.

"That's right, and I don't want that to happen to you. You should feel sad that your dad is gone, and it's okay to be angry, but in time, like a good boy, you'll let the anger go, continue to be a good person, and one day a good man."

Officer John wasn't ever sure his explanation made any sense but his kids but like all the others Bobby seemed to be calming down. He knew what Bobby needed next. "Can I give you a hug?"

Bobby dropped his lunch bag and gave his friend a big hug. He felt relief like he hadn't experienced since he'd been given the news that his father was gone. They embraced for a while as if Officer John knew it was what Bobby had needed, and he wanted him to feel safe again.

Officer John and Bobby ate lunch together after Officer John completed his routine. In these situations, he brought his kid a carton of milk and an ice cream sandwich, which he had arranged with his superiors would be reimbursed.

"If you need anything," Officer John said. "And I mean anything, all you have to do is ask." He also said, "I promise you, I'll never let anything happen to you or your family again."

Bobby felt a huge sense of relief, hearing his friend saying those words, but it wouldn't last long.

Just when Bobby finally began to feel better, it was time for recess and a million questions from his friends. The minute he got outside, his they ran up to him and it began,

"What did Officer John say?" one wanted to know.

"Did Officer John threaten to kill you, too?" another asked.

"How could you talk to a police officer when they killed your father?" another asked.

The questions persisted until the gym coach intervened, demanding they fall in line for exercises. It was what Bobby needed—a way to get away from his friends and resume some sense of normalcy.

Gym class, unfortunately, seemed to fly by, and the enjoyment he usually felt doing exercises and playing sports and games was lost somewhere between worrying if his friends were right, or if Officer John was right. Was Officer John really his friend? Could he trust him?

Believing that Officer John was his friend and wouldn't hurt him was something he forced himself to believe.

When the final school bell rang, Bobby skipped the normal gathering in the schoolyard, didn't sit and talk about homework or play. He didn't go to any of his friend's houses or invite anyone over to his. He didn't even stopping when he saw Brian. He kept his head down and walked out the doors, down the four blocks to his house, and straight up to his room, laying on his bed without taking his shoes off, he fell asleep the moment his head hit the pillow.

Officer John had a unique task to do, and it unfortunately wasn't the first time. He gathered all the teachers, the guidance counselors, and the principals in an assembly relaying his observations about Bobby's first day back.

"I know that we spoke to all of Bobby's classmates prior to him coming back but some children aren't as popular as Bobby or their parents aren't as well-known, but this is a case where I think almost all the kids are aware of what happened to his father. I think it's a good idea that we have all the teachers speak with their classes to explain what has happened and explain that they should be patient with Bobby and not ask him questions unless he brings it up.

"Bobby was visibly upset that kids were corralling around him, and it wasn't only the kids in his class. We initially thought that it was best to focus on Bobby's classmates but after today I think we have to involve the entire school."

The teachers agreed they would all communicate with their homeroom classes the following day. As they left the auditorium they spoke about how sad and unnecessary Bobby's father's death was. One of Bobby's teachers said the obvious, "It won't be the last time."

After his nap, Bobby had his usual conversation with his sister, Nancy. "Officer John told me that he will look out for our family." Nancy looked at him with skepticism, "what do you mean? When did he tell you that?"

"At school. We had lunch together and he told me he was sorry about what happened to Dad. He said he would look out for us."

Like Bobby, Nancy felt a sense of relief because they had someone on their side. She thought about what Bobby had told her the day of their father's funeral.

"See, you must have misunderstood what the men had said after the funeral. If Officer John's looking out for us, we'll be okay," she said.

Nancy also knew Officer John. He'd been at John Marshall Elementary School when she went there, and she thought he was a very nice police officer."

"I didn't misunderstand, that's what they said, but they don't know Officer John. I have homework," Bobby replied. He cut their conversation short and left annoyed. Thelma called her children down for dinner at the usual time. She had prepared a meal of leftovers, she thought food always tasted better the next day, after the flavors had time to set.

After dinner, his mother had her children stay at the table even though their plates were empty. She had something to say to them.

"I know it's been hard on all of you since your father died. You've all been very brave. I know you miss him, and so do I. Everything will be all right, but money will be a little tight until I get a job. Your father took very good care of us, so you shouldn't worry, but we need to be smart, and that means not wasting anything."

"Mom, do I need to get a job now that I'm the man of the house?" Bobby asked.

His mother smiled. "No, baby. You don't need to get a job. Like I said, your father took very good care of us, and we're going to be okay. We just don't have money to waste. You all understand?"

They said, yes, in unison, though they didn't really understand. Bobby was happy that he didn't have to get a job.

"Hey, Bobby," Brian said the next day at school. "Meet you in the cafeteria for lunch?"

Bobby wasn't sure he wanted to answer all of Brian's questions, but he answered yes anyway. He had to eat with someone, and Brian at least knew enough that he wouldn't keep asking the same questions.

Despite Officer John and Bobby's teacher's best efforts, the questions came nonetheless, but it wasn't as bad as the first day.

Bobby was relieved when lunch was all about normal kids' stuff and his father never came up.

Over the next few weeks, things slowly started to feel like normal again. Bobby started to forget the pain he'd felt upon hearing the news of his father's death. He started to play again, engage in class, and sleep normally. He even fully trusted Officer John again. Everything seemed to be back to as normal as possible.

Things would remain that way until a man came to his home to talk to Bobby's mother about the trial.

Chapter 3

It was about two months after Bobby's father had been killed that the man came to the door, right before dinnertime. By then, Bobby's mother was working full-time and raising three children on her own. Her time was limited. Though, she would have never wished for the circumstances, she actually enjoyed her job. She and her husband, Jimmy, had decided long ago that she wouldn't work once they had children, Jimmy like his father spent four years in the Army, mostly abroad. That brief experience taught him the importance of family, so after they were married, they anxiously waited for their first child. As nature would have it, they didn't have to wait long. Nancy was born exactly eleven months after their wedding, and the rest followed suit.

They couldn't have been happier with the way their life was going. Jimmy's career was progressing nicely. After changing jobs, a couple of times, he found his home in a company that valued him and his talents. They'd moved from the modest apartment in which they'd lived when they'd started their family to a nice home just outside of downtown Hampton, not far from the Hampton Institute, which would, years later, grow into Hampton University. They'd purchased at just the right time, before the housing market in the area had inflated beyond their budget.

After ten years in their home, they'd invested in improving the yard and adding a guest house in the backyard, sure that it would provide additional funds for their retirement when it sold. It was a worthwhile investment. Their neighbors also had children, which was a great convenience. When they first moved in, they noticed the neighbors across the street had a pool, and they wasted no time introducing themselves and making friends.

After only a few months, they were so entrenched in the community, people new to the area thought they'd lived in the neighborhood for years. They were the family everyone liked, their home was always a hub of activity. Be it the neighborhood kid, who they were always happy to babysit, or the mothers in the area who stopped by to chat with Thelma. She was known to have a recipe for everything, and a home that always smelled of some tasty dish. With time on her hands and a loving family, she always had something on the stove to make the end of the day a happy one. She wanted her family to look forward to coming home for dinner.

The fun times diminished after Jimmy had passed away, but they would come back again. Unfortunately, they hadn't yet. On that particular night, their visitor wasn't there to socialize, he was a lawyer.

Shortly after her husband's death, Thelma's head had begun to clear. She'd slowly transitioned from insurmountable sadness to anger, and she knew she needed a lawyer. She had other immediate priorities, however. She had to get her life and the kids' lives back in order. She'd worked in healthcare prior to getting married, so she knew a lot of people and easily found a job once she'd started looking.

The hospital she'd selected was ecstatic to have someone with her experience, and the position of Charge RN was perfect for her. She would work seven days every two weeks, so she had a lot of time for her children. Due to her experience, she was able to get the morning shift.

She wasn't there when the kids got home from school on the days she worked, but Nancy was a big help, and Thelma was lucky that she no longer had babies. She was also fortunate that her children were good kids—they got good grades and had active lives at school with friends and after school activities.

Thelma had an understanding with her neighbors, when you are home, you keep an eye on all the kids outside at all times. Their neighborhood wasn't perfect, and it didn't need to be. They understood that the world was full of different kinds of people, and that's what made it an amazing place. They didn't look down on people who were different or had more or less than they did. They appreciated everyone for who they were and the uniqueness they brought to the world. Everyone had their struggles to bear, and Thelma and Jimmy decided long ago that they'd accept people as they were.

However, Thelma wasn't foolish. She was well-traveled and had experienced enough in her thirty-five years to know the world wasn't always friendly or welcoming to brown people like her and her family. She was acutely aware of the dangers of living in the American South, and she made it a point to keep her family close by and out of the spotlight.

Regardless of the situation, she knew that a racist in Virginia or some other Southern state could cause immeasurable harm to her and her family's happiness, so she did everything she could to make them invisible when in public. She made it a point to treat people with dignity and respect, which tended to make things better, especially due to her profession.

Once she felt like things were in order, and the trial for the police officer that killed her husband was still a few months away, she felt it time to talk to a lawyer. Because her time was limited, she arranged for him to come to her house around dinnertime.

A young ambitious Black man that worked on many cases in the community.

He'd been referred by a friend and was already aware of Jimmy's death. Their planning would start on that day and continue until the day before the trial.

The young lawyer's appearance had an immediate impact on Bobby and Nancy. Each day, before he arrived, Nancy would spend hours in front of her mirror combing her hair, keeping it in place with her favorite barrettes. She brushed her teeth and dressed herself in her favorite dresses and in case he was to ever come into her room, she put all of her dolls away.

Once he arrived, she made an immediate dash for the door, greeting him with wide eyes and a smile that showed all of her teeth. She would walk through the living room where he and her mother talked for hours, what about Nancy didn't care. She shook as she asked him things like "can I get you some more lemonade" standing inches from his seated arm and leg.

It was inevitable that her mother would grow tired of Nancy's constant interruptions and look directly into her daughter's eyes and ask "don't you have homework to do?"

Bobby glared at the young man that sat too close to his mother and spoke to her too long into the night. He interrupted their polite but professional exchanges when the lawyer arrived and left and if they engaged in any type of light hearted exchange that lasted more than a few moments, Bobby would walk into the living room and pick up a picture of his father that sat on the night stand and pretend to look at it. Thelma would pick up her son and put him on her lap or in between her and the lawyer, understanding what her young son was not doubt thinking.

These new family rituals would continue every night as the lawyer knew their planning was a must as the cards were stacked against them because police did not go to jail for killing black men and boys.

⁓*⁓

By the time the trial date arrived, much of the talk about Bobby's father's death had come to an end, and things were getting back too normal. He no longer had nightmares about all the scary and unknown things awaiting him without his father there to protect him. His relationships with his friends and Officer John were back too normal, he and his siblings played like normal kids. Their mother—who was busy with the trial preparation—no longer cried in front of them because she was determined to help them get their lives back in order.

Everything was as normal as it could be and similar to the way things were prior to their father's death. All of that changed on the day the trial started.

Chapter 4

Everyone in the city knew about the trial. Once it was set to start, an uneasiness settled around Bobby and everyone he came into contact with. At school, some teachers that usually engaged every student with a smile, whether in their class or not, avoided eye contact with him. Some of his teachers who had that called on him whether his hand was raised or not, avoided him altogether. Bobby wasn't sure whether his experience was real or not and asked his sister Nancy if she noticed anything weird going on.

"The crooked cop is going to go to jail for what he did to our dad," she said.

Bobby had thought the crooked cop was already in jail. His parents had told him that bad people get arrested and go to jail for stealing and lying to police. He'd assumed that after shooting and killing his father, the crooked cop was already paying for his crime.

Bobby was confused. "Is that why teachers at school are acting strange, because he isn't in jail?"

"I don't know, maybe they are embarrassed that he did go to jail before," Nancy replied honestly. Bobby felt a sense of relief that the crooked cop was finally going to jail and would not be able to harm anyone else.

Bobby approached Officer John at school the next day. Officer John smiled as he always did and knelt down as Bobby got close, "what can I do for you Bobby?"

"Why didn't the crooked cop go to jail after he killed my father?" He asked the ground unable to look Officer John in the eye. It had been on his mind since talking to his sister.

It was not a question Officer John had ever gotten before despite the many officer-involved shootings that resulted in death. He thought for a moment and explained.

"Well, Bobby, the way our judicial system works, when someone is accused of a crime there is a trial, and a group of people decides whether they committed the crime or not. You see, sometimes bad things happen, but they are not on purpose, it could be an accident. We have to assume people are innocent until proven guilty, so the crooked cop was going to have a trial before going to jail."

Bobby thought for a moment and finally looked at Officer John, "so the crooked cop will go to jail after the trial?"

Officer John knew that there was a real possibility that the crooked cop would not be found guilty. He had to think about his words to Bobby because if he said the wrong thing, he knew he would forever lose Bobby's trust, "well Bobby, it is possible that the shooting was an accident, if Crooked Cop #1 thought because your father had a gun and might shoot, people in the jury might unfortunately, think that it was all just a very unfortunate misunderstanding and not send the crooked cop to jail. It may not seem fair to you and me, but we have to go by what is presented in court at the trial and accept whatever is decided but remember, I will make sure that nothing happens to you and your family, so you don't have to worry, ok?"

As Officer John explained the reality of the situation, Bobby was confused but said, "ok."

Officer John reflected on how he knew the American system was unjust, and that racism and sexism played a large role in who was considered innocent and guilty. *None of that is going to be solved today,* Officer John thought. His only goal was to put Bobby at ease as much as possible.

_*_

In the cold stale environment of the courthouse sat the familiar Black congregation, it could have been church. Fellowship and support surrounded the family that needed it, old brown faces tired and burdened in their Sunday best sat in weathered cherry wood benches facing a judge and jury that did not reflect them. A Themis stood in proud American symbolism standing for everyone except those that truly needed it, and at the center of it all a white officer and his team opposite a grieving family in a situation far too common. The trial started exactly as the lawyer had said it would. The police officer's defense was that Jimmy had failed to stop fully at a stop sign, and he'd pulled him over. When he got to the car, Jimmy refused to supply his license and registration, as the officer had instructed. Things escalated, and without warning, Jimmy pulled a gun on him. The officer had no choice but to protect himself by firing his weapon.

He'd shot at Jimmy five times. Two of the bullets struck and killed him. It was, unfortunately, the word of a dead man against the officer, and there was no evidence to the contrary. The police officer's record wasn't admissible, even though it was known in the community that he didn't like black people, he'd had many complaints of using excessive force, and he'd arrested black people more often than any other race.

In that part of Virginia, that type of racism was considered normal. Black people were said to be more likely to commit crimes, according to anyone whose opinion mattered. Those same people never mentioned that many laws had been put into place so minorities and the poor could be confronted without actually doing anything wrong.

In Jimmy's case, there just wasn't any hard evidence, and there were no witnesses to the incident.

Many of the people the crooked cop had arrested arrived at the station with bruises and other injuries and were accused of resisting arrest. Most were released, because they were, of course, not guilty of that of which they were accused. So, as not to cause any more trouble for themselves, they pressed no charges against the officer because they knew the other officers had his back. No one cared about another Black man.

The lawyer had prepared Thelma for this unfortunate reality. Without evidence that the officer was lying, the only thing the lawyer could think to do was to have as many people testify on behalf of Jimmy as character witnesses as he could. They planned to end the case by putting Thelma on the stand to tell their story with the hope that it would put questions in the jury's mind about the officer's story. It was a long shot, considering there were seven men and five women on the all-white jury. They hoped the men would relate more to Jimmy, a young man trying to take care of his family, than the officer. They also hoped the women would fear the possibility of something similar happening to their husbands.

When the day arrived for Thelma to take the stand, the lawyer had convinced her that Bobby and Nancy should come to the trial. This way the jury could see their whole family without a father, only Michael remained at home, knowing he was old enough to understand what would be said but young enough to not fully understand. Bobby and Nancy were nervous, looking around at all the people present and the officers sitting on the other side of the room, it was surreal.

It was time Thelma took the stand.

"Be good, I'll be right over there," she quietly whispered to her children, pointing to the stand. The courtroom was completely silent, and all eyes were on her.

"He'd purchased the gun legally, for his family's protection," she began. "It had become obvious that during this so-called 'War on Drugs' that minorities were the real targets and seemingly, every black man was suspect number one. Police no longer needed real evidence to search your car or home. It seemed there was always a suspect for which black men fit the description, and there was no defense against search, detainment, or arrest.

"However, the police weren't the reason Jimmy purchased the gun. We saw with our own eyes what racist white people do the unarmed Black people and other minorities in the South and Black people had no means of legal protection.

"Jimmy decided to buy a gun after seeing that people on television were lobbying for gun ownership and open-carry laws as a right of every citizen. Jimmy was well aware of how blacks were treated if they were thought to have committed a crime, and there was a very good chance that people would take the law into their own hands. This could only lead to many more men of color being killed for crimes they didn't commit, especially in our neighborhood, where all the families were black, but law enforcement and neighboring communities were not.

"It seemed whenever there was a crime committed near our neighborhood it was blamed on one of the Black people in our neighborhood or community. If the police didn't act, racists took the law into their own hands, oftentimes without any knowledge of the real details of the crime or who was actually at fault."

Thelma continued her recount of events. "Word of crime spread like wildfire. Vague sketches appeared on the nightly news. Innocent victims gave interviews, which to him, seemed like a strange thing to do. Jimmy had said—on many occasions—that there was no need to post the faces of wanted men on the news, like we lived in the Old West. We lived in a modern world, and modern technology was a much better way of tracking criminals than plastering vague sketches or descriptions of Black men on the news. All it did was to create suspicion and distrust of all of them.

"Never had he seen the public shaming of white people even though they committed crimes, too. We had three children, a good life, we had a lot to lose if someone broke into a house because Jimmy fit the description of a suspect on the news. He worked hard to get what we had. He was content and happy with his life, so when owning a gun became legal, he felt the need to get one for his family's protection. He felt that we had the right to feel safe, that everyone should feel safe.

"He filled out all the paperwork and was given the legal right to have the gun in his home and in his car. He spoke with me about it at great length, and we gave it much thought and prayer," Thelma said in a voice no higher than a whisper. "Ultimately, we decided to move forward with the purchase.

"We never imagined that a police officer would pull him over for no reason, kill him in his car, say that Jimmy drew a gun on him, say that it was self-defense. This should never have happened. The officer pulled him over because he was Black. He committed no crime and should never have been in that situation."

Thelma wept as she continued. "These laws are a trap for Black people. We all must abide by the same laws. If having a gun in your car is legal, then police have to be prepared for that fact, and if they cannot, then the laws have to change. They use these legal guns as reasons to kill Black men. When everyone around us had a gun the only way to feel safe is to get a gun. Then they use them to justify killing, they are trying to use a legal gun to justify killing my husband," Thelma said, her soft-spoken mouth wet with tears.

Thelma was asked no questions by the defense because it was clear the jury was on the fence, and the defense attorney didn't want to be seen as the bad guy. He knew that one wrong word could send the trial in the wrong direction.

He'd defended officers before, in circumstances far worse for his clients, times when there had been witnesses and testimonies about what had happened, not to mention accusations about the police force. He knew how to work a jury to his client's advantage. He coached his clients before the trials, telling them what to do and what to say. He was so good at it that most of the crooked cops in the city considered him the go-to attorney when they were being held accountable for their illegal actions, and he'd become rich defending them and getting them off.

He had a proven recipe for success from which he refused to deviate. He would present many character witnesses and his client's record, which was exemplary because the complaints against him were not a part of his official record. The "cleaned" records highlighted the years he'd served with distinction and the fact that he'd put his life on the line in the noblest way.

Whenever one of his clients protested to the way he conducted his defense, he always gave the same response. "You do the killing, and I do the defending—I don't tell you how to kill, and you don't tell me how to defend."

When the crooked cop looked at each of the jurors, it would be with a confident stare. These were his people, and he'd risked his life to protect them against the animals in the community. It only made sense that they would protect him in return. Few members looked at Bobby and his family as they adjourned to decide the fate of the officer that had killed his father. He looked at each one. Instinctively trying to capture their gaze but it was for naught.

The jury took little time to deliver a not guilty verdict, and that was that, the trial was over. The crooked cop had killed Bobby's father. Jimmy was just another Black man, and the officer would not suffer at all. Instead, he would go back to work. He and the officers celebrated the verdict with cheers of joy despite of the fact that a wife and mother with her children sat across from them, crying for the loss of a husband and father. Bobby and Nancy had no idea what the not guilty declaration from the jury meant, but they knew based on the reaction that the officer won, and they had lost not only their father but their chance to make the crooked cop pay for what he had done.

Chapter 5

Michael was sitting at home playing and enjoying the innocence of childhood, when his family, the lawyer, and friends burst into the house.

Aunt Roberta, called that despite the fact that there was no relation, immediately knew what the verdict was before anyone had said a word. She instructed the kids to go to their room, but their mother interjected, "You all come with me" she said reaching for her children. Michael jumped to his feet recognizing the tone in his mother's voice.

As they walked briskly into her room, she turned towards them, knelt in the privacy and silence and embraced them tightly. Bobby and Nancy were still processing what had happened in the courtroom and in the car home, their mother sobbed the whole way. She looked at them and especially Michael searching for a way to tell him the news that she herself didn't want to believe was true.

Over the years, Thelma had seen news reports of Black people being killed one way or another, and she always said a silent prayer for the families. Sometimes the killer was a neighbor, sometimes a stranger that was apparently in danger even though the black person threatening them didn't have a weapon, and sometimes it was one of the many crooked cops on the police force.

The person killed was, more often than not, a black man but black women and children were not exempt. In her eyes, when Black boys were killed, their physical appearance was used to hide the fact that they were babies. Looking at her own son she could not imagine how the family left behind could cope with the loss. She prayed for all of them not knowing what was to come.

This time it was her beloved husband, and she was the one who needed prayers. *How am I going to explain this to my kids?* she thought.

Yet, there she was, on her knees, embracing her children, trying to figure out what to say. How could she explain racism to her young children? What could she say to keep her children protected from the injustices of the world but not paralyzing them with fear? She knew what awaited them when they'd leave the room, a different world for them now. She knew that the crooked cop was out there free, and she feared that he would hurt her family again. The world would never be the same for them, and it was her job to prepare them for this injustice so that they wouldn't be next.

"I want you all to listen to me, and listen good," she said. "In this world, when you have brown skin like we do, people treat you different. You know that already, we told you that right? About racist people and the K.K.K?"

"Yes, ma'am," they all responded in chorus.

"Well, that's good but there are other dangers out there, and you need to be careful of them too. The police are just as racist as everybody else, and they will kill you simply for living your life. And they get away with it by lying about you when you're gone. That happened to your father. Those police lied. That crooked cop that killed your father got away with it."

The kids stared at their mother with tears welling in their eyes. Bobby spoke with tender confusion, "why did daddy have a gun? Papa Martin said daddy had a gun. Did daddy try and shoot at the police man? Officer John at the school is a nice man. Why would the crooked cop shoot daddy?" Bobby's face was full of tears, fear, and confusion.

"Not all people, and not all police are racist, but you don't know which ones are and which ones aren't 'til sometimes it's too late. You have to be careful and not trust people 'til you know their true nature. Some good people have guns, and some bad people have guns. Black people sometimes have to have guns because of the racist people that want to do us harm. Your daddy didn't do anything wrong. He had a gun legally for our protection. Understand?"

Bobby looked at his mother confused. "What do we do momma? How do we keep the bad people from hurting us?"

It was a question that had no easy answer. As Thelma looked at her kids, she told them the only answer she knew and as she spoke, she knew it would not mean their safety. She saw the fear in their tear-filled eyes.

"You must be careful to never to do anything wrong. You can't be in the wrong place at the wrong time, so you can't be out late or alone. You can't trust police officers because the officer that killed your father is free, and he doesn't work alone. There are a lot of crooked cops, and they hate black people like us. The officer that killed your father is out there on the streets, and you have to be extra careful. When you see police, you go the other way!"

"Police are everywhere, at school, the mall, what are we supposed to do?" Nancy asked.

Thelma didn't want to punish her children, but she needed to keep them safe.

"You need to go to school and then come home. Spend as little time walking the streets as possible. Those streets out there aren't safe for you. So, you'll stay right in here. Your friends can come over here. or you can go to their house, but you can't be walking around by yourself or with your friends because it's not safe. Those crooked cops are out there, and it isn't safe."

Thelma held her children for a long time that night and they all cried together until she, exhausted, took them to her bedroom and slept with them for the first time in a very long time.

Bobby's mind couldn't get past the fact that the crooked cop that killed his father was out there. Things would never be the same. How could he continue to play, to skip, or laugh? He had to watch out for the bad people; for the bad crooked cops. Officer John could protect him at school, but what about when he left school? What would he do? What about his family? He was the man of the house, but he didn't know what to do.

In his parent's bed, where he used to feel so safe and secure, he cried himself to sleep.

Chapter 6

The next morning, Bobby decided never to feel as helpless and weak as he did the day before, in his mother's room, again. He cried himself to sleep for the last time that night. After hours of confused thoughts, his mind transformed the sadness and frustration into anger and a life's mission that had no time for tears.

Bobby was no longer a child. He was a man now—the man of the house.

When he woke up the next day, he used his out-of-control emotions as fuel for one singular focus, to be stronger and smarter. Not book smart, but street-smart. It was a term he'd heard his father use many times before, and he'd asked what it meant. His father was never one to mince words with his son, and he explained how street-smart was having the knowledge necessary to deal with potential difficulties or dangers in life because life was hard, and too many people were ill-equipped to handle it. He explained to an eight-year-old Bobby how he couldn't get it from books but rather, from watching and listening. He would get it from watching people—both good and bad—and learning from them what to do and what not to do. He would get it from listening to people—everybody.

You listened to the rich hustler who made his money on the street. You listened to the drunk on the street because he'd tell you how to not end up like him. You listened to teachers and professionals because they understood how to play the game. Most importantly, you listened to your family because they were the only ones who would tell you the truth.

Bobby always listened to what his father had to say, but he was totally confused by what his father had meant by street-smarts. He got it that night, and he was determined to be strong and always street-smart.

The next day, and for the rest of his young adult life, Bobby was more likely to listen than speak, more likely to volunteer to do what was needed than sit and relax, more likely to run to where he needed to go than walk, and he spent more time reading than watching television. His father was not a big fan of television—he often referred to it as "the idiot box"—and he didn't like it when the kids wasted more than an hour watching TV. Bobby took his father's attitude to the extreme, spending all of his time either playing outside with his friends—a pastime his father assured him would prepare him to be a strong man—or inside, reading all kinds of books. To the outside world, Bobby was an active, thoughtful child without a care in the world. The truth on the inside could not be further from that.

Bobby constantly put more and more pressure on himself—to run faster than his friends, hit the ball farther than anyone on the team, and play longer than anyone else. Tormented by the possibility of being weak, his anger surrounding his father's death, and the knowledge that crooked cop was out there somewhere, not in jail where he belonged, drove him never to give less than one hundred percent.

He grew into a young man obsessed with strength, sports, and competition. The obsession transformed his body into a lean, muscular machine, honed to perform physically challenging exercises with ease. In the back of his mind, he still clung to the constant fear that something would happen to his family, he would be too weak to protect them, and the bad people in the world would hurt them again. This self-proclaimed position as protector drove him to become a physical specimen admired by both kids and adults, but they had no idea what was going on inside his young mind or often to his developing body.

This obsession came at a cost—cuts, bruises, broken bones, and blood-soaked bandages became commonplace in his life. So, too did the practice of hiding them, as much as he could, from his mother. She understood that sports, especially football and baseball, came with their share of injuries, and so, she for the most part accepted the occasional broken bone as a part of growing up. She would never know fully how much pain her son was in, but she knew it was more than he let on.

Thelma developed an obsession of her own, being sort of a detective when it came to her son. She often spoke to Bobby's coaches without his knowledge, looking for clues as to what was going on in his mind at the dinner table. She would talk to his friends after practice, and as they were leaving her home after visiting.

She would engage in games of cat and mouse with Bobby, having the same conversations with him over and over again. They would all start with a simple knock on his door and a gentle hand on his shoulder with the same question.

"Are you okay? It looked like you got hit pretty hard out there today. I know you want to win and I'm proud of you for that, but I don't want to lose you in the process."

Bobby would rub his calloused hands together focusing on them and not the pain, wherever it was at the time, or his mother's gentle touch, telling her the same answer each time.

"It always looks worse than it is."

It was his response to everyone, not only her, no one could know about the nights it hurt to lay in bed, or the tears he cried when he was alone, because the over-the-counter pain medication was insufficient relief from the injuries of the day.

Thelma would sit next to Bobby, consoling him, knowing the cause of all of his pain she would try to hold in her tears. She was usually unsuccessful, and Bobby would console her instead, trying to convince her that his lie was the truth.

Neither of them able to bring his father back or ensure the family's safety. So, Bobby continued his push to be strong enough to protect them, if it were ever needed, saving the medication he received for relief from a broken bone whenever he could, using the leftover pills for the days when the pain from hidden injuries was unbearable.

This was Bobby's routine. This was the price he paid for being strong and tough enough that he didn't have to worry about the crooked cop hurting his family. Many nights his pain would lead him to a sleep filled with dreams of confronting the crooked cop in some dark alley. Graphic images of fights, blood, and death would ensue. Each time the dream ending with Bobby killing the man responsible for his father's death, his pain, and fear.

When his coaches became concerned—partially because of the collisions Bobby seemed to enjoy regardless of the pain they caused and partially because of his mother's questions—they would confront Bobby and get the same reply.

"I know my father is watching, and I want him to know that his son is the best."

It was a statement they empathized with and could not argue against. It was well-crafted by Bobby for that exact reason. He couldn't let them know his real motivation was fear. They had to be on his side, and it worked like a charm. Bobby was given leeway around injuries because he would insist, he was okay. Only when he was really hurt, was he pulled from practice or games.

His teammates looked to him as the standard they should aspire. Bobby's team and winning first attitude and work ethic inspired them to work harder and his teams enjoyed winning seasons as a result. They all knew his mantra; my father is watching. They all knew his story and they didn't want to let him down lest they let their own fathers down.

Just as Bobby had planned, everyone was fooled, and everyone let him keep to his obsessive behavior because the reason they all knew. Only Bobby knew the reason he preached was a lie. A noble lie that allowed him to push away the fear of a little boy rather than deal with it. Bobby became an expert at not dealing with emotional or physical pain. It also ensured that he had no close intimate relationships with anyone outside of his family and teammates.

Most of the friends he made on the field, remained friends at school, the gym, and at practice. Only the strongest few made their way into Bobby's circle. No after school phone calls or hanging out or going to parties, Bobby and the elite few in his circle were all about work and winning with Bobby leading the charge day and night. This was pleasing to Thelma but not for the reason she thought. Bobby's tight group of friends were fueling his unhealthy obsession.

In her mind, her son was following the instructions she laid out for all her children, unlike Nancy and Michael, who enjoyed active social lives and often argued with her about boundaries. Bobby, she thought, understood her concerns about the safety of Black men in Virginia. But she would never know the toll that put on her son, or his obsessive nature.

Chapter 7

When Bobby was close to finishing high school, he had the same decisions to make as the rest of his classmates surrounding what would come next. He knew he wanted to get out of Virginia to start his life anew.

He often thought about what would come next, what to do with the anger and frustration that he had developed at such a young age. To him, everyone seemed to have it all figured out and all he was doing was wasting time preparing for a battle with crooked cops that might never come. He worried all that time, energy, and muscle that resulted from preparing for that fight might be in vain, was it all for nothing? It wasn't until he saw a commercial with the tagline, "The Few. The Proud. The Marines" and the strength of those soldiers, the training they'd received, and the way they'd carried themselves with such strength and bravery, that he thought there might have been a purpose to all his work after all.

At night staring into the darkness in exhausted sleeplessness he often thought about beating the crooked cop till every bit of life had left his body, with tears welling up in his eyes he'd think about being a soldier and helping people all over the world fight against evil people. These dreams made him more determined to join the ranks of those strong, determined, brave men. He'd thought about it a lot over the years and had even looked into joining the army or marines in his junior year. Now a senior having passed the tests required he could go into any branch he wanted, he just needed to let the recruiter know his decision.

During one of his long phone calls with Nancy he confided his plans, since she had been trying to convince him to join her.

"I understand why you love Virginia Tech so much," he said. "It really is a unique place. I'm sure it's not perfect but there's a generally positive feeling and it is refreshing. Everyone seems focused on the same things and not the differences that exist between them. Disagreements seem to be viewed as opportunities to understand, not hate. I'm happy you found your path in life there, but to be honest I don't think college is for me. I've been thinking about it a lot and I feel I need to do something else, that there's another purpose for my life."

Bobby explained gently but with conviction. "For as long as I can remember, I've had a calling to use my life to protect others, to protect the innocent and make sure that those in the world that are hurting others are held accountable. Ever since Dad was killed, this need to serve those who can't protect themselves has been the one constant in my life. It's what drives me to get up in the morning, to be the best Bobby I can be."

Nancy sat listening to her brother without judgement. "I know, Bobby, I've watched you change into a person I admire and worry about. Clearly something is driving you to spend your days running, my worry is that you will never slow down, never live in the moment and enjoy the good in your life. If you can't find that inner peace here, I understand, but I do worry you will never find it."

She still knows me better than anyone else, he thought, and with a deep breath told her, "I'm going to join the Marines." Nancy remained silent, processing, trying to reconcile the danger that her little brother could potentially be putting himself into. "Are you sure, Bobby? That path can be really dangerous or not, you never know til it's too late. Is that really what you want to do?"

Bobby was already convinced of his decision, so he answered simply. "Yes."

That was all Nancy needed to hear, and with that came the only answer she could give her little brother. "Then I support you. You're going to be the next G.I. Joe."

With a chuckle, the only person that could have persuaded Bobby to change course had given him the support he needed. His decision was made.

Just days prior to final exams, Bobby focused on his studies and prepared for his military career. His mother and little brother were proud of him but worried because neither Nancy nor Bobby had shared his plans after graduation. By this time, Michael had joined Bobby at high school, becoming popular with the teachers and other students. Their family was well-known at the school, both for their father's death and their success in sports; to most they would always be known as the family whose father had been shot.

They missed out on a lot of the experiences their classmates got to enjoyed, especially the white teens but the same was true of a lot of black kids in the South whose families had to balance the dangers of southern living and the desires of teenagers. They lived under the veil of racism. This meant they had to be sure their lives didn't interfere with the lives of whites.

As the school year came to an end, Bobby's graduation day arrived. Bobby had planned to share with the rest of the family that he planned to join the Marines, making the announcement at the graduation party his mother had been planning for months.

It was quite the celebration, aunts, uncles, and cousins were all there to celebrate his accomplishment. His mother had prepared all his favorite foods, and the party lasted well into the evening. When it came time to deliver his speech, he was excited to share his thoughts and appreciation.

"I want to thank everyone for coming to celebrate my graduation. I know my father would be proud of me for graduating at all."

The partygoers laughed.

"I feel his presence and love, just as I feel all your love. Mom, I know it hasn't been easy for you. We had some hard times, but you always found a way for us to have food on the table, shoes on our feet, and a warm house to come home to. I can't imagine my life without your love and support. I love you, Mom."

Thelma's eyes teared up along with everyone else's. It was time for the news.

"I've decided that I'm going to be a Marine!" he said.

Everyone cheered flooding him with hugs, proud of him, and happy to see that he had found his path. They wanted to give him the support his father wasn't there to give him. It wouldn't be an easy path, but nothing about his life had ever been easy, and if others could do it, so could he.

Chapter 8

Bobby knew that he would have had a difficult time with college. While he wasn't a bad student and loved to read, he was more comfortable doing than learning. In his mind, knowledge was secondary to being strong and hard. Despite that fact, he was nervous about what lay ahead where basic training was concerned. He'd heard about how hard basic training was, and he didn't want to fail. For him, failure was not an option.

However, he loved the idea of being away from home and seeing the world. This would be the first time in his life, since his father's death, that he wouldn't be focused on protecting his family.

Nancy was safe at Virginia Tech, and Michael was equally as strong and determined as Bobby. Whatever Bobby did, his little brother was right behind him. They'd wrestle and challenge each other to the point of frustration for their mother. He knew that Michael would protect their mother and that he was free to go on his new adventure.

Bobby had never left Virginia up to that point in his life, so when he learned he'd begin his service at MCRD San Diego, he was thrilled.

His first impression as he flew into LAX wasn't exactly positive, seeing as there was very little of the greenery to which he'd grown accustomed in his home state. He'd expected LA to be much lusher, more of a paradise than what he was seeing. Disappointment dissipated as the sight of palm trees along the wide sand beaches and endless blue of the Pacific came into view as the plane approached LAX. The endless beach from LA to San Diego mesmerizing in its beauty put a spell on Bobby like so many before him, convincing him that he had made the right decision, never hinting at the challenge that lay ahead. The feeling wouldn't leave him until he'd settled in and began bonding with his unit, in an instant he was no longer a young man, no longer black, no longer distracted, no longer afraid, no longer anything other than a Marine.

In Basic, Bobby discovered he was a natural leader. He was always getting on those in the unit when they didn't do what they were supposed to. It was his way of keeping them and himself out of trouble. When one of them screwed up, they were all punished.

He made little time for goofing off, going out with his unit, or pursuing women, which were the only source of strain within the group. They thought Bobby a Momma's boy, a goodie two shoes, or worse, but they never pushed him too far because they understood him, and he understood them. They knew about his father and the fear and strain that put on his life. This sharing of his intimate secrets was part of the process, and they all did it. It helped them to form the type of real bond Bobby and the rest of his unit needed.

Together they honed their physical skills and trained their already impressive bodies to develop a level of endurance and precision that they did not think possible. The men in his unit supported and accepted each other and this made basic training a labor of love. Bobby's dedication and sharp focus led to him often getting lost in his work and not hearing what was going on around him. It was also why they'd given him the nickname, the hawk.

Bobby's completion of Basic was bittersweet. He was used to the routine, and he'd developed friendships he hoped would never end. At the same time, he was excited about Camp Lemonnier in Djibouti Africa, the destination to which the Marines would take him next. He had never seen so many Black people and it made him feel safe.

His distrust of most white people he didn't know had taken a toll on him, forcing him to be on alert at all times.

However, in Africa, most people looked like him and that was a source of real comfort. It allowed him to relax a little, let down his guard, and start to build more pieces of a social life. It was the first time Bobby had a relationship that lasted longer than a few weeks. His girlfriend knew that the relationship would not result in marriage. Bobby was honest about his desires and intentions, so they were able to just have fun. Something he really needed.

Bobby would have all kinds of adventures in the twelve years he spent in the Marines. He'd travel the world, participating in conflicts from the Gulf War to the Somali Civil War, and the Intervention in Haiti. Like all marines, he put his life on the line to protect Americans and American interests. He was there to protect all Americans, but every day before going to bed, he'd think about his family, friends, his father, and their lives. No matter how hard the daily task, he would complete it so they could have better lives and his father, whom he was sure watched over him from the beyond, would be proud of him.

He'd understood there would be challenges when he'd joined, but there were more good times than he could count, and he'd found a brotherhood he'd never be able to forget or replace. The challenges, however, made him look forward to going back home to visit his family.

When Bobby went home to visit, he would spend most of his first day back sitting with Thelma, Nancy, and Michael, sharing his adventures and listening to what was happening in their lives. Even though they communicated often, nothing could ever replace sharing with them, face-to-face. His time away from Virginia only made him appreciate the life he'd left and the simple goodness of the people there. His path in life had taken him around the world, but on the flight back to Norfolk International Airport after his career in the Marines was over, he looked forward to welcoming the next chapter of his life—or so he thought.

When he touched down in Hampton Roads twelve years after he'd left, as a decorated sergeant major, he felt relieved to be somewhere familiar, comfortable, and safe. The war and conflicts he took part in were horrific making him forget all the challenges he'd faced prior to joining the Marines. The loss of his father aside, he couldn't remember the bad times of his youth because they paled in comparison to the experiences he had as a Marine.

The training and missions had changed his mind and body. He stepped off the airplane a soldier in every sense of the word. Tall and muscular, with a broad chest more pronounced by a slim waist and thick thighs. Clean shaven with a tight fade that accentuated his dark handsome face.

His eyes, which had developed a permanent squint that exuded both predator and prey, had seen a lot of amazing things. They'd also seen things he couldn't forget even when he tried. Suffering and inequality, he learned, was not unique to the Southern part of America, and he had seen things that could not be unseen. He realized the world was full of evil and good and that evil people somehow seemed to be connected to each other. He'd had many experiences he wouldn't want to forget.

He'd joined the Marines to protect America from the evil in the world, but it hadn't taken long for him to realize that American politicians caused a lot of the problems in the world, and their evil deeds had a lasting impact. He romanticized his simple life in Newport News and was ecstatic to be back.

After twelve years, he was done!

Chapter 9

Bobby settled into an apartment not far from the warehouse in which he would end up working, providing security services. He knew from the many conversations he had with retired military personnel that it wouldn't be easy to acclimate to civilian life. For him, the key would be to keep busy and face the challenge head-on. He was no longer afraid of a challenge.

A few months after moving into his apartment, he'd turned it into a modest but comfortable home. He had many mementos from his travels and was pleased to be able to incorporate them into his decorating. One night while walking into his apartment after a leisurely day off, he was made aware of the fact that fall had arrived, the chilly night making his apartment cool and comfortable. It reminded him of the autumn evenings he'd experienced as a child, as well as, the many things he loved about the area and why he felt so lucky to live there. Nights like that made him nostalgic for a time when his family had all been together, and he didn't have a care in the world.

As he lamented times past, his mind wandered back to when his father had been alive. Thinking about the love he felt and the fun they had together. Even after the many years that had past, those memories were still vivid in his mind. He quickly realized he wasn't doing himself any good, remembering a time full of sadness and fear, like so many times before when thoughts of his father came to mind, he shifted his thoughts toward something else.

Bobby needed something to occupy his mind. He turned the television on and was confronted by an all too familiar story on the local news.

"A soon to be identified Black man has been shot by local police..." the reporter began. "The man whose name is not being released pending notification of his family, had been a local resident for many years." The news reporter continued, "Earlier tonight, a robbery occurred at the local BB&T Credit Union ATM. The victim described the perpetrator as a large Black man, approximately five-foot-nine and one-hundred and eighty pounds. He was wearing a brown, hooded sweatshirt.

"The victim didn't get a good look at the perpetrator, and security footage is not yet available.

"The officer was on routine patrol when he spotted someone fitting the description. He turned on his lights and pulled over to talk to the suspect when the suspect ran away. The officer pursued the suspect ordering him to stop several times, following the suspect through this neighborhood in the 7800-block of Roanoke Avenue, an area known for drug related crimes.

"The officer was not available for an interview but did offer concern for the suspect who is now on his way to Southland Hospital, it is unfortunate that the suspect did not heed officer instructions. We can only guess as to why the suspect ran. Apparently pulling something out of his pocket and turning toward the officer, the officer was forced to fire for fear of his safety.

"We'll continue to cover the story as more information becomes available." The image of Black families standing outside police tape looking for answers ended the news report.

Typical, Bobby thought, *what Black man in this neighborhood wants to be harassed by the cops, they seem to always find a reason.* Thinking this wasn't doing him any good, he had had enough television for one day and decided to read in bed. He didn't need to get upset, not on a night like this, he thought with a content smile, and with that thought retired to his bedroom with a book and looked forward to what the next day would bring.

Bobby was up early the next morning for work. He arrived a few minutes before his regular shift began and greeted the nightshift workers as they left. For the security guards, the routine never really changed, small talk about nothing in particular until the change of shift, and clock-in and out after exactly eight hours. Overtime was not allowed, so next shift always arrived a few minutes early and waited till the earlier shift hit eight hours. On that day, however, the conversation was anything but small talk.

"Did you hear about Johnny?" one of the security guards asked. Johnny was one of the guys from Bobby's neighborhood. He was well-liked and known by many. He'd been a standout basketball player in his high school days, playing at the local community college. He stayed local and got a job after completing school. Although he hadn't accomplished a lot—he hadn't gone to a major university because he didn't have the grades, nor did he play for the NBA—he was somewhat of a local hero because of his success in high school, leading the high school team to a state championship in his senior year.

"No," Bobby answered. "What did he get into? Thinking that he had gotten into some sort of trouble.

"Shot last night. He died in Southland Hospital."

"What?" Was Bobby's only response as his nostrils began to flair and his gaze focused.

The security guard nodded, "yep, don't make no sense."

Bobby's thoughts ran a mile a minute, Johnny had a wife and a young son, and he never got into any trouble. "What happened?" he finally said.

"Cops claim they thought he was a suspect in a robbery or something from earlier that night. Said they tried to stop him, when he supposedly pulled a weapon, so the cops shot him."

Bobby stared off into space, thinking for a minute. "You mean the robbery at the ATM?"

"Yeah. You know about that?"

"I saw it on the news. The suspect was my height, like 5'9"—Johnny's almost 6'7". How the hell did they confuse him with that guy?" Bobby was too caught up in his thoughts to hear the reply. He didn't need to hear anymore, because he knew exactly what had happened. The crooked cops at the police station had struck again. They saw a Black man, probably recognized Johnny, and thought they would give him a hard time because he gave those white kids a beatdown so many times on the basketball court.

Bobby returned to the conversation to hear what he was thinking. "They shot the wrong guy, with Johnny. He never got into any trouble and definitely didn't rob anyone." Bobby spoke his thoughts. "Maybe this time, things will be different. They shoot first and ask questions later, but you're right about Johnny. People will see right through their BS and aren't going to buy the crap these crooked cops are gonna try to sell this time.

"Johnny's height alone is gonna kill their noise about fitting the description of the suspect. And that bull about him running, they shouldn't have been approaching him in the first place so they still on the hook."

Bobby clocked into work and continued his mental account of what he was sure would happen as he said his goodbyes to the night watch. Throughout his eight-hour shift, Bobby's mind never left Johnny, his basketball games, the celebration after leading the local high school to the state championship, the articles in the paper. Bobby's shift, which normally seemed to move as slow as molasses in the winter, flew by and he was startled by his relief when it was over.

Bobby left work after exactly eight hours and headed to the gym, hopeful that the news would be on so that he could get the latest update on Johnny's death. It was all the chatter at the gym as Bobby tended to his workout with his headset on. It was his way of getting a full workout in on consistent schedule without having to engage with the other gymgoers sharing his workout time. He viewed them as obstacles to his goal of being in and out in one and a half hours. He was stopped mid-routine when Johnny's face flashed on the television, removing his headset he got closer to the tv so he could hear.

"Chief Dolan has offered little explanation about the mistaken identity of the officer involved shooting of local basketball star Johnny Rey. Community leaders are demanding the officer involved be suspended without pay and are looking for an explanation as to how the 6'7" tall Johnny could be confused for a 5'9" suspect."

Bobby turned to the gymgoer next to him, "apparently we all look the same height in the mind of these crooked cops." The other man responded to Bobby's comment with a head nod never taking his eyes off the screen. The reporter turned to one of Johnny's former teammates, while Bobby decided he'd heard enough and went back to his workout putting his headphones on but not turning on the music he thought about what he knew would come next, based on his experience when his father died. He thought about the endless conversations about Johnny's death and the outrage so many people would express. He wondered if the officer would continue to get paid in light of this new evidence? On the way home Bobby called his sister.

"I was just about to call you but wanted to wait till you were done with your workout. Did you hear about Johnny?" Nancy said without even saying hello.

"Yea, that's why I was calling. It's one thing to say that it was dark, or they were wearing similar clothes, but how are they gonna explain the height difference, there's no way."

"I know!" His sister said. "They screwed up this time. They're not even close to the same height, but you know they're going to make it about Johnny running from the cops, not following his instructions. That bullshit about turning and pointing something at the cop, good luck with that, there was no gun at the scene. The only thing he had on him was his wallet and keys. How do either of those look like a gun?"

The entire conversation with his sister centered around Johnny's height and how the crooked cop wouldn't be able to get off this time.

Chapter 10

Bobby attended Johnny's wake, along with many others, most in attendance didn't know Johnny well or at all, but they came, nevertheless. They were there to pay their respects. They brought flowers, pictures, and newspaper clippings of Johnny in his prime. *The repass is sure to be an extended affair full of stories about Johnny,* Bobby thought. He looked forward to sharing his with the many high school classmates of his in attendance.

The scene was something out of a movie, with so many people dressed in black, gathered over the cemetery's grassy knolls, surrounded with ironic beauty. Many of Johnny's state championship teammates were there. Bobby's focus slowly drifted from the people he knew to Johnny's young son, who stood near his mother lost in grief. He looked at the young boy who stood no taller than his mother's waist, holding onto her leg, crying with a look on his face that Bobby found all too familiar.

Bobby was taken back to his father's funeral and the emotions he'd felt that day. He knew exactly how the boy felt. A long-repressed flood of anger and sadness washed over him. All of a sudden, he was that nine-year-old boy again. The boy whose father had just died. The empathy he felt for the boy was something only someone who had gone through it could feel. There was confusion, helplessness, anger, fear, powerlessness…Bobby's anger grew. As the feelings from his childhood resurfaced, his eyes began to tear.

"I'm not powerless anymore," he told himself. "I will do something to stop this if the courts won't."

Bobby decided to skip the repass, not wanting to add his own emotions, now spiraling out of control, to those of the family.

***

As the weeks went by, more details were released about Johnny's shooting while the officer in question was given paid leave. The local media covered the story as if it were a major news story because of Johnny's relative celebrity. One of Bobby's favorites was a retelling of Johnny's glory days, referring to his four years in high school that culminated into the basketball championship. They also broadcasted several interviews with Johnny's widow, who questioned why the officer was on paid leave, and why he'd drawn his gun when no weapon was recovered from the scene, to which Bobby yelled at the television screen. "Exactly!"

Over and over, there was the video surveillance from the ATM, showing someone much smaller than Johnny and the same question, how such an obvious case of mistaken identity was possible.

***

As weeks turned to months, the police officer's fast-approaching trial stirred up another media frenzy, which had died down some time before.

Bobby was so interested in the outcome of the trial and his need to see and feel the atmosphere in the courtroom, that he went to the first day of deliberation. He sat as close to the front as he could next to an older woman whom he recognized, short and stout, nicely dressed in a fashionable hat.

"Mrs. Jones, do you mind if I sit here?"

"Of course not. How are you, Bobby? Did you know Johnny well?" she asked.

Bobby smiled a mischievous smile. "No actually, I just wanted to see justice served. I was at the funeral and saw Johnny's family. It made me think about my father's trial. I was too young to attend that one, so I wanted to be present for this one."

As Bobby spoke, the lawyers and officers came into the courthouse, Mrs. Jones grunted under her breath, "he's going to get off now."

Bobby was surprised by the assertion, "what do you mean?"

"Do you recognize him?" Mrs. Jones looked at him, pointing to the lawyer representing the officer.

"No, should I?" Bobby responded after looking at the old man sitting next to the officer on trial.

She looked at him, surprised. "You were so young, that lawyer represented the officer that killed your father, God rest his soul," she said as she pulled a handkerchief to wipe sweat from her brow and the tears that were welling up that she tried to hide.

Bobby looked at the professionally dressed man in an expensive looking pinstriped suit, immaculately kept grey hair, and mustache. *The man doesn't look that old, at least not old enough to have been a lawyer that many years ago,* Bobby thought. "Are you sure?"

Putting her handkerchief back as she responded without looking up, "I'll never forget that evil man as long as I live."

As the trial and arguments started Bobby sat in the courtroom hoping that something would happen to solidify the officer's guilt. Each time a witness was introduced, and testimony given, the lawyer for the officer delivered eloquent statements with grand gestures that Bobby likened to some sort of performance art.

Do people actually fall for this? He thought staring at the attractive older man. Bobby looked at the jury that was all-white with the exception of a middle-aged black woman who didn't take her eyes off the lawyers once. He couldn't tell if they saw through the performance or not. At noon the proceedings broke for lunch. Bobby decided sticking around was a waste of time.

"Mrs. Jones I'm going to go. It was good seeing you again.

"You too," she responded in kind. "And when you talk to your mother, tell her I said hello."

Bobby left the courtroom, wondering if the jury would finally hold this officer accountable for his actions? Bobby would follow the trial with the news like everyone else, but when it was announced that closing arguments were to take place the following day, he could not stay away. He expected the courtroom would be packed, so he asked a coworker from the night shift to switch shifts with him, which they happily did, allowing Bobby to arrive at the courthouse two hours before the trial was set to start and there were still a few people in line to get in.

Although there were plenty of seats ahead of him, Bobby sat in the middle wanting to blend in. He was used to exercising patience and finding a way to occupy his time. So as people shuffled in over the next two hours, he immersed himself in a book and was perfectly content till the trial started.

The attorneys and their clients came in, and Bobby couldn't help but notice the smug look on the face of the crooked cop's attorney, this was not a good sign.

When it was his time to speak, the attorney got up and began closing arguments.

"Imagine running down a dark street at night chasing a subject, who is ignoring your command to stop," he looked directly at the Black woman juror. "Challenging place to be in, you don't know who this person is or why he is running. Is he a danger to the community? Is he a danger to you? Does he have a weapon? You are not in a position to stop and call for assistance, because just as you do the subject makes an aggressive move, and you have a split-second to make a decision. To ensure your safety and the safety of the community, you fire, to protect everyone, to uphold your sworn oath. That's what this brave officer did on that faithful night." He pointed directly at the crooked cop who sat with his head held in regret.

The lawyer spoke to the crooked cop who did not look at him. "Imagine the surprise when you run to the aid of the man that is now on the ground, you run towards him after he had run away from you, you run hoping that he will not fire upon you, finally while risking your life again to attend to a suspect that refused to follow your commands you realize you may have the wrong man.

"You call for backup and an ambulance wondering why this young man did not follow your commands and why he made such an aggressive move towards you. That is what this officer did, and now we want to judge his actions as unnecessary, send hate mail to him and his family, causing him many sleepless nights, extreme guilt, and had thoughts of suicide."

"Johnny had an impressive basketball career and was a hero to me and the police academy, and most in the community who were old enough to have witnessed his inspired play but he, unfortunately, did not find a profitable career playing professionally and settled in a part of the city plagued by guns, drugs, and violence."

He turned to Johnny's grieving widow and spoke directly to her. "We may never know why Johnny ran from the officer, but we do know that this officer was acting to protect the public, himself, you, and your son."

As he turned toward the jury one last time, he explained, "Had Johnny not run away from the officer, acted so erratically, and used threatening gestures, he'd still be alive today; innocent men don't run from law enforcement."

Bobby stared at the jury who were all looking at the officer and not Johnny's widow, he wondered what was going through their minds? Were they thinking about why he pursued Johnny in the first place instead of calling for backup, were they wondering why the officer confused Johnny for someone almost a foot shorter than him which ultimately led to the situation, were they thinking that this type of mistaken identity could result in their lives or their family's life being taken.

Bobby knew he would never know. He stood up to leave as they adjourned the jury to deliberate the verdict. He hoped that the attorney's performance, however grand, didn't change their mind about the facts. This officer grossly misidentified an unarmed suspect and shot him dead, leaving a mother and son without a husband and father.

The case was now in the hands of the jury. Bobby looked around as he walked out at the numerous African Americans in the courtroom whose faces said they thought the case was over and the officer would get away with murder. Did they think this because the jury would likely assume that Johnny had run because of some mysterious crime he'd committed elsewhere, one for which he'd never stand trial? The jury wouldn't think that he thought, Johnny had no criminal background at all, so they'd have no facts to support that assumptions this time, Johnny wasn't guilty of anything.

Bobby hoped that he and the African Americans in the courtroom would be wrong. He assured himself that times had changed since his father's murder at the hands of a white police officer, that there weren't as many racists as there used to be when he was a child, and that people of different backgrounds were getting along better than ever. He assured himself that this time, things would be different.

His naiveté and optimism were quickly squashed when, as many had expected, the jury returned a not guilty verdict in less than two hours after retiring to review the case. It was over—for everyone—except Bobby.

Bobby was livid.

He was home when he heard it on the news. He watched in shock as the courtroom exploded in chatter, and reporters pushed their way to the front of the courtroom to get pictures and statements as if it was some sort of show and not real life. Bobby stared at the television, his rage causing his eyes to tear as anger engulfed his body.

Chapter 11

Bobby needed to get some fresh air. He went for a walk, looking around his neighborhood at the people he loved and those he didn't know. They seemed to live in a war zone now but were completely unaware. The enemy created a narrative about them to justify the hostility against them. Weapons of war were used against them. The offenders receiving no punishment for their hostility, because in war, there were casualties. Abandoned and dilapidated buildings surrounded by rubble and vacant lots, corner stores instead of supermarkets, liquor stores and check cashing, fast food instead of health food, he looked again at his neighbors and their struggle, and his adrenaline began to flow through his body like the mighty Mississippi. Was this America or a war-torn ghetto in a place he thought he had escaped when he retired his salute. Bobby knew what war looked like, and it wasn't so different from his neighborhood.

His days in the Marines had been filled with tours in the many parts of the world where America was fighting. Were the members of the KKK so influential in America that they had waged a secret war against Black people? In the Marines, it was not his job to question the reason—it was his job to protect Americans, and he wasn't going to let them down. Neither abroad nor at home his oath to protect was like a steam engine fueled from the new energy boiling within him, "this enemy will not win."

He was surrounded by law-abiding citizen who paid his taxes and contributed to his great nation like everyone else but that didn't matter, they were being targeted by the powerful who wished to exterminate them while they, like drones, went about their day totally aware but unable to change the environment around them.

He looked at all the nationalities of the people around him and wondered when the racists and bigots had taken charge. Why hadn't leadership put them in their place, let them know their unfounded hatred would not be tolerated. Ensure that the country he loved, the one that was supposed to stand for everyone, could thrive under a banner of diversity? When did Americans turn a blind eye to injustice? More importantly, how had he been so blind to it for so long?

Racism wasn't new, but Bobby was taught that racists who had systematically infiltrated positions of power to corrupt and destroy diversity had been dealt with in the 60's and 70's. He decided right then and there to keep his silent promise to Johnny's young son—he would catch the crooked cops on camera and expose them for the criminals they were. Someone had to, and if no one else was willing to answer the call, he would. He vowed to do whatever it took to bring the crooked cops to justice.

Recording their evil would leave no doubt as to the crooked cops' guilt and their sham trials would be a thing of the past. The juries would see their encounters with law-abiding citizens living their lives committing no crimes when the police engaged in acts of brutality or murder. They'd no longer be able to lie to juries and get off, not if there were video evidence. They'd pay for their crimes, and people would see the crooked cops for what they were, racist criminals. Walking by a storefront window, one of the few not boarded up, he looked at himself instantly transported back to a place and time when he was extremely dangerous, when he was the power that took control, when he patrolled and protected … he was his old self again, his back muscles cracked as the slump of a common man began to erase, his nostrils reacted as his lungs increased their intake, his eyes reacted taking on the focus of predator not prey, his mind let go of jingles and jokes of chores and appointments, he turned in lock step exercising complete control of his body and its sizable frame, he was a marine again.

Bobby went and bought a police scanner and the smallest camcorder he could find at the local electronics store, questioning the store clerk many times about the availability of smaller models regardless of the price. He ended up with a model that would be relatively easy to maneuver but looking at the device he would have to make some adjusting if he wanted to avoid being seen.

Sitting down at his small dining room table with tools in hand he removed the large microphone and handle and created a makeshift handle on the side with duct tape and cardboard and removed all nonessential casing securing his new smaller camcorder with more duct tape which he spray-painted black. Looking at the finished product he was pretty happy, at least seven pounds lighter and significantly less conspicuous, and after several tests recordings he was relieved that it still worked.

Shortly after 8:00pm he affixed the scanner to his dashboard and placed the camcorder in the passenger seat and drove to a deserted street in his neighborhood, not wanting to be seen sitting in his car by someone he knew. He waited with excitement. Now he only needed to wait till the sun went down and for the scanner to supply some action.

The first time he heard an officer call in a 10-38 (traffic stop) he was so excited he started the car and shifted into drive before he got the location. It was far but he was too excited to not got investigate. If a crooked cop was involved, it might take time to escalate things to the point of excessive force and that's what he wanted to capture.

The incident was in a mostly industrial area near the shipyard. There wasn't a lot of traffic in that area at this hour, as most of the businesses would be closed, so, if one of these cops wanted to act up, it was a good place. His adrenaline was pumping as he weaved his way through the city streets, avoiding red lights but not exceeding the speed limit. As he turned on Warwick Blvd about a mile from the location of the stop, he heard the officer report a 10-24 and 10-76. The stop was over, and the officer was going to another assignment having to do with a domestic disturbance.

A little disappointed, Bobby reminded himself that this wasn't a game, and someone could have been seriously hurt.

"What the heck am I thinking?" he asked to himself. He should be happy no one was unnecessarily arrested or attacked by police. He turned back towards home, deciding that next time he would wait until there was a stop in his neighborhood. There was no need to run all over the city looking for trouble. He lived in a predominately black neighborhood and trouble found itself in black neighborhoods, he didn't have to go searching. He couldn't get upset if there weren't any incidents, it meant he and his neighbors were safe.

Returning to his spot he opened his thermos and took a sip of his still hot tea. When he heard a call for a 10-31 not too far from him, as he shifted the car into drive, he had a realization, they might implicate him in the crime, wonder why he was in the vicinity if he were to be seen. He needed to be patient, wait for a 10-23, 26, 27, 28, 29, 37 or 38, and he couldn't be tempted to respond to every police code. These general codes of an officer arriving at a scene, detaining a suspect, license information, registration check, check for warrants, investigating a suspicious vehicle, and stopping a suspicious vehicle were general enough for a crooked cop to use to their advantage and stop someone who wasn't doing anything worse than driving while black.

Just as stale pain was beginning to develop in his legs Bobby had heard the police trap, he was waiting for, a 10-94 on Jefferson, not too far away from him. He shifted into drive, wondering why in the world someone would drag race in a residential neighborhood at 10:27 at night. Probably some dumb kids exercising poor judgement.

As he approached the intersection, he saw the patrol lights flashing so he quickly pulled over. He was looking for a place to hide and record but there just wasn't any good options, he would have to stay in his car. He turned off his lights and slowly inched forward along the curb until he was close enough to see the interaction.

Just as he suspected, 4 cars with large tires and sports striping were surrounded by 3 patrol cars and 6 kids of mixed races were standing along a wall while officers spoke to them. Bobby pulled his camera and began recording. They seemed to be talking to one white kid more than the others, he was clearly the leader of this group, the others smartly looked at the ground appearing to hang their heads in shame.

To Bobby's surprise there was a Black kid in the group. *What was he thinking?* There are some rich Black families in the city. *Clearly these kids lived there and were not from around here*, he thought. After a lengthy conversation, Bobby was shocked to see everyone get into their cars with no citations given and no one arrested. He was relieved that no one got hurt and silently hoped that whoever that Black kid was, he recognized that he was not like those other kids. He better not try that stuff when he was alone. Bobby decided he had seen enough and called it a night, heading home more determined than ever.

It was on the third night after he'd begun that it happened. He'd been sitting, waiting, and listening for over three hours. His determination and anger keeping him alert and attentive, even after the long day he'd put in at work. The cop from Johnny's murder, *Crooked Cop #2*, as Bobby thought of him, reported a possible 502—or drunk driver—at the corner of 25th and Orcutt.

Bobby knew the intersection, just a few blocks away. If *Crooked Cop #2* started any trouble, he'd be there to capture it. As Bobby approached, he saw *Crooked Cop #2*, out of his car and walking back to the patrol car. He might not harass the poor guy he'd pulled over, but Bobby wasn't taking any chances.

Quickly and cautiously, Bobby got out of his car, ran behind some bushes, and crouched down, as *Crooked Cop #2* went about his usual routine. Bobby slowly moved closer until he found a good spot from which he could clearly see and record any inappropriate behavior.

Bobby watched and recorded as *Crooked Cop #2* got out of his car and walked toward the suspect's car. His adrenaline pumped and his breath increased. It was the same reaction he always got when he was about to engage the enemy.

Bobby noted how *Crooked Cop #2* walked as if he didn't have a care in the world, meanwhile the driver of the vehicle was no doubt paralyzed with fear. Bobby felt sorry for the driver, he didn't recognize the car, could not see who the driver was, but he knew enough about him. He was a Black man that was stopped by a crooked cop, one with a history of excessive force.

Crooked Cop #2 was at the passenger door for what seemed like a really long time. He was no doubt playing cat and mouse with the driver, screwing with him in some twisted game, Bobby thought.

Bobby zoomed in to get as clear an image of *Crooked Cop #2*'s face as he could, when it seemed like he looked directly into the camera.

Crap, he saw me, Bobby thought. He knew the area, so if he needed to, he could make a quick escape down the alley.

Bobby noticed what seemed to be a change in *Crooked Cop #2's* behavior.

"He definitely saw me!" Bobby said, silently to himself. He thought about making a move for it, but he would definitely get caught. *No*, he thought. *Don't panic, the best move is to stay hidden and not make my presence known.*

Crooked Cop #2 dropped the driver's license, which made Bobby wonder if the driver were someone important that *Crooked Cop #2* didn't immediately recognize. Bobby wondered why he was taking so long and beginning to act weird. Was it his camera, was he seen, Bobby was getting nervous again?

Just as Bobby's nerves were getting the best of him, Crooked Cop #2 handed the driver his information and tapped the roof of the car and turned to walk back to his patrol car.

Bobby was shocked that he didn't give the driver of the car a ticket. Bobby watched as the car pulled away noting it was a moderately priced Buick, certainly not the type of car of someone famous or with power or influence would drive. Bobby began to question if he had gotten it all wrong. Maybe this was not one of the crooked cops on the police force.

Bobby began to live in his unwarranted judgment looking into the nothing of the night his heart slowed its beat and the frown that adorned his face for much of the night softened with regret. Maybe he had been wrong and the victims as he called them were actually criminals, and this cop was just doing his job. *I should check my prejudice lest I become as bad as the crooked cops I hate so much*, he thought,

As Bobby completed his thought *Crooked Cop #2* abruptly changed course and instead of walking to his patrol car began sprinting toward Bobby.

Although not fat, he was no runner, so Bobby had time to react. His heart beat immediately increased as he jumped up and started to run down an alley away from Crooked Cop #2, struggling not to drop his camera as he gathered his balance and ran.

Crooked Cop #2 followed quickly behind him, drew his weapon, and fired a shot down the alley toward Bobby…and missed.

Bobby's eyes were rapid and decisive as he made his way down the alley scanning every aluminum can, deserted tire, and discarded plastic bag. He approached the corner where three buildings met and stopped, thinking if he continued to run, he would get shot in the back. Planning his next best move, he put the camera down.

His pounding heart tempered by a conscious effort to slow out of control breathing, in equal parts from the rush to safety and the adrenaline of the moment, Bobby stood in momentary safety in the T of the alley.

Bobby's eyes scanned for escape, A large spiders web in the corner of the building crossing an old pipe used as a water drain, *too weak for an escape,* he thought.

Broken glass catching the light, shimmering on a litter filled ground broken down into small unrecognizable pieces because of a constant stream of the foot traffic of the unjust. *Best to be still*, Bobby thought as he closed his eyes, *listen rather than run.*

Dirty brick buildings that long ago lost the beauty they had when newly erected in a part of town that was not supposed to be a neighborhood of mostly Black residents, protected Bobby from the bullets from a weapon designed to kill.

Waiting, listening, waiting, then the crackling of garbage, faint but sufficient. Bobby opened his eyes to the shadow of what was now the prey, first a gun, then arms extended with a tight grip by steady hands, bold and confident.

With the precision expected of a well-trained Marine, a swift tight grip onto the top of the gun and a forceful elbow to the arm and chest of the crooked cop that sent him flying into metal garbage cans creating a loud clatter that in other neighborhoods would normally elicit attention but not in this alley.

Suddenly the confidence in his prey turns to fear and for Bobby the training of a soldier kicks in as the weapon now in his control is flipped around and a single, altercation ending, shot frees him from danger... BANG.

Chapter 12

Bobby woke up the next morning, not sure if what he remembered had actually happened or if it was a nightmare. A pile of dirty clothes and a brown paper bag with the exposed handle of a gun lay in a pile, out of place in the immaculately clean room. Every picture was at the correct angle, masculine furniture accentuated by freshly painted walls decorated with memorabilia collected over a decorated military career. As he recalled the previous night's events, he was unsure of what to do, and he began to get a headache. He knew he didn't have a lot of time to get himself together—it had been four o'clock in the morning by the time he'd gotten home.

After the loud shot Bobby knew there'd be people coming to windows and down the alley with flashlights any minute. He walked briskly out of the alley trying to avoid the light. His mind racing, he thought hard about what his next move should be.

Upon arriving in his neighborhood, he went to a local bar to supply an alibi if needed. He had spent a good three hours there, ordering drinks and pretending to have fun. Rather than imbibe, he poured the drinks down the drain in the bathroom and acted as if he were wasted, counting on his friends at the bar to call him a cab home, which they did.

A loud "thanks for the ride" and a heavy-footed climb up the stairs, a slam of the door, and a few more heavy stomps on the floor were not completely uncommon coming from the apartment of the retire marine but were definitely not common.

Now, the dawn of a new day, he had to figure things out. He had to get rid of his clothes, but how? He needed to be sure that no one had seen him or knew anything about what had happened. Bobby had to play things cool.

First things first—he'd walk through the neighborhood to see if there was any talk of what had happened. He also needed to go get his car. He dared not go back last night for fear he would be seen. Saturday morning was a good day to be out and about, as there would be a lot of people on the street. He went to the Denny's close to the alley for breakfast. Everyone seemed to be acting normal as he slowly ate, even though he had no appetite.

His hair stood on end when he heard a couple a few booths over talking about the cop that had been shot only a few blocks away. Bobby responded, "Really? A cop was shot?"

They happily told what they knew. "It was that same crooked cop that shot Johnny. From the neighborhood. He harassed everyone and acted like he owned the city. He got what he deserved!"

The waitress refilled his coffee and added to the conversation. "Yeah. I see him all the time, pushing people against cars and kicking their feet apart so he can frisk them," she said. "He beat this one kid really bad a few months back, and what you think happened to him? Nothing. He doesn't like black people, so when he pulls us over, he's gonna cause some trouble!"

Bobby knew all of that, but he acted as if he didn't. "Really? "Why didn't someone do something about it?" he asked rhetorically.

"They did. Last night," the waitress answered. "There are some crooked cops in this neighborhood, for sure."

Bobby thought he'd asked enough questions. He finished his *Moons Over My Hammy* and calculated his next move.

Sitting there, looking around at the comfortable surroundings of the diner chain, he wondered when his actions would catch up with him. He needed more information, and he knew exactly where to get it.

He needed to stay as far away from the alley as possible to avoid sending himself into a panic attack. Luckily, his next destination, the barbershop, was in the opposite direction. He knew that if there were information out there about what had happened the night before and his involvement, he'd hear about it there.

Esquire Barber Shop was as busy as Bobby expected. He entered to the familiar sound of the bell ringing and the welcoming hellos from the people he'd gotten to know after years of going there for a trim. Before leaving to join the Marines, Bobby had gone there for his last haircut. He had also gone there for his first haircut after his return.

Nothing had changed in the twelve years he'd been gone. The place was clean, neat, and smelled fresh. A broom sat waiting in the far corner, ready to collect hair on the floor; 5 stations to the left and 3 to the right stations were immaculately clean, organized and professional-looking. Solutions and sprays organized in front of a large mirror opposite each chair. Combs and pics in jars of Barbicide, clean white towels draped on racks perfectly positioned for easy access next to large Black chairs staffed by barbers dressed in slacks with trimmed beards and mustaches and tight fades that perfectly accentuated handsome brown faces. Bobby appreciated their professionalism, and their leadership in the community.

Fred, his barber, was surprised to see him.

"Hey, Bobby," he said. "What're you doing here?"

"I have a hot date tonight, so I want to look my best. No rush. Just fit me in whenever you can," Bobby—who wasn't due for a haircut for another week or two—replied.

He sat down and pretended to read an old issue of *Jet* from the organized magazine stack. A number of people were talking about the crooked cop that had been shot the night before. There wasn't any new information until Teddy walked in and casually said, "Y'all hear that cop that got killed last night?"

Killed?

"You sure he died? I heard he got shot, but I didn't know he died," Bobby asked.

A few people chimed in.

"Heard he was in the hospital."

Another said, "Heard he wasn't doing well. When did he die?"

"He died early this morning. Better be careful out there cause every cop in the city is on the lookout for the killer!"

"They act like he was some kind of saint. Couldn't be further from the truth! Crooked-ass cop got what he deserved."

Bobby thought about his car, was it far enough from the alley for him to go get it without causing suspicion?

"You know, he put Doug in the hospital. Claims he resisted arrest after he pulled him over for running a stop sign," Fred lamented. "How you gonna resist arrest when you didn't do anything but run a stop sign? That's supposed to be a ticket and then on your way. They're all liars, do whatever they want and think they can get away with it. Well, somebody had something planned for their asses last night."

The chatter continued, but Bobby tuned it out. He had worried that *Crooked Cop #2* would be able to identify him, but he didn't have to worry about that now. Instead, he had a whole new set of worries. It was bad enough to have shot a cop—even a crooked one—but to kill one? He was beside himself and deep in his own thoughts when he was brought back to reality by the sound of his name being called.

"Bobby! You hard of hearing all of a sudden? Get in the chair. Ain't gonna take no time to give you a trim, so let's go!"

"Sorry, Fred," Bobby said getting up and sitting in the barber's chair. Fred didn't need to ask how Bobby wanted his hair. He already knew and went right to work.

Fred was talking, but Bobby wasn't listening. He was too busy thinking about what to do next. Bobby wouldn't find his answer at the barbershop. When his haircut was done, he paid Fred and headed for the door.

"See y'all later," he said. With that, he was outside and heading for his car.

As Bobby walked, he contemplated his next move. He felt like his time was limited, sure that someone had seen him leaving the alley. How could he know for sure that they weren't looking for him right now? He'd been careful, but someone might have seen him after he'd left the alley. He'd acted normal enough, having walked away in no big rush, so he wouldn't draw attention to himself, but someone might have had enough time to get a good look at him. Should he have gotten into his car? No, his car would be easily recognizable. There were too many Black men walking the streets to identify Bobby at night. He just wasn't sure.

He needed help, and there was only one person he could think of that could actually help him. Bobby wasn't sure how he might react, but he had no choice. He changed direction and began walking down the familiar streets of his city, deaf to the occasional hello, the noises of a typical Saturday morning, honking horns, and idle chatter. He didn't stop to pet any of the local dogs being walked by neighbors he'd known for a lifetime.

Bobby walked the full five miles to his house. He paused before walking up the stairs—there was no turning back once he'd made his presence known. He wondered if it was the right next move as he felt his legs move him up the stairs, and his hand raised to ring the bell.

Less than a minute later, the opportunity to change his mind evaporated when the door opened, and the friendly face welcomed him in.

"Well, this is a surprise!"

Chapter 13

"What brings you by—not that I mind at all," Officer John said. "Come in!"

Officer John was happy to see Bobby. He didn't get a lot of visitors, especially on an early Saturday morning, so he was pleased to have the company. Since his wife had died of cancer a few years before, Officer John's social calendar was pretty wide open. He tried to keep himself busy by working at the school and keeping in touch with friends. Finally, he was beginning to get used to being in the house alone. He still wasn't happy with his life, but he was beginning to feel somewhat content, settling into his new life without his beloved.

The two men walked into the living room. Officer John was a distinguished, fifty-nine-years-old now, but looked older. His hair peppered with grey, was thin, and receding, which prompted him to keep it cut short. His thick full beard was also mostly grey but well groomed, a requirement dictated by his now departed wife when he decided to grow it. He kept himself in shape and was always well-dressed but never fancy.

His home was warm and comfortable, thanks to his wife. He hadn't changed anything since her death, unsure of what he would change if he wanted. The living room was decorated with pictures from school and of the extended family. The furniture was old but well-kept and comfortable. He'd added a few pieces since the last time Bobby had been there.

"The coffee table's new," Bobby said, trying tried to engage in small talk.

"Yes, it is," Officer John's said. "Do you want some coffee or water?"

"Coffee." Bobby nodded his acceptance. "What happened to the old one? It was nice." He followed up with more useless conversation while Officer John disappeared into the kitchen to get their coffee.

"To tell you the truth, I put my foot through it last week. I was frustrated about nothing important. It wasn't one of my brighter moves," Officer John called from the kitchen. "I was feeling sorry for myself, I guess. I'd had too much to drink, and the table got the brunt of it. Sometimes it creeps up on me, and I do something I regret later."

Officer John returned with their coffee. "You hear about the officer that was shot? It's all everyone is talking about. A routine traffic stop ends with an officer dead, makes me happy to be at the school. It's dangerous out there, always has been, but lately there are more shootings than ever before." Officer John continued, his attention on his coffee as well as the coffee table he'd destroyed. He'd done it after getting home from work and trying to reconcile the son of a colleague, another crooked cop, who'd come to school with fresh bruises on his arm.

He'd seen the bruises before, and he knew what caused them. He knew the boy's father well. He also knew the temper the man couldn't control, along with the drinking habit that only made things worse. If it wasn't the boy that had bruises, it was his mother.

This frustrated Officer John to no end, but there was little he could do about it. That had been the real reason he'd kicked the table and not alcohol. He had to figure out how he'd deal with this one.

His attention returned to his living room and Bobby. That was when he finally saw the expression on Bobby's face. "What's wrong?" he asked.

"I'm not sure you're ready to hear this, but I'm going to tell you anyway," Bobby said. He hesitated for a split second before he was out with it. "I shot that crooked cop last night. I was trying to record him. Catch him in the act of some sort of police brutality. You know that these crooked cops are always harassing someone, arresting people for no reason. By the time people get to the station, they're so beat up, they can hardly walk. Lord knows what he's done in his time as a cop, Stuff I can't even imagine.

"He killed that sixteen-year-old boy seven years ago, and nothing happened to him. Then, he put another one in the hospital, and again nothing happened. Well, I wanted to get some evidence, so I was listening to the police radio I bought a few month ago and heard him say that he'd pulled over a guy on 25th and Orcutt. I went over there to make sure that nothing went wrong, but he saw me and came after me. I tried to run away, and he began shooting at me. One thing led to another and…I shot him. It wasn't my intention. It just happened!"

He took a deep breath and continued to explain. "Something had to be done. Crooked Cop #1 killed my father. They've shot and killed too many people in this community. They brutalize every minority they come in contact with, whether it's a man or a woman. Something had to be done," he repeated himself. "So, I tried to do something about it. I tried to catch him in the act." Bobby continued telling his story and defending his actions.

Officer John listened as Bobby recounted the horrible encounters, he and his friends and family had experienced with the crooked cops. Although he had no reason to believe the stories weren't true, Officer John couldn't believe his ears. His heart raced, and his only thought was that of concern for his friend.

He finally interrupted Bobby. "What are you talking about? Did you just say you killed Crooked Cop #2? I don't want to get things confused!"

"Yes," Bobby tentatively replied.

Officer John stared for a moment in disbelief. "Regardless of what those cops do, you can't take the law into your own hands. When did you become judge, jury, and executioner? America isn't a place where we tolerate vigilante justice. Laws matter, here.

"What were you thinking, Bobby? I understand your frustration, the sadness, empathy, and anger. I understand feeling powerless to change things, but that's murder, and I'm a police officer, and now, I have to arrest you.

"You knew I'd have to bring you in—why did you tell me this? Do you want me to take you in and protect you?"

Bobby seemed surprised at Officer John's response. Thinking about things from Officer John's perspective, how could he not expect to be arrested after confessing?

"I was defending myself," Bobby said. "He shot at me! What gives him the right to draw his gun when his life isn't in danger? I have the right to feel safe in my own community and country. I have the right to be on the street recording whatever I want so long as it's not in someone's window.

"When you see a Black man running away from you, is your first thought as a cop to draw your gun and fire? These assholes treat Black people like animals, like we aren't people, like we don't have the same rights as everyone else. You know it's true whether you admit it or not, and you're one of them, so what are you doing to stop them?"

Bobby regretted saying the words as soon as they came out, but it was too late now. He was somehow emboldened to confront Officer John about feelings he had for many years.

"I'll tell you what you're doing, you aren't doing anything, and people are getting killed. Arrest me! Fine! But any more deaths mean blood on your hands because you know what they're doing, and you aren't doing anything to stop them. You haven't *done* anything to stop them. You've been a cop since the day I met you—what have you done to prevent these senseless murders that your department is responsible for?"

Officer John had had enough of Bobby's lecture. He could no longer contain his anger and exploded. "You don't think I feel the same way? You don't think any of us see what's going on? You think the rest of us, the good cops, aren't fed up? The difference is we don't go around killing people. You can't just go around killing people!"

Bobby's eyes were fixated on Officer John's, shocked at his response. "Why haven't you done anything?" he asked. "What are you all waiting for? These cops are criminals with a badge. Why should I recognize or respect the badge they wear when they break the law? Funny thing about America is we love labels but not the responsibility that comes with them. People say they hate discrimination but don't interfere when they see it in practice. People say they respect Mother Earth but don't do anything when industry pollutes and destroys. People say they love children but don't do anything to stop child suffering. People say that they love America because it is the land of the free and the land of opportunity and diversity, but they don't stop oppression and racism. Well I am done with the hypocrisy, I DO love this country and everything it represents and these crooked cops are undermining everything I love about this country and I will risk my life defending what America is really all about because unlike those crooked cops I made an oath to this country and I plan on keeping it. I'm just a fed up Nigger that isn't going to sit by and let these racists kill my brothers and sisters anymore."

Officer John lost the blood red color from his face and the bulging veins from his neck as he turned to Bobby and met his eyes with the look of a father to a son he had disappointed, "I won't let others use that word to about you and I won't let you use it to describe you. It is the word cowards and the weak use when they have nothing else to say to validate their views. It is used by the weak to appear strong and the uneducated to hide their ignorance. It's a made up word used to describe a people so strong that they endured and survived legal enslavement, so smart that they educated themselves out of ignorance, and so determined that they changed a country that was against them. Describing Black people with a word with such negative connotations is an insult to humanity."

Officer John sat and put his hand on his on Bobby's shoulder, "you like many black people are fed up, that is true, but the one thing I know about you, all of you is when you are fed up you go into action. Too many innocent people have been hurt or—worse—killed and us so-called good cops have done nothing."

Bobby's elevated tone calmed as he asked the question again, this time not out of anger but confusion; Why haven't you done anything all these years? He continued.

"When a good cop covers for a crooked cop, it makes you all crooked. You're all guilty of assault and murder. You're all guilty of the subsequent cover-up, you're all guilty. Which makes us, the powerless caught in the middle with no allies and no way to defend ourselves. What about us, the regular people just trying to make it through the day? What are we supposed to do?"

Officer John responded in frustration and defeat, "What are we supposed to do? Tell our superiors? So, what—we get labeled troublemakers and get accused of turning our backs on our brothers? Our fellow officers stop trusting us; that's what unfortunately happens, I've seen it happen. We all put our life on the line, and we need someone to watch our backs…who's going to do that? You know how it is, you were a Marine in combat.

Funny thing is I think the police union knows it. They're the ones making and enforcing the rules, recruiting and protecting dirty cops. Ensuring the worst of us either get rewarded when we harm the innocent without getting caught or get a slap on the wrist if we do get caught.

The fucking union, there to make sure the fires of racism, sexism, and homophobia continue to burn like a wildfire in a dry forest in every new class of recruits. Promoting officers that have mastered the art of hiding their awful prejudices in places where prejudice isn't supposed to exist while spewing the vilest speech to young offices with the sole purpose of continuing the cycle of hate.

"It's not easy for officers on the streets, so we try and stick together even though some cops are the problem."

Bobby and Officer John stared at each other in anger and frustration, knowing it was a no-win argument because neither had the power to compel the police department or union to change.

Both men stood. They were silent for a moment, neither of them knowing what to say or do. Officer John signed, thinking Bobby was a dead man. The police would not let a cop killer roam the streets free, they would need to punish him.

"I need to think," Officer John said, breaking the silence.

He needed to figure out what he'd do next. He also thought about what the crooked cops on the force might be up to. He paced around the living room, trying to figure out what he might do to keep Bobby safe from the consequences of his actions. He'd been trying to keep Bobby safe for longer than he could remember. The need to continue doing so surprised him. Bobby wasn't a little boy anymore, but whenever Officer John saw Bobby, he remembered a scared little boy whose father had been killed by a crooked cop. He thought of that little boy needing his protection.

Chapter 14

Officer John's mind took him back to when he'd first joined the force, useless memories of a time that no longer existed. He heard himself talking, not really knowing. It didn't seem to be appropriate, given what Bobby had just said. But it explained some of his actions.

He talked about being a young man who was determined to join the police force. The application process had seemed to take forever. He had, like Bobby, considered going to a local community college or to UVA. It wasn't expensive back then, which was good because as farmers, his family wasn't well-off. Problem was he never really liked school that much. He knew that living on the family farm wasn't the life he wanted. He'd considered going into the military; but there was so much needed in his local community, it seemed crazy to put people he didn't know before the friends and family he loved.

Officer John had been born in 1945 and grew up hearing about the struggles of people in town, the immigrants, Black people, and rich big-city bankers that had caused so many problems. His parents had commented every day about how things had changed, how dishonest people had become, and how crime and injustice had taken over what used to be a really great place to live. He was so excited when he applied to the police academy, ready to make a difference in his quiet Virginia town.

A year went by, and he'd heard nothing, but he'd needed a job. He went to work at a family friend's body shop but hated every minute of it. He wasn't afraid of hard work or getting a little dirty, but his heart just wasn't in working on cars, he wanted something more for his life.

He used to work on his first car with his father, but the joy had been in spending time with his dad and not fixing an old car. Every time he looked at his hands, soiled with grease, the lines in his hands black with oil, his nails harbors of grease and gas that he could never fully remove, he became a little more disappointed in himself.

He'd blamed himself for not doing well enough on the police entrance exam to get into the force. He vividly remembered when he was called in and found out that he had, in fact, passed the test and background checks…and he was in!

The Academy would be the best six months of his life. He'd genuinely liked his squad. They were a good group with a lot of comradery and appreciation for the job. There were no slugs, as they called them, in his group. Everyone had been committed to being the best. They'd taken pride in finishing first or second in every competition. Even their uniforms had to be perfect. If you showed up to the Academy and your uniform wasn't perfect, someone in the squad was sure to let you know about it. The Police Department was a distinguished group of well-respected men and women in those days.

His favorite part of Academy had been the Emergency Vehicle Operations Center— EVOC—because he was a skilled driver. He had a lot to learn at the Academy, but driving was something he'd learned at a young age when he and his father would take their old Oldsmobile Rocket to the local track to race it when he was as young as fifteen. When he'd gotten his license at sixteen, his dad had shocked him by giving him the car for his birthday. Driving meant two things to him from that point on, independence and prestige. There weren't many of his classmates at school who had a car, so he was instantly popular with the girls, even those that would have otherwise been totally out of his league. The experience led to a lifelong love affair with cars.

When it was time for EVOC, he excelled above everyone else. At graduation, one of his squad had been valedictorian, which was a huge deal. He'd been chosen as Most Inspirational, which gave him an enormous source of pride. His parents had also been proud of him at graduation, having driven to Hampton for the ceremony. His mom kept commenting on how handsome he'd looked in his uniform and constantly took pictures of him and all of his classmates with her new Kodak camera.

He'd been so nervous on his first day of patrol that his partner could easily tell. They'd spoken for hours that first day, his partner taking him under his wing and sharing his own experiences. By the end of it, he wasn't as on edge as when he'd started. His sergeant had been a decorated police officer, respected by everyone. Their captain was a good guy who understood his officers and the job. He was realistic with his expectations, and he had their back as long as they did their best and went by the book. The chief had a bit of a hard-edge to him and wasn't seen as approachable. John would avoid getting on his radar at all costs, but he understood the chief and respected him. The chief had to stand in front of the press and deal with things John had no interest in. He'd often see him on television, explaining the actions of his officers, and he always had their back and supported them. John grew to appreciate and respect that about him...until he discovered the force's dark side.

Chapter 15

The first time John realized that every officer didn't do things by the book was a few months after he'd arrived at his station. He was there doing his paperwork when he heard one of the officers talking about an arrest he'd made and how that black piece of trash would be feeling his nightstick for a while. He was proud he didn't take any lip from those animals on the streets. This was John's introduction to crooked cops.

His first year on the force had caused him a lot of internal conflict. It only got worse from that first encounter. He became aware of suspects with bruises or bleeding and women sobbing, it was almost a weekly occurrence. Then there were the arrests that made no sense. Simple infractions escalated, resulting in charges of resisting arrest, followed by brushing the whole thing under the rug and letting the victims go without charges being filed. There were, however, fresh, new bruises.

There were deaths. Dead suspects with no witnesses other than the officer or two who had identical accounts of what had happened. The story always seemed to be the same, a minority had gone for one of their guns or had pointed a gun at them, and they were forced to shoot to kill. John had no idea what to do about it. At times, he regretted being a cop. He wondered why no one was doing anything about these crooked cops?

John had noticed that many of the crooked cops stayed close to Assistant Chief Brice—who everyone called A.C. Brice—and to each other but no one else. They also seemed able to do whatever they wanted without question or consequence. The year A.C. Brice had joined the force, the department began to change. He was an active member of the Ku Klux Klan and heavily recruited its members to join the force.

Officer John was almost at the point where he couldn't take it anymore when the position of police officer at John Marshall Elementary School came available, and he jumped at the chance. Because he was so well-liked and had a perfect record, he was given the assignment. He felt like the kids were his own, and he was determined to keep them protected.

John had never wanted kids—he thought it would be a shame to bring a kid into the world he knew, a world that was mean and cruel and didn't care. He was pretty sure he'd never get married because of his lack of interest in having children, but then he'd met Jennifer. She was beautiful, athletically inclined, and driven. He was sure he'd marry her the first time he'd laid eyes on her.

After a long, two-year courtship, they decided to get married. They were both in their thirties, and neither wanted kids. They had a good life, traveled often, and didn't want for anything. John and Jennifer's love for the kids at John Marshall filled their hearts and gave them the joy of having kids of their own without the burden or responsibility.

They thought of the kids as an extension of their small family. He wanted them to think of him as their uncle. He also wanted them to trust him because if their parents weren't treating them right, he wanted to know about it. He kept an eye out for bruises and broken bones if they happened too often, and he made it a point to talk to the shy ones to ensure everything was okay.

Wanting to excel at his job he had taken courses at the local college on Social Work and Psychology. This helped him when it came to his little girls. He paid the most attention to his girls and looked for changes in behavior as they started to get older because he knew how sick people could be.

When he heard Bobby's father was killed by that crooked cop, he knew he had to reach out to Bobby to make him feel okay.

Bobby listened to his friend as he shared pieces of his past in between long pauses. He was surprised to hear that Officer John had been aware of the crooked cops on the force for so long and hadn't done anything about it.

Bobby interrupted his friend's seemingly automatic confession by asking if he remembered the first day he'd gone back to school after his father had been killed.

"I do," he said softly but confidently, much to Bobby's surprise.

"Do you remember what you told me that day? It was something I'll never forget."

Bobby could see it all quite clearly, his young self, crying and afraid. The trust and love he usually felt replaced with fear and confusion. He remembered Officer John as he kneeled in front of him.

"I said that everything was okay and that I was sorry a police officer had shot your father. I said that if there were any way I could've stopped them, I would've. I told you that if you ever needed anything, all you had to do was ask."

Bobby responded, "These men cause so much death, horror, and despair, not just to Black people, but everyone. When they go about dehumanizing Black people, they're also destroying the minds of white children. When they teach them hate and racism, they destroy the goodness in them. Those kids grow up not learning or fully understanding compassion or fairness.

"These evil men don't only devalue black lives; they devalue women and the disabled. They see everyone as less than they are, and no one is doing anything about it." Finally, Bobby confessed as to where this all came from, "seeing Johnny's young son at his father's funeral told me I needed to do something. I'm done watching! Marines don't just watch injustice and wait for someone else to do something about it, we take an oath to be the ones to act."

Officer John looked at Bobby as he considered his words. He thought about that other crooked cop, the third that they had front of mind, the one who had abused his wife and child. He thought about the awful racist things he heard children say, knowing they were repeating what their parents had said at home. He knew that hate could spread and hate unchecked could destroy quicker and more permanently than either fire or flood. He knew that Bobby was right, and something had to be done to show everyone in the city that good men would not stand by and let it to go unpunished. The crooked cops had to be held accountable for their actions.

Bobby looked at Officer John and said, "I'm asking for your help to make them pay, not for killing my father but for all the awful things they do every day. I'm asking you to help me prevent any more kids having to go to their parent's funeral."

Chapter 16

As the two men stood in silence in the comfort of Officer John's living room, they were anything but comfortable. Bobby was watching Officer John, who was looking out the window as if there were answers somewhere out there. Both of them, it seemed, were trying to figure out what to do with the information they had just shared.

Officer John began to feel a weight on his shoulders—had he been at the school hiding from the truth of the force for too long? He lowered his head as his eyes closed from the weight of humiliation, all the years of making excuses for his lack of action suddenly felt like 500 pounds.

He wondered how many people he could have helped if he'd done something years ago instead of hiding at the school, protecting children that, for the most part, didn't really need his protection? The handful of kids he'd helped paled in comparison to the people in his community in need of a strong, honest cop. For the first time, he acknowledged to himself that what he was doing at the school was hiding like a coward.

Bobby broke the silence. "We have to put an end to this. We have to stop these crooked cops since no one else will."

Officer John turned to look at Bobby. "I'm not the person to help you, Bobby. You need someone young and strong. I've been out of the fight for so long. I'm not even sure I'd know how to fight anymore." Saying his fears out loud made Officer John grow even more disappointed with himself. What had he become?

Bobby walked over to his friend. "You may not be young, but you're not old either and you're still an officer, and I need someone on the inside if I'm going to make a difference." Bobby put his hand on Officer John's shoulder and stared into his eyes. "John, I need you!"

Officer John wasn't sure he wanted to hear what Bobby would say next, but he also didn't want to ignore the truth anymore.

"We can't let them terrorize the city and turn a blind eye to the murder of innocent people," Bobby continued. "You and I both know who these crooked cops are, and we can catch them in the act—"

John interrupted, "You mean like you did last night? Is that what you call catching them in the act?"

Bobby looked at Officer John. He didn't see the fear of a weak, old man, Officer John projected a fire in need of stroking to a flame.

"*Crooked Cop #2* drew his gun and fired at me for recording him," Bobby said. "In the Marines, many a man fired at me and didn't live through the day. Just like those evil men, *Crooked Cop #2* messed with the wrong marine. I know you don't think the death of an enemy soldier halfway around the world is my fault—how is this any different?

"You may not be willing to admit this, but to the minorities in this country, it feels like we're at war with an unjust system made worse by racists and worst of all, crooked cops that seem to be trying to kill us all."

Bobby exuded adrenaline and control calmed by the many years of combat, fighting for his country. "*Crooked Cop #2* was out for blood last night, but I'm sure he never imagined it would be his own. Last night was just the beginning. This soldier is ready for war—the question is John, are you ready to do what needs to be done?"

Officer John sat on the couch in silent thought for what, to Bobby, seemed like an eternity. Would he side with the crooked cops and turn him in? There was no way to know what he'd do or think, so Bobby sat beside him in silence and waited.

He had no choice but to trust that his friend would finally see what the juries had not. He would have to see the crooked cops' actions for what they were and not blame the victims. He would prove that not all cops were crooked. He would prove that there were good people willing to fight for justice. Not only in comic books or halfway around the world for reasons unknown to most Americans, but right here, and right now.

Officer John finally spoke. "What happened last night wasn't your fault. He shouldn't have shot at you because he was in no immediate danger even if you were running away. You had committed no crime, so he could not have reasonably thought you were a danger to society. If what you told me is true, you killed him in self-defense. You did what needed to be done."

Officer John continued, "If I were the man you are, Bobby, I'd have done something a long time ago."

Bobby didn't know how to respond. He empathized with the defeated look he saw in Officer John, and he hadn't expected him to shoulder the blame himself. Bobby knew that leadership determined the actions of those they led when it came to soldiers, so it was no doubt true of the police force. Bobby had seen more than one racist marine sergeant in his twelve years. He also saw the impact it had on the soldiers and the horrible things some of them did overseas. It was a learned culture that could have easily been checked by strong leadership, and he knew the police were the same.

"Officer John," Bobby said. "The chief and assistant chief are responsible for the culture of the police force. If they allow racists and crooked cops to break the law, what is one officer to do? I guess I can understand you not doing anything before, but that's in the past and cannot be changed. I'm asking you to do something now."

Chapter 17

Officer John got up from the couch and walked into the kitchen. He didn't spend a lot of time there; he considered the kitchen his wife's. Going in there reminded him of her.

It was exactly as she'd left it, her favorite cast iron skillet sitting on the stove, her apron hanging from the decorative knob on the door of the small pantry, and the jar of used grease on the counter. What she did with it, he had no idea.

He avoided the room because the thought of her no longer in it overwhelmed him, but he needed something from it if he were going to continue his conversation with Bobby.

He picked up what he needed along with two small glasses into which he put a couple of ice cubes, returned to the living room, and set everything on the coffee table.

"Glenfiddich 18? Isn't it a little early for that?" Bobby asked as Officer John poured two fingers in each glass.

"If we're going to have this conversation, I need a drink, and if I'm gonna have a drink this early, it's not gonna be crap!"

Officer John raised his glass and waited for Bobby who reluctantly complied, "cheers I guess." After a sip and a look at the determination in Bobby's eyes, Officer John knew he needed to put his police skills and training to work. "What happened, exactly, and where were you when it happened? Spare no detail, regardless of how insignificant you think it is."

He might have been slightly out of practice, but he wasn't as completely useless he thought. He knew that crimes rarely happened without at least one witness, whether they came forward was a different story. So, his first thought was that Bobby might be in custody within twenty-four hours if he didn't figure out what the police knew and how much trouble Bobby was in.

Officer John explained his need for answers. "You can't kill a cop, even one like *Crooked Cop #2,* who is known to be dirty, and just walk away; everyone on the force will be out looking for you, so I need to get ahead of the situation, ASAP."

Bobby smiled as he realized his friend was on board with his plan.

Knowing what Bobby was no doubt thinking, Officer John threw a quick dose of reality to Bobby's premature smile. "I'm afraid you're a dead man walking. I wouldn't be smiling if I were you. I don't know what I can do other than try to find out as much as I can in the hope that you weren't seen, or if you were, it wasn't reported to the police.

"I understand why you did what you did, and I'd have probably done the same thing given the situation, but if even one person comes forward with a description of you and these crooked cops find you, they'll no doubt kill you on the way to the station or in your apartment before I have any chance to protect you. So, what happened?"

As Bobby spoke, Officer John listened, but he wrote down nothing. There could be no evidence of their conversation.

After Officer John had heard enough details, he told Bobby to go get his car and go home and wait for word. "If the police approach you at your car or come to your door, cooperate with every request they make because they're going to want to punish a cop killer, and you do not want to piss them off more than they already are. Come by in the morning if I don't hear from me, and we'll talk more. We'll see if we can keep you alive."

Officer John walked Bobby to the door and gave his friend a genuine hug. "We'll get through this situation and then talk about what's next."

After Bobby disappeared into the neighborhood, Officer John headed out the door, knowing he needed to get answers, and there was only one place to do that. He was headed to another place he'd avoided for the most part.

As he walked into the police station, he was overcome with memories of a life he'd left long ago. He remembered what the place had once meant to him and how different he felt about it now. To him, the station was a place of contradiction. "To Protect and Serve" was just a catch-phrase without meaning. The words were supposed to apply to everyone and offer reassurance that the people in that building wearing a badge were there to make things safer or better for everyone, but there, in his city, they didn't.

He was greeted by the officers at the reception desk. He knew them well and appreciated the work they did; they were two of the good ones. There were many in the station that did good work, but unfortunately, there were far too many who did not. He hadn't been to the station for a while, and they knew exactly why he was there—or so he thought.

"So, you heard what happened?" one of the officers asked.

"Yes, I heard," Officer John said. "Any leads? We gotta find that bastard."

"We will," another replied.

"How you holding up in that house all alone? You, okay?"

The last time Officer John had seen the two officers was at his wife's funeral. He remembered how somber everyone had been, and the many people in tears and those who had comforted him. Jennifer, his departed wife, had been popular and had a large extended family who adored her. She was active not only in the school but the local civic club and her sorority, even after graduating from Hampton University. She loved AKA and her AKA sisters, and they loved her. She was always looking to get involved, whether it was lending help to Officer John's school's bake sales or car washes or raising money for some cause or person in need—whatever she could do for the less fortunate.

That had been their lives until her cancer diagnosis. In the end, cancer had taken most of the life out of her, and she was bedridden. Toward the end, she was in such pain that she and John prayed for her passing. It was a shared prayer they'd never admit to each other.

John was both destroyed and relieved when he'd woken up that hot July morning, eager to help his wife with her medication before her pain had become unbearable, only to find her lifeless body at peace. He'd cried over her for hours before calling the coroner to report her passing.

The funeral was beautiful with its pink and green wreaths. He knew she was at peace, and that was all he cared about.

He slowly came back to the present, the station, and the officers at the desk who were still talking, seemingly unaware that Officer John had left the conversation.

"The chief in?" he asked them.

"Yeah. Go on back," came the answer. "He'll be happy to see you."

John headed further into the station, noticing that the crooked cops who normally hung around A.C. Brice's office weren't there. They were, no doubt, out trying to figure out what had happened the night before. Officer John needed to figure out if they knew anything, and the chief was the best, safest place for information.

He approached the door and saw the chief get up from his desk. He opened the door and extended a hand to Officer John.

"How are you, John," he asked.

"I'm good, Chief. I came as soon as I heard. How are you, and what can I do? What do we know?" John asked the questions the chief would expect, getting straight to the point, knowing the chief had no reason to withhold information.

"We don't know shit!" He returned to his desk, motioning for John to take a chair on the other side. His office was impressive, with its large, cherry desk and matching furniture. It had a comfortable sitting area by the window where the chief would have informal conversations with his officers, but everything of a serious nature was done at his desk.

The chief, it seemed, had no suspects, no leads, and a press conference in an hour. Officer John offered his support. "Chief, if you need me, I can work extra duty after the school, whatever is needed to help us get this guy."

"I appreciate the offer and will let you know. In the meantime, of course see if you can uncover any information from parents at the school. Someone may have seen something."

"Of course, Chief."

With that the Chief stood, which was a professional way of letting Officer John know that he needed to leave. Officer John immediately stood up and shook hands and excuse himself. He exited the station without delay, giving a nod and warm smile to the officers at the desk on his way out and headed for home.

As he walked out, he was reminded of what Bobby had said. It was high time someone did something about the crooked cops ruining his station and his city.

I could take Bobby's idea one step safer, he thought. It wouldn't take much to set up some traps, station some cameras around the city so they could get information without confrontation. The thought put the first smile of the day on his face.

He had surveillance equipment to prepare. Everything he needed was back at his house, but that just one part of the equation. The hard part was to make sure that everything was in good working order and would do its job because once he set up his trap, he could never go back. Although he was at the Elementary School and wasn't in harm's way, he was still a very capable police officer, even though he never gave himself much credit for the fact. He'd spent a lot of time keeping his skills sharp through training sessions at the academy and police station. He had everything he'd need, and more, to do his job and protect his neighborhood and kids in his backyard shed. He had a lot to do before Bobby came over in the morning.

Officer John felt sorry for the position his chief was in, but that didn't alter his plans. The chief was a part of the problem. The more Officer John thought about the situation, the more he realized the police union—and everyone in a position of power on the force—were to blame for the current situation. They worked hard to protect the crooked cops; no doubt due to their racist agenda.

It was an agenda that Officer John would no longer support. He knew things would only get worse for the chief, but it wasn't his or Bobby's fault—it was the fault of the crooked cops that had been left unchecked, and those who protected them.

While Officer John gathered his information from the station, Bobby approached the corner of the shooting, his heart pounding. His car was further away than he had realized. He saw police tape and officers blocking the two visible entrances to the alley. He forced himself to not look away as he crossed the street and headed for his car. He knew that to look away would be unusual, he looked with fake curiosity at the officers and the scene.

He noticed an officer look over at him, he slowed and took steps toward the officer who immediately spoke up. "Unless you have information, keep moving!"

It was just what Bobby needed. He nodded his head and turned toward his car, got in, and drove away. He hoped that the officer was just reacting to him as they would any Black man and did not make any special note of his car. His heart pounded the short drive home. Although it provided no safety, he couldn't get there fast enough.

Chapter 18

As Officer John headed back home, he thought it best to page Bobby to meet him there. *Crooked Cop #2* was dead, and there had been no useful information gathered on the murder; hopefully, it would stay that way.

The two men arrived at Officer John's at the same time. Bobby was noticeably shaken as he leaped up Officer John's staircase and waited by the door.

"At the moment, they don't know anything," Officer John said, as he unlocked the door.

Once inside, Officer John updated Bobby on what he'd found out.

"You're extremely lucky because a lot of citizens hated *Crooked Cop #2*. Even if they saw something, they aren't likely to come forward with information about his killing. Dead men tell no tales, as they say, so we'll see what the next few days bring. In the meantime, you need to be invisible, and thank your lucky stars if you don't end up dead or in jail."

"Just so you know, I'm going back out there. This soldier's war is far from over. It's just beginning. I'm going to continue recording these crooked cops in the act, and when I do, I'm going to get the recording in front of every news outlet out there to make them answer for their crimes.

"This has to stop, and if everyone—including you—wants to turn a blind eye to what these criminals are doing, I understand, but I'm not. I'm committed to being the one that brings them to justice, alone if I have to.

"I'm not afraid of them. Marines aren't afraid of bullies. I swore an oath to support and defend the Constitution of the United States, and these racist, crooked cops are the biggest threat to the U.S. in the entire world," Bobby said.

Officer John listened to Bobby's speech with pride. It reaffirmed his commitment to help him. He listened as Bobby continued.

"You know, I went all over the world when I was in the Marines, and I saw all kinds of conflict, but none of it compares to what our government and police do to the poor and Black people. Nothing's really changed since slavery's abolishment. It may look different, more covert and in the back rooms and shadows but it's the same hate. It's still our blood that is spilled. They still want us to live in fear. If the citizens don't believe in our great country, it doesn't matter what foreign countries do—our democracy and freedom die. The only question left unanswered is if you're going to help me or go back to hiding at your school."

Officer John smiled and thought back to his first days at the police academy, his oath to protect and serve, and how he'd known the crooked cops on the force were doing everything but that. He finally spoke up.

"You know what, my friend?" Officer John said, after a deep breath that relaxed his whole body. "You're right! I've spent a career looking the other way, trying not to get into trouble instead of doing the right thing.

"It's true that the Chief and Asst. Chief set the culture and the tone for the department, but I could have gone to Internal Affairs or the Mayor or Governor if I wanted to, but the truth is I was more concerned about myself and my wife and friends than the corruption in my department. I have to admit, in order to forgive myself, that I could have done more. I'm just as much to blame for the way things are as the crooked cops, but I'm done. I'm with you, and together we're gonna change things or die trying."

Bobby smiled, relieved that his friend wasn't about to let him or his community down.

The same community that had supported Officer John and his wife for many years was the same community who had put their trust in his hands.

"We have to be strategic and smart because if we aren't, we'll be dead in no time, and that's not going to help anyone."

Officer John had some ideas he needed to share, he was all in, but he was not going to proceed without a clear understanding between he and Bobby.

"We need to begin by laying out some rules for engagement with the police. Officer John paused and waited for Bobby to respond which he did, "ok, what do you have in mind?"

Officer John thought for a moment and wondered what would make him confident that they didn't turn into the crooked cops they were trying to hold accountable. "Ok, first things first, we don't draw blood unless our lives are in danger. Officers have the right to use whatever force is reasonably necessary to make an arrest or protect themselves or others from imminent harm, we don't have that protection and we will not be the bad guys."

"I'm no cop killer, but if our job is to stop the killers in the department, we can't kid ourselves, we will need to most likely operate outside the letter of the law in order to complete our mission."

"I know," Officer John responded. "I'm fully aware but I want to make sure that we understand each other, which brings me to number two, nothing happens without my knowledge. If I'm going to help you, there can be no secrets."

Bobby looked intently at Officer John, and he said what John knew to have been true since Bobby had started elementary school, "I trust you. I have no reason to lie to you because you've never given me a reason to."

Officer John would help Bobby any way he could and make sure that Bobby had a rock-solid alibi, should there ever be a question about his whereabouts. John also knew that as an officer himself, he'd be the last person suspected of recording officers or bringing officers to justice who were breaking the law. He also knew that if he was ever discovered, the crooked cops on the force would immediately kill him.

Officer John thought for a moment, then spoke. "I think we need to start by setting up some cameras to catch the drug dealing cops, they will be an easy target.

"The best place to set them up is on 16th Street near the Chesapeake Bay." The area was crawling with drug dealers and addicts, and Officer John knew that several crooked cops frequented that part of the city. His first-hand knowledge of the area was a story he would not tell Bobby at this particular moment, but his experience told him this was the place to get drugs.

"If we want to find crooked cops, that's a good place to find them," Officer John confided in Bobby. "No one would dare go there if they weren't buying or selling drugs. We'll set up a camera tomorrow morning, when the dealers have gone home to sleep, and I'll make sure that no cops are in the area."

Bobby smiled again.

"What are you smiling about?" Officer John demanded.

"We're finally gonna do something. You have to be excited about this. We're gonna get their crooked asses."

Officer John again brought Bobby back to reality. "We haven't done anything yet."

After Bobby left, Officer John went straight to his shed. He opened a door that he hadn't been through in a while, pulling the string to turn the light on to illuminate the modest space before getting to work. He opened one of the many drawers lining the wall to his left and pulled out three 720p HD night vision intelligent spy cameras and checked them. He'd need to increase the battery life.

As he opened more drawers to gather more equipment, he began to feel like he did when he first went to the police academy; he felt like he was about to make a difference. He worked the entire day away without stopping until everything had been squared away. When he finally left his shed, he was starving and tired.

He decided to walk down the street to the Church's Chicken for food—it was a familiar place where he ate often since he never cooked, and his departed wife wasn't there to make his dinner.

There was an uneasiness as he entered and ordered his usual three-piece meal, speaking casually to the cashier at the register, whom he did not recognize.

"How's it going?" he asked with a slight smile.

"Pretty good. Thank you for asking," she replied.

"I don't think we've met. I'm Officer John. I live right down the street."

She smiled a little as she replied, "I know who you are. I haven't seen you in a while. A couple of cops were here earlier, asking questions, and I told them I don't know anything, and I'm sorry, but I still don't," she said nervously.

Officer John realized the uneasiness he was causing. He'd been so preoccupied with his work that the reality of what was going on had escaped him. "I'm just here to get something to eat," he said with a comforting smile. "I can imagine that must've been pretty scary for you."

He sat near a booth by the window and was just about to let his mind wander again when a patrol car pulled up. The officers got out of the car, talking loudly. Their behavior continued as they entered the restaurant. "Fucking cop gets killed in a busy neighborhood, and no one saw a fucking thing. They're all working together against us, you know."

As they approached the counter, Officer John looked at the cashier who was giving him and the other officers nervous looks. He knew she probably had reason to be nervous, given the situation. Officer John didn't want to deal with any crooked cops that night. He got quickly up and headed toward the counter.

"What's up, boot?" he said.

The officers' heads turned, upon hearing the derogatory police academy term—they hadn't expected to hear that there, or at all, since leaving the academy. They replied courteously upon recognizing Officer John. "Hey, John—what you doing here this late?"

"Just grabbing some dinner from my friend here. Best chicken in the city, if you ask me." John extended his hand to the officers.

"I guess, I don't need to tell you about the food, otherwise you wouldn't be here. It's been a long day, but I can stay and eat with you if you like?" Officer John was more concerned about the cashier getting hassled than chatting with the officers, she was visibly nervous.

"We're gonna take our food to go and eat in the car. We're still on patrol. No word on our cop killer so we don't have the luxury of hanging out. Nobody saw anything, heard anything, or knows anything. 'Course if it was one of them, referring to the cashier and the many black residents, who got hurt, there would be a thousand witnesses." The officers genuinely believed this not thinking about the reason behind their statement.

Officer John's bag was presented to him, as he extended words of encouragement, he hoped would not come true. "We'll find the killer soon enough, they always trip up!"

He gave the cashier a smile, hoping to relieve the tension created by the other officers.

"Thank you, and please take care of my friends here like you always take care of me." He turned toward the door and advised the other officers. "There are lots of good people here, enjoy your dinner, guys!" He hoped that there wouldn't be any issues after he'd left, as that was all he had the energy for. The next day would be busy, and he needed to get some sleep.

Though he was exhausted, he felt better than he had in a really long time as he got into bed. He needed to feel good about his job and the force again, and Bobby had given him hope that it was possible. For the first time in a long time, Officer John fell asleep with a content smile on his face.

Chapter 19

Officer John awoke to a loud knock at his door. He jumped out of bed, with a single thought, someone must've found out about Bobby and seen the two of them together. He tried to decide what he would tell the officers, how he'd protect Bobby, and how he'd protect himself.

John looked at his clock. It was just before five a.m.

As he hastily put on his slippers, he noticed the light of day had yet to show its impending presence. It was almost a full hour before he normally woke up, as he did every morning—six sharp and out the door by six-thirty to be at the school and ready to greet his kids a little before seven.

He wasn't required to be there until seven-thirty after the crossing guards had ensured everyone's safe entry into the building, but he liked to be there to welcome the kids and their parents. It had been his routine for more than twenty years, even on weekends and holidays.

John approached the door and gave a sigh of relief when he saw Bobby through the glass, standing under the illumination of the porch light. Truth be told, it was tinged with a bit of frustration. He opened the door quietly but deliberately and greeted Bobby. "What the heck are you knocking so loudly for? You trying to wake everyone in the neighborhood?"

Bobby smiled as he walked past his friend and into the house. "If you'd answered my calls, and my previous attempts at knocking, I wouldn't have had to knock so loudly. You must sleep like a log."

Officer John followed Bobby to the living room. "I don't keep my phone in the bedroom. It keeps me awake," he said with a hint of frustration. He knew that Bobby was most likely telling the truth, and he'd most likely made several attempts to get him to wake up and answer the door.

"The coffee will start to brew in a few minutes," John said. "I'm going to get dressed. Everything we need is ready and in the back of my van. Help yourself."

Officer John joined Bobby in his living room to the smell of fresh coffee. He filled a travel mug, and Bobby rose and followed him out to the van, and they were off. John explained the plan once again, in greater detail this time. "The cameras need to be put in an inconspicuous place but with a clear view of the street. I have monitors in the back, so I'll let you know if the view is obstructed. Place them as high as you can reach, and then try to cover them with dirt or something to make them blend in. No one will be looking for them, so don't worry too much about them—you'll see, they're already pretty inconspicuous."

As they drove toward Jefferson Avenue, Bobby was struck by how their plan would not have worked when he was a kid.

"When I was young, probably the same for you, kids played outside and climbed trees and were apt to notice anything new or out of place. This just wouldn't have worked back then."

Officer John chuckled. "Are you kidding, no way would we have missed cameras hidden in our neighborhood. We were outside from the moment we got out of school until dinnertime, exploring and creating a world out of our imagination that encompassed every inch of their neighborhood and sometimes beyond. Things were different back then. We didn't know what was going on or at least our parents knew but not as much as we do now with 24-hour news and access to information that we didn't have before.

"I don't think we were any safer, kids didn't end up on milk cartons because the world was safe, it was dangerous, but I don't think we understood the extent of our problems. Now we know and it's up to us to do something about them."

Bobby listened. *He gets it! We are going to do something,* he thought.

He added to the conversation, "a lot of kids were inside, playing video games or outside but involved in organized sports rather than playing in the streets, at least, in their part of the city."

It was an unfortunate reality that served Officer John and Bobby well. Their plan could work, because things were different now.

After they stopped and scanned the neighborhood, John got out and acted as if he were on his phone, engaging in conversation while he listened to his police radio. While John was engaged in his charade, Bobby placed the cameras in the best spots possible, making sure they were out of view. They worked quickly because they wanted to be done before dawn, and their time was running out.

They finished their work at 6:30 a.m. and decided to part ways once they got back to Officer John's house. They'd meet that night at nine to watch the monitors and see if they were able to gather any evidence.

Quickly gathering their tools, they jumped in the car and headed back.

Once in the quiet of the car, Officer John silently reflected on what had gotten the department to this point.

"You know, the police force I'd been so proud to join all those years ago is gone, transformed into something else, maybe it was never what I thought it was. I guess my ignorance really was bliss."

Bobby sighed, "I know what you mean. All the sacrifices I made as a marine to protect my friends and family from threats all around the world while the crooked cops in my own neighborhood are their biggest threat. They not only cause physical harm, what's worse of all is they kill our spirit a little bit every day. I didn't see it before, but I see it now."

"Yeah," was all Officer John could think to say. They pulled up to Officer John's house and with little said, but with a genuine heartfelt embrace, parted ways.

Chapter 20

Bobby had an anxious Sunday ahead of him. He didn't want to spend the whole day thinking about what their video recorder might be capturing, but it was all he could think about. He was up and had nothing to occupy his time.

Pacing around his apartment and engaging in chores, the clock finally struck 9:00 a.m., and he could engage in his normal routine and call his sister, Nancy. She was all abuzz because Virginia Tech had been scheduled to have their opening game against Georgia Tech the day before but had been canceled due to lighting. She was excited about the upcoming season, as Tech was coming off of a national championship run, having come just short of winning the title in the previous season. They were ranked eleventh and expected to do well that season.

Bobby listened as his sister recounted the previous season with such enthusiasm—as if she hadn't done the same thing every game the previous year. He always chucked to himself when listening to his sister, who sounded more like an undergrad than the mother of a seven-year-old daughter.

He admired his sister greatly. She'd graduated from Virginia Tech and had begun working in healthcare like their father. She'd married Jeff shortly after graduation, a man that Bobby liked and respected, and settled in Williamsburg, Virginia. Bobby thought it no coincidence that she lived an easy, four-hour drive on the 460 to Virginia Tech.

Nancy, Jeff, and their daughter Alisa were huge fans and season's ticket holders. Her stories of their trips to see the Hokies play in stadiums all over the country amused Bobby. He promised to join them for a game one day, thinking to himself that it would be more amusing in person than over the phone.

After an hour of talking to Nancy and a brief exchange with Jeff and Alisa, it was time to call Michael and then his mother.

Bobby's little brother, Michael, had settled in northern Virginia, just outside of Washington D.C. He worked as a warehouse manager and enjoyed a comfortable life. They spoke about their grandparents, who lived close to Michael. Bobby hadn't been up there to see them in a while, so he'd get regular updates from Michael. Although Bobby spoke to them often, he knew they weren't always forthcoming with the struggles they were having, now that they were in their eighties. Bobby was grateful that Michael was close by and kept an eye on them so they wouldn't be alone.

He hung up the phone and looked at the clock to realize he still had a long day ahead of him; it was not yet 11:00 a.m. He'd spend the next hour catching up with Thelma and making sure she had what she needed. His mother, ever the independent woman, didn't like her children to worry, but she did like them to visit her often.

Bobby hung up with his mother and realized he still had a good nine hours to kill before he could go to Officer John's house to put his mind to good use and do some good. He'd get his clothes ready for work in the morning and prepare food, even though he wasn't hungry. He watched TV, and when he became bored with that, he tried to read a book, but to no avail.

He decided to take a nap, but after setting his alarm and checking it twice, he resolved himself to lay there, lost in thoughts of the crooked cops going to jail. He had images of them being in court where the prosecutor would play his videos before the guilty verdict was finally given, and they were put in handcuffs and taken off to jail where they belonged. As he imagined justice being served, he finally dozed off to sleep.

In his dreams, Bobby's mind took him to a place he didn't want to go. He saw the face of the *Crooked Cop #2*, dead in the alley. The face without life was suddenly alive again, spattered with blood from the gunshot wound in his chest Bobby had delivered.

He spoke to Bobby, wanting to know why Bobby had taken his life and left him in such a state. Bobby tried to run, but his legs weren't working. The face grew larger as it threatened to tell everyone what Bobby had done. It got closer and larger and began screaming loud thunderous threats at Bobby with calls of lynching. Images of the bodies of Black men and boys hanging from trees filled Bobby's sleeping mind, suddenly *Strange Fruit* played in Bobby's mind as he saw himself swinging from a tree, his sleeping body began to sweat as he tossed and turned.

The face was now huge, with bloodshot eyes. Seemingly everywhere Bobby turned, he was filled with fear as the images filled his mind.

What had he done?

Covered in sweat, Bobby was jolted back to reality by his alarm as it rang, waking him from his nightmare at 8:30 p.m. He surveyed the room. His wet, sweat stained shirt and sheets making him realize it had been a dream.

His fear left in an instant as he was flooded with memories of the events of that night and the criminal actions of *Crooked Cop #2* that led to his death at Bobby's hands.

Shaking off the mental effects of the dream, Bobby got up, changed his shirt, and was out the door and into the night, on his way without another thought of the dead.

He found Officer John sitting on his porch, waiting for him to arrive. It was a nice fall night, cool and comfortable, but the men had only one thing on their minds and relaxing on the porch was not in their plans.

They entered the shed, sat in front of the monitors, and reviewed the recordings, not believing their eyes. During the day there was a lot of activity, but it wasn't until after dusk that the crooked cops started their work. There, clearly on the screen was a crooked cop and his partner buying drugs. A little fast forwarding and there again, two crooked cops hassling a group of homeless people before confiscating their drugs without arresting them.

"I know all these officers," Officer John confessed to Bobby.

Officer John did not expect the range of emotions he was feeling, from embarrassment to shock, disbelief, and finally, anger. He was beginning to understand why there was such distrust of the police. He was seeing it with his own eyes. Out in their community for everyone to see but powerless to stop were crooked cops acting like criminals.

He wondered how many complaints had been filed against crooked cops in the department with nothing done. What must people think, knowing the truth but the department and chief doing nothing to address what was going on.

The only thing people could assume was that all cops either knew what they were doing or were doing the same thing. He sat in silence after that, processing what he was seeing.

Bobby, however, did not. "This is bullshit," he exclaimed. "That's exactly why no one trusts cops anymore. The crooked ones get away with murder and all kinds of illegal shit, and the good ones turn a blinds eye to it. These are the same fuckers that are trusted to uphold the law and testify in court as if they're to be trusted." He looked at Officer John. "Can you believe this shit? We're gonna nail their asses to the wall!"

He got up to pace. He was mad and needed to do something with his energy.

Seeing his friend's frustration, John offered some advice. "Maybe I should watch the rest of the tapes and send them to the newspaper, and you just head home."

Bobby's initial reaction was to argue that he had every right to be there. He had taken the risk of putting the cameras out there, after all, and they were in it together. They'd agreed they wouldn't have secrets where stuff like that was concerned. Bobby questioned if he could trust Officer John, but as quickly as those thoughts came, he knew that Officer John was right, no good would come of his watching the crooked cops break the law. It would just make him angrier.

"Okay," he responded.

As Bobby turned toward the door, Officer John got up and put his hand on his friend's shoulder. "Don't worry," he said. "We'll get them.

They won't get away with this stuff anymore. We'll make sure these guys get what they deserve."

Bobby left, and Officer John began gathering the damaging footage to send to a friend he had at the local newspaper. He couldn't let anyone know he was involved, so he'd have to put it in an unmarked envelope, and then he and Bobby would have to wait until it showed up in the paper or maybe on the nightly news.

Officer John got to work. By 1:00 a.m., he was exhausted, but he had everything he needed to get at least three officers arrested for possession of narcotics, and one of them slapped with an added charge of police brutality if the letter of the law was followed. It was a good start, he thought. Hopefully, it would shake things up enough to force the officers on the force to act right. Some of the officers he knew needed help. Maybe this would prompt them to get the help they needed. He understood the pressures of the job and hoped that this would be enough to scare some of them straight.

When he finally lay down in his bed, he had one final thought, was he betraying his brothers? He closed his eyes, knowing he wouldn't be asleep for a while and that there was no easy answer to that question; he just knew he had to do something.

Chapter 21

Bobby and Officer John didn't communicate over the next few days, not wanting anyone to see them together. They both took the time to focus on their jobs, which for Officer John had suffered slightly. His reports were not as thorough as they usually were, so he promised himself that when he got the time, he would go back over them. No one would know the difference but that is what made him good at his job, his accountability to himself and his kids.

Bobby went about reengaging his coworkers, spending more time off the clock chatting with them and strengthening their connections. Bobby learned the value of relationships in the Marines, and he knew the stronger they are the easier it is to get things done. It was also a great way to get information about what was happening with the company, if there were changes that may affect him, and the latest neighborhood gossip which was especially important given what he had done.

Everywhere Bobby went, there was talk about the officer that had been shot, however the news reported little information other than how much of a tragedy it was, and that the killer was still at large. Patrols were everywhere, talking to folks, trying to get a sense of what had happened to one of their own. Every time Bobby saw an officer on patrol his heart began to race. His years of Marine training kept him calm and composed externally but he could never fully control what was happening internally, he was a soldier through and through but a human with fears and emotions.

He had an overwhelming urge to go back to the alley and check to see if the police were still there. He wondered if they had spoken to all the people in the neighborhood yet. Although he wouldn't go—he had been once to get his car and wasn't going back—his curiosity about what was happening was overwhelming at times.

He curbed his curiosity by constantly watching the news for updates, fearing that one day his picture would pop up.

There were press conferences and news stories each day, but luckily, all that came of them were people making bold proclamations about justice being served. Each time he heard someone say it, he thought to himself how justice had been served.

After his shift at work, Bobby wondered how long it would take before anything would come of the video they'd taken. He prepared himself a late lunch of pasta with cream sauce and sausage, one of his favorites. His normal routine was to eat dinner after work and the gym, usually getting home no later than four o'clock when he worked the morning shift, and it was a good way to keep his expenses down, saving for a future that was a complete mystery to him.

He sat in front of the television, hoping to enjoy the distraction while eating, wondering to himself what Officer John was up to. He trusted that his friend would deliver the videos as soon as he could. It was his responsibility to be patient and wait.

He took his first bite of pasta and turned on the television, shocked to see that their video was being aired. Bobby couldn't believe his eyes or ears, as the reporter spoke in detail about the tape and the officers involved.

"You can see, here, Officers Bryant, Wade, and Kilpatrick obtaining what appears to be drugs," the reporter said to the three other people on the panel and the viewers at home. The typical news setup had been replaced with banners in bold colors and large fonts announcing that he was watching breaking news. Bobby tried his best to focus on what was being said. He didn't know the officers, but he'd obviously seen the video before. He paid keen attention to the parts of the video he'd missed at Officer John's.

One of the panelists replied, "The validity of the video is still being determined, according to Chief Dolan, who also said that a full investigation is underway. It's important not to jump to conclusions too quickly in situations like this, as the officers involved have all been protecting the city for some time now."

The reporter was interrupted by another on the panel. "Officer Bryant has been on the force for nine years, Officer Wade three years, and Officer Kilpatrick five years, all of them serving with distinction. Stay right where you are and get the latest news on this developing story as details become available."

As they switched gears to other news, Bobby flipped to other channels, hoping for more information but the few local news channels that ran the story reported the same—the video was shown multiple times with few details and a promise of more news to come. One local reporter however suggested that the video "could be documenting some sort of sting operation" which made Bobby's stomach drop. He wondered would they be able to spin this like it was the police doing their job and not engaged in any illegal activity? Bobby was leery of the police and their allies in the city but that didn't curtail his shock that things had happened so quickly, and he was abuzz with excitement and energy.

As the news broke, Officer John was watching his kids getting picked up by their parents. As the last of his kids was leaving school, a teacher approached him. "Did you hear the news? So disappointing," she said.

"What news?" he replied.

"The three officers caught on tape buying drugs. It's all everyone is talking about!"

Officer John tried to look surprised, unsure how good of an actor he was. "Really? Who? Do you know their names?" His heart pounded.

"I don't remember, but it's pretty shocking."

John stood there, shaking his head as the teacher turned and walked away, not at all satisfied with the interaction. *Here we go,* John thought.

He thought about what would come next, and for the first time ever he considered leaving his post at the school early to see what was happening. He made his way into the office and signed out as normal, only 45 minutes earlier than he had ever before. Exchanging pleasantries with the office staff as he made his way to the door skipping the teachers' lounge where many of the teachers were watching the breaking news.

He called Bobby on his way home, driving as fast as he could without speeding.

"Can you believe this?" Bobby said as his greeting.

"Just wanted to make sure you knew, I'm on my way home." With that the conversation ended.

Officer John pulled into his driveway and went straight to the television. He and Bobby in their separate homes would follow the same routine, running to get food and tending to chores during commercial breaks but keeping their full attention on the television not wanting to miss a single detail.

In a press conference later that night, Chief Dolan assured the public that a complete investigation was being conducted and that the officers involved were on administrative leave.

The next day, the stories turned to the failed drug tests of the officers involved and the suspensions without pay they had received. These stories were followed by the officers being arrested and charged with illegal possession. With each break in the story, Bobby and Officer John were on the phone with each other processing what was happening and discussing the latest update. Bobby was the first to bring up the surprise and complete shift in news coverage.

"There's little to no talk about *Crooked Cop #2*, That became old news pretty quickly."

Officer John tried to give Bobby a reality check. "It may be old news to the media, but it's not old news to the department. They're still very focused on catching the killer, you may not see it, but I do, it's being heavily investigated."

That was all the reminder Bobby needed. He wasn't out of the woods yet. There was still a lot of people focused on what had happened and their work would continue in spite of this new scandal. He would never say, but deep down he hoped that the officers might think it was an inside job. Why else would someone kill an influential officer who had been on the force a long time and was very well connected?

The next day presented a cool evening during Bobby's favorite time of year. The prospect of being in jail increased his appreciation of Fall even more than before.

The day was full of the usual sounds of fall, people were aware that their evening rituals would soon be interrupted by the cold and possibly snow of winter, so they took advantage of what time they had left by spending more time outside, walking and talking to friends and neighbors on the street. Walks to the corner store or ice cream shop were a source of enjoyment because they would soon be put on hold for at least five months.

It was on that day that the silence between Officer John and Bobby was broken by a quick call from Officer John.

"Hey, finally I have some updates, I assume you saw the news?"

Bobby excitedly said, "yes!"

"Good, meet me at my house at 6:00."

Bobby arrived on time, eager to celebrate their victory over the crooked cops. He was also eager to see what they might have recorded on their hidden cameras. When he entered the house, John seemed in no mood to celebrate their success.

"We have something to discuss," he said as they entered the living room.

Bobby saw two glasses with cubes of ice and a bottle of Glenlivet sitting on the coffee table. "This must be serious," Bobby said.

"It is, and I'm not sure we are up for this yet," Officer John explained as he poured his friend a drink.

Bobby sat and listening. "I figure if we are going to do this, we can't rely on being lucky. We need information that we will not get from cameras because these cops aren't that dumb, they are going to be more careful about what they do and where.

Also, I am leery of us being seen together, the more we are out and about together the more attention will be paid to you.

I need to get into the Crooked Cops circle, it's the only way to know what is going on and be able to stay ahead of things and be as safe as possible."

Bobby looked at Officer John with skepticism and concern. "Are you up for that? I don't mean any disrespect but hearing you say it makes me worried."

"Me too, but it's the only way. I need to spend some time at the station finding out what's going on and how I can get in. The death of *Crooked Cop #2* gives me a reason to be more active than I was so there is my cover."

Bobby still wasn't convinced but he knew Officer John was right. He was worried, nonetheless. "When was the last time you did anything like this? I only remember you at the school and to be honest, there isn't much real police work going on there."

Officer John smiled. "It's supposed to look that way. The school has helped me prepare for this. I see the smallest detail because it's my job. I see the bruises and can tell the ones that are the result of a fall and the ones from a hand. I keep a file on every kid that displays any erratic behavior and try to find out why. When you all go home, my work just begins. I have files on as many family members as needed once I see a child in need. Uncles, aunts, older siblings, their parents. My job isn't so much to protect the kids when they are at school, it's to protect them… period."

Bobby was surprised and impressed. "I would never have thought that were the case."

"It's not as dangerous as being on patrol, I'm not saying that, but it has certainly made my surveillance skills top notch which is what I need. The same way I get what I need from parents without causing suspicion, I need to figure out who can get me into this ring the crooked cops are running, inject myself in," Officer John acknowledged. "We need to be in control of everything we do otherwise we will be discovered. I've been thinking about it, and I think I know where to start. I'll be in touch with you when the time is right so until I reach out, lay low where the cops are concerned.

"We'll also need these," Officer John pulled out the latest in technology, two surprisingly small cell phones. Bobby had seen them before and was aware of how popular they were becoming but he considered them a luxury item and a waste of money. "Cell phones?"

Officer John explained, "we need to be able to communicate at all times and pages aren't gonna cut it. These are only for you and me to use when absolutely necessary, you have to pay for minutes and messages, but they will definitely be an advantage for us."

Bobby took the phone and looked it over. "I don't even know how to use this?"

Officer John laughed, "which one of us is the young buck and the old fart again?"

He gave Bobby a quick tutorial.

Chapter 22

Then next day, Officer John waited until the last of his kids were picked up by their parents like he did everyday but instead of going to update his files at his school office he headed for the station.

The best place to start would be the locker room and the shooting range. Officers tended to spend a lot of time there, mostly out of necessity so it was a good place to chat.

Walking into the locker room he began scanning for the right person to target. Someone that he knew was relatively new but also in with the crooked cops. Someone that had an ego that he could use to his advantage. As he walked between the lockers, he heard the perfect candidate, Officer Waller.

Waller was in his second year on patrol and had quickly picked up the habits that would endear him to the crooked cops. A known racist, he was a member of the KKK, and his father was a cop, so he was in from the start.

Officer John approached him and the other officer he was speaking to. "Hey, you headed to the range?" Waller turned and extended his hand. "Yeah! You heading there, I'll wait for you."

As John put his incidentals, keys, and wallet in the locker next to Waller's, he started to lay the foundation for what was to come.

"Still no word on a suspect I understand. Somebody had to see something." Waller shook his head. "Give it time, we'll figure it out. How are things going over at the school?"

"It's going, you know."

The two turned and headed toward the range. Officer John continued, "I started a side hustle to make some extra money. My wife's funeral and other expenses really put a dent into things."

"Couldn't imagine what you're going through. I know it's been a few years since your wife died, how are you adjusting? I know it happened before I started patrol but if you need anything let me know man," Waller replied.

Officer John nodded. "Appreciate it. Things are going okay. Keeping busy helps. I was thinking about moving out of the house, too many memories ya know, but it's home. I could definitely use another night out once in a while so looking for a league or something to keep busy but everything's so expensive these days."

Officer John was interrupted as they arrived at the counter.

"Three and four are open," was all that was said by the officer running the range who was distracted by the small television on the left side of the counter. Handing them their guns, bullets, and targets without looking up, he pointed to the sign in.

Officer John and Waller filled out the extensive form, picked up their equipment and headed to their stations. Officer John left the conversation alone for the moment and focused on what he was doing. An impressive round would open up more conversation, so he cleared his mind of distractions as he hung his target and sent it zooming 15 yards towards the wall.

He, for the first time noticed that all the targets were black figures on a white background and wondered if it was Bobby's influence that made him notice it now and never before.

Taking a deep breath, he measured his weapon and began to fire.

John was always a good shot. He excelled at the things that make a good cop so when the target came zooming back towards him, he was not at all surprised at his results. He removed the target, attached another, and lost himself in his routine.

He continued until he felt a tap on his shoulder. Nodding, he finished his last round, and brought his target back. He gathered his supplies and followed Waller back to the counter and returned everything but his targets.

Stepping out of the live area they began to speak. "That always gets my juices going," Waller said.

Officer John laughed. "I'm just the opposite, it gets me more focused and centered. Helps me to put aside everything that is on my mind."

Waller reached for Officer John's targets and began looking them over. "I would say so, you're a damn good shot. I was thinking about what you were saying, and I might have something for you. Let me talk to some folks and get back to you."

Officer John hoped he knew what Waller meant. "I won't hold you to anything, but I appreciate the thought."

The two men headed towards the locker room.

"What are you up to?" Waller asked.

"I have to do some paperwork at home. I usually finish my reports right after the school day is done but was distracted today so needed to clear my head a bit, thanks for the company." He extended his hand after emptying the contents of his locker.

"Anytime," Waller said. "I'll be in touch."

Officer John was counting on it. He was counting on *Crooked Cop #2* needing to be replaced and Waller might recommend him after he raised concerns about money. The leaders within the department with close ties to the union would have to meet, if they hadn't already, to discuss the situation, assess the need for any damage control, and replace their crooked soldier and the best place to start is an officer in trouble.

Officer John headed home feeling like he had achieved his goal. He was putting his plan into motion, and if Waller was respected at all it wouldn't take much for him to bring Officer John in for consideration.

The next day John was completing his paperwork from a busy day at school and starting to think about what he was going to eat for dinner when his phone rang.

He looked and did not recognize the number. "Hello." The voice on the other end was familiar from the first word, "Hey John, Waller here. Have some people I want you to meet, you free this evening?"

This was exactly what Officer John was hoping for. "Yes, whatever you need." He wondered if he sounded too eager.

"Perfect, meet us at this address. You have a pen?" Officer John responded in kind and took down the address.

"I can be there in an hour."

Waller's response was a quick, perfect, see you there and then he hung up.

The address was in Oyster Point, a rather nice area of Newport News. Officer John wondered whose house he was headed to as he put his paperwork away and headed for the door. The residence was in a cul-de-sac at the very end. It was the nicest house on the street and there were several cars in the circular driveway.

Officer John was just clearing the last step when the door opened, and Waller greeted him.

"Thanks for coming, John, come on in."

Officer John entered the sparsely decorated home noting there were no pictures on the walls or rugs on the bamboo floors. The furniture was old and rather worn but not in a comfortable way.

He followed Waller into what would be the dining room, though he doubted that anyone regularly dined in the room even though there were tables and chairs. The owner was either single or this was simply a meeting place. It definitely didn't feel like a home.

Waller introduced Officer John to four crooked cops who were sitting around a table with chairs that didn't exactly match.

"Have a seat John," one of them instructed after they had exchanged handshakes and pleasant smiles. "Waller has been talking to us about your financial situation, and we may be able to help each other. We are looking for a reliable man to help us with a little side business. We heard about the work you have been doing down at the school. Pretty calm over there, some might say boring. You ready for some action?"

Officer John was on alert but calm. He knew very little would happen in this neighborhood, any unusual noises like a gunshot would draw immediate attention. "I'm just looking to make a little extra money; any action would be a bonus. He smiled, boring doesn't begin to describe the school, he said and I'm not getting any hazard pay over there."

Officer John decided to go for it and cut to the chase, "we talking about running guns, drugs, or am I dating myself? I'm not as young as I used to be but that was the game when I was fresh out of the academy, and it was a good way to make extra money to get my house and pay for the very expensive wedding I had."

Waller laughed first and the others followed. "It hasn't changed, John. A little of this and that, right?" He motioned to the crooked cop at the head of the table, now further convinced that Officer John wasn't working with internal affairs on a sting operation.

"No, it hasn't, I guess. I like this guy, Waller, no bullshit. It's a pretty easy gig, just do what you're told and be on time and if you do its easy money. With *Crooked Cop #2* going down and some of our guys becoming tv stars we need another man. I guess their misfortune is your gain."

He spoke looking directly looking into Officer John's eyes trying to read his strength. "We've got jobs coming up, and we need warm bodies. There's a little heat right now but we've seen way worse over the years. We have to keep our commitments so that means pressing forward and that's where you come in."

Officer John's gaze didn't waver as he nodded. "With what they pay us, I'd like a little easy money. What's next?" he asked, looking around the room, trying to make eye contact with the other three crooked cops at the table, who, after making contact with Officer John, looked to the head of the table for an answer.

"We'll be in touch, just a quick meeting to make sure we are all on the same page." The crooked cop at the head of the table looked at Waller who then immediately stood up. "I'll walk you out John."

Once outside, Waller tried to put Officer John at ease. "They just want to make sure you're cool. You handled yourself well, didn't come across shaken or nervous. I wouldn't worry, I think you're in."

Officer John smiled extending his hand to Waller. "I hope so, I guess I'll find out soon enough. You better get back inside."

John walked to his car, confident that the men were watching him and that his years on the force would make him a shoo-in. Now he needed to wait.

Chapter 23

It had been three days since Officer John had spoken to Bobby, and in that time, the crooked cops and Waller had been in touch with bits of information gauging his trustworthiness and interest, allowing more and more information to come to light.

Officer John knew he needed to reach out, otherwise he risked Bobby going mad with curiosity about what was happening.

When the two men met at Officer John's request. Bobby was eager to hear what was going on as he sat in anticipation on Officer John's couch, Glenlivet their other companion.

"Well, the time I've spent at the station making sure there isn't any heat on our tail and reestablishing relationships has paid off as we had hoped. One of the crooked cops I've known since my days at the Academy was an Officer Waller, well his son is now on the force and befriending him has presented me with an opportunity that might be exactly what we need." He reviewed his meetings and conversations with Bobby who listened relieved that there was movement.

Bobby's felt his facial expression changing from shock to worry to relief as he listened to Officer John's recount of the past events. "I know that crooked, racist cop? He's been a fucking jerk ever since he joined the force, harassing and arresting innocent people on BS charges …he's become one of the worst in a really short period of time. I guess like father like son."

Officer John nodded as he knew Bobby was right. "He's in with the guys that will get us all the information we need to execute our missions.

They know what's going down and may even be planning some of it. I'm not sure who is in charge and who is following orders yet, but I'll figure it out soon enough.

"It's just what you'd expect—they're a little freaked out by what's happened the last few weeks, but they won't stop. They have people on their payroll, and they aren't going to stop with the drugs. It's way bigger than we thought. The other night, we didn't catch someone buying drugs. They were checking to make sure that the drugs on the street were theirs. They were protecting their turf! They're recruiting people to replace the men they have lost, and the pay must be good."

Bobby said, "Did he just come out and tell you this? That's pretty risky!"

Officer John took a sip of his drink. "They've been giving me bits of information over the last three days.

"I'm sure they checked up on me and discovered I wasn't always the person I am today. Waller Sr. knew me at a time in my life when I was experimenting and trying to fit in. I'd gotten into drugs a bit, nothing too heavy so I never got hooked, thank God. It was during a dark period, and I knew it was just an escape, which was often quicker and quite frankly easier than alcohol, quick and dirty, hated myself every time I did it.

"Back then, I was on the outskirts of their circle, not knowing everything they were doing.

"I quickly learned some things about the department. The police union really does facilitate an unhealthy environment. I definitely did some things I'm not proud of, and once I was clean, I distanced myself from them. Spending all my time at the school kept me just far enough that I was able to get out of that circle. Connecting with Waller, was just the way for me to get back in.

Last night I got the details of my first job."

Seven chimes sounded from the grandfather clock in the corner, a reminder that it was getting late, but the two men weren't concerned, even though they had to get up early the next morning.

Officer John filled Bobby in on the details of the job and the location. While he was proving to those in charge that he was serious, helping with a drug deal on Saturday night, Bobby would get more of them on tape with the drugs.

John voiced concerns he was feeling ever since he was informed of the job and realized that Bobby would be in a really dangerous position if he did what needed to be done, "you ready for this?"

Bobby gave his friend a confused look and proudly replied, "Man, I'm a marine! I've dealt with way worse than these small-time thugs."

Bobby knew how to do reconnaissance, knew how to take care of himself, knew his way around a gun, and he was ready to take on the challenge. "We need to make a plan," he said. "What time is it going down?"

John replied, "It's going to be at the dock, not far from Anderson Park. You know it? It's where the Battle of the Monitor and Merrimack took place during the Civil War."

Bobby knew the park. He nodded as Officer John continued.

"The drugs will be brought by boat, and we'll pick them up and take them to the processing house. I figure if you can record what's going on, we'll be able to take down a few more of these bastards."

"Sounds like a plan. I'll go to check it out and get better understanding of the layout of the park and make sure I'm prepared for whatever might go down. Nothing I haven't done before.

"Once you know the exact location, I'll get there and get into position. It might be a good idea if you don't know where I'll be, so you don't inadvertently look my way."

John looked at Bobby with suspicion. "The last time you attempted this, you ended up being spotted and killing a cop."

Bobby paused. He had to admit the truth. "I sort of wanted the cop to see me. I wanted him to start some trouble with me, but I didn't expect him to start shooting. I'd had enough of their bullshit."

Officer John looked at Bobby for a minute before breaking the silence. "Don't get caught. These guys will be heavily armed."

Bobby left Officer John's house around nine o'clock knowing he had a lot of work to do. He needed a failsafe; it was something he'd learned in the Marines. While there was the overt mission, the work being done that everyone could see, then there was the covert mission that happened in the shadows and out of sight.

Bobby had his covert mission to prepare for. He'd have to get familiar with the area Officer John would be working, every bush, tree, hill, and without raising suspicion. He had two days to get everything in order.

The camera was the least of his worries, he needed to be prepared if anything went wrong and have a plan of escape and support for Officer John if needed.

Bobby started to feel the adrenaline that came with every mission as a Marine. The rush that long ago replaced the fear that existed when he was young. He was a war machine and a soldier now, had been for many years, and he was ready to put his training from his many combat missions to use. As he walked to his car, he confidently thought to himself "I would be ready."

Chapter 24

The darkness of night enveloped Bobby's bed but supplied little comfort or rest, he had something weighing on his mind.

He wanted to appear strong and confident to Officer John when he bragged about Crooked Cop #2 but in the darkness of his bedroom, he had serious questions for himself.

"Did I lure Crooked Cop #2 down the alley that night?

"If I were to be honest with myself, did I want something to go down with the hope that I'd have the opportunity to engage him… beat the crap out of him… kill him?"

Bobby had enjoyed his military training. He took it very seriously as had everyone in his unit. He took pride in his body as it got stronger, and his mind as it got sharper. His basic and combat training had transformed his body into a weapon, and even though he'd been out for what seemed like an eternity to him, it had actually only been a little over a year.

He was as combat ready as ever.

He spent hours at the gym five days a week and frequented the firing range.

He wondered to himself if, without knowing it, had he been training for that day his entire life, a day when he'd confront the crooked cops, hurting them the way they'd hurt him and so many others.

He wondered if that made him as bad as they were. He wondered if, deep down, he wondered silently had he secretly wanted to kill Crooked Cop #2 in the same way as Crooked Cop #1 had killed his father.

It had been a long time since his father's death had weighed so heavily on his mind. He thought about playing with his father in the yard, of his childhood home, and quiet nights alone with his family. They were memories he'd fought never to forget because it had happened so long ago. He never wanted to forget his father's face, the feeling of being picked up and put on his father's shoulders. The hugs he'd get from his father. He'd carried these memories with him ever since his father had died.

Were they the fuel for his rage that night? The reason he was committed to bringing them to justice one way or another?

Bobby realized only good men question their actions, he spoke to the empty room "You crooked cops are not worried about me, why am I worried about you?"

Bobby pounded his head with his fists trying to get the guilt of his actions out of his head by force, but his blows were in vain.

There, in the loneliness of his dark bedroom, Bobby did something he hadn't done in a very long time, he cried himself to sleep with the final thought that no matter the cost, the crooked cops had to be stopped. He swore aloud to his father—whom he was sure was watching over him—"they will pay for what they did to you and the rest!"

Bobby woke up the next day energized and at peace. He would never admit to himself that the tears from the night before were the release of emotion he needed. After a quick breakfast he was off to work with an exuberance that had nothing to do with work and more to do with what lay waiting for him after work.

As soon as his shift was done, he headed for Anderson Park. He walked the park casually, leaving dictated messages on his phone about his thoughts and observations. After surveying the area, drawing a thorough mental picture he headed home where with his notes and a map of the park, he'd map out his plan of attack. This would remain his routine over the next few days refining and adjusting his plan based on the days survey.

He also cleaned his rifle, a memento from his days in the military, adding his silencer to ensure his location would not be discovered.

By the time Officer John had texted him the exact address, he knew where to hide, where Officer John would be, where his exits were if something went down, and several routes to take to get home if his police scanner alerted him to officers coming his way. Looking at his map he picked a brush of shrubs and trees just off of Hampton Drive as his temporary hunter's perch.

This was the best spot possible. Using his military-grade infrared camera, he would be able to get adequate images of the perpetrators.

Bobby arrived at the park a little before 9:00pm. Surveying the area from his car, when the coast was clear, with his rifle hanging over his shoulder in its duffle case and camera in hand, he quickly walked the path that led to his perch. Bobby set up his camera and removed his rifle from its case and an extra magazine just in case. He peered through his binoculars and waited for signs of activity.

Just as Officer John had said, a boat approached the dock at 9:30 on the dot, well after the park had closed but not late enough to draw suspicion.

Bobby began to film, looking around for Officer John and the others. He saw them at last, getting out of a dark van in the parking lot, not too far from the dock. As the crooked cops and Officer John approached the three guys that had just gotten off the boat, Bobby zoomed in to get a shot of everyone's face—except for Officer John's.

He made sure to film as much of each of them as possible while avoiding his friend. He had the perfect view with which to record the faces of the crooked cops. As luck would have it, the back of one of the guy's heads from the boat perfectly blocked Officer John's face. Bobby marveled that it could not be going any better, everything was going according to plan he thought as a sense of pride and fulfillment came over him. He couldn't help but smile to himself. He had all the footage he'd need to bring all the assholes involved to justice.

After they had been engaged in chatter for what seemed like an eternity, Bobby began to wonder what they could possibly be talking about. Would they shoot the shit and engage in small talk in the middle of a drug deal? It was a secluded park, but it was still a public place where people could see them. The longer the exchange lasted, the more uneasy

Bobby felt, but there was nothing he could do except stay put, continue to record, and hope for the best.

The exchange finally seemed to be happening and it was like something out of a movie. They had small briefcases in which they kept money or drugs. When one of the men from the boat finally opened the briefcase, exposing what Bobby assumed was cocaine, "gotcha!" the smile returned to Bobby's face. Having never actually seen it, he made that assumption based on what he saw in movies and not any personal knowledge.

Bobby watched as Officer John and the others finally headed back for the van. Each of them suddenly reaching for their backs as if they'd been bit by a mosquito or stung by a bee. Immediately Bobby shifted his focus to Officer John and almost in slow motion he saw the all too familiar sight of a bullet entering his friend's back as he fell to the ground. The smile and every ounce of pride melted from Bobby as he fought the urge to scream out for his friend.

"No!" he said silently to himself.

Feelings of guilt and remorse flooded Bobby who through tear filled eyes and intense worry had to focus on the broader scene and not just his friend. One of the guys from the boat ran to pick up the briefcase which was now on the ground. After securing the briefcase, the three men lowered their guns which were still pointed at the officers and began to retreat back to the boat.

The reality of the situation was like a bolt of lightning that shifted Bobby attention away from the momentary guilt over putting his friend in the situation that could have possibly just taken his life and alerted him to the fact that these mobster guys whoever they are were getting away.

Again, Bobby had to work through tears as he drew his weapon, got his targets into focus, and fired three quick shots. Two of the guys went down. The third looked around before running toward the boat.

Bobby followed him through the scope on his gun, sniffling like a child with a cold, he locked his target in sight and took another shot.

Down he went.

Bobby packed up his gear and ran towards the coast where everyone lay on the ground. His mind was overwhelmed with concern for Officer John, but his military training had his legs moving towards the mobsters near the boat. He had to ensure they were no longer a threat before he could attend to his friend. They weren't breathing.

He rushed over to Officer John and the other crooked cops. He didn't want to reveal himself to them, but he had to help John.

One of the crooked cops wasn't moving. The other looked directly at Bobby. "You motherfucker," he said in a weak but angry voice. "You'll pay for this."

Bobby realized the crooked cop thought that Bobby was to blame for his being shot instead of the mobsters that he was doing business with. Bobby tried to wrap his mind around what had happened and what he'd do now that the crooked cop had seen him. This would put him and Officer John at risk if he was even still alive. His concern distracted him for a moment, long enough for the crooked cop laying on the ground to unholster a pistol and begin to pull it up to fire. Bobby instinctually pulled his pistol from his hip holster and shot him dead.

Without wasting another second, Bobby rushed over to Officer John and gently but anxiously checked his heartbeat and listened to see if he were still breathing. Silent whisper of "I'm sorry, I'm sorry" kept coming from his mouth without thinking or processing the words. His tears paused, by a glimmer of hope, when he realized Officer John was alive. He again moved as gently but quickly as he could, using every ounce of strength to deadlift Officer John from the ground. Groans of pain came from Officer John causing Bobby to again whisper "I'm sorry."

Turning and running towards the van, Bobby gently put Officer John's feet on the ground and propped him against the side of the van so he could free his hand and open the door.

He gently laid Officer John in the 2nd row face down so that the blood coming from Officer John's back that had already stained Bobby's shirt would not stain the seat.

"Please, please," Bobby said as he checked Officer John for the keys, to no avail. He'd have to go back.

He rushed over and checked the other cops for keys. "Yes," he found them, turned and raced back to the van. Jumping into the driver's seat, they were off.

"Please hold on!" Bobby repeated over and over as he sped towards his car.

He pulled up behind his car and again. "Hold on, hold on," he said, as he moved Officer John from the van to his car. "I'll be right back, hold on." Assuring Officer John, not knowing if he was hearing him.

As Bobby grabbed a ballcap in his passenger seat, put there in case he needed to hide his face, he looked once again at Officer John one last time, "hold on!" and ran back to the van to take it back to the park.

As he got closer to the park, his mind shifted from Officer John to the image of the dead crooked cop's open eyes, seemingly staring at him as he searched for the keys. The image escaped him before but now that he was heading back, they flashed in his mind like a ghost in the night.

He'd had similar experiences in the Marines in which he had to kill the enemy, but he'd never come that close to them or seen their dead eyes looking at him.

His heart pounding; worried what he'd find once he got back to the park even though it had only been a few minutes since he left.

The scene was exactly as he'd left it, but he knew it wouldn't be long before one of the residents on Walnut or Blair Avenues or someone walking by would see the men on the ground and call the police.

He had to move fast.

Bobby wondered if anyone had seen what had happened. The trees weren't that dense, but it was dark, and that helped to hide what had gone on. Bobby parked the van and quickly surveyed it for Officer John's blood. Not seeing any he placed the ballcap lower on his head and got out of the van.

He tossed the keys at one of the dead cops laying on the ground and ran as quickly as he could back to his car and Officer John, keeping his head down to hide his face, making sure not to look up in the direction of any of the homes adjacent to the park. He got back to his car and checked that his friend was still breathing, "please, please. He was breathing but was still unconscious. Bobby didn't know what to do or where to go. He couldn't go to the hospital, and he couldn't take him home—although Bobby had a lot of training in the Marines, he was no doctor. "Think, think," he said as he hit himself in the head trying to make it work up a solution.

He sat there with the car running and his heart pounding, wondering what to do. His friend's life was slipping away, and he had no idea where to turn for help. Then "please, please," he shifted into drive and took off down the street toward the Hampton Roads Beltway, turning onto the Beltway, and quickly accelerating to sixty miles an hour through the tunnel into Suffolk. Bobby prayed his friend would survive the ride, speaking the only words of encouragement he could muster, "hold on, hold on".

Would she be home, he thought. His fear intensifying, he adjusted the rear-view mirror so that he could see Officer John, he whispered to himself, "please be home."

Bobby continued his prayer that she'd be home the entire way.

He thought about the last time he had seen her. It was shortly after he'd gotten out of the Marines. He had gone by to say hello and thank her for all the love and support she had shown him while he was serving.

She'd gotten his address from his mother at his party so many years ago, when he'd announced he was going into the Marines. She, like everyone else, was so happy for him. She'd been one of the few friends from home that had kept in touch with him the entire time he was in, sending care packages for him and his squad when he was overseas and in harm's way and letters when he wasn't. They'd developed a friendship over the years, and he never thought he'd need her for anything other than friendship. However, on that night, he was eternally grateful to have a friend who was a doctor.

He turned into the dirt and gravel road that led to her Victorian-style farmhouse noticing that a few lights were on. "Thank you, God, thank you God." Hopefully, she was home alone.

He pulled up, putting the car into park before it was fully stopped causing a jolt as it came to an immediate halt.

He took one final look at Officer John, "hold on one more minute!" he asked his friend as he leaped out of the car, ran past the mailbox and through the white picket fence, leaping up the four stairs without touching them, he rang the bell, stopping his momentum just before running into the front door screen. "Please be home, please be home" he quietly prayed.

Then the porch light came on and the door opened, a slim woman in her sixties with mostly grey hair in a short modern style, wearing a satin thigh length housecoat, and comfortable attractive slippers stood there. A look of shock and confusion on her well maintained and moisturized face. She had only one thing to say, "Bobby?"

Chapter 25

"Dr. Chien, I need your help!" Bobby said. "Officer John is hurt!"

"What?" was her only reply before following Bobby to his car, where she saw Officer John, unconscious and in the backseat. "Let's get him inside," she instinctually said, opening the door so Bobby could pick him up.

Dr. Chien was well acquainted with Officer John from the years that her daughter had attended the elementary school that he patrolled. Officer John had made it a point to get to know her given her status as a very popular pediatrician that cared for many of the kids at the school.

Bobby followed Dr. Chien into her house, though the living room filled with ornate, stylish, and comfortable furniture and then the dining room passed a long table suitable for dinner parties and a China cabinet full of well used China and into the kitchen.

"Lay him down there," she said, motioning at the kitchen table. "I'll be right back." She left the kitchen, leaving Bobby alone with Officer John.

Bobby stared at his friend, hoping he was strong enough to make it. "Hold on buddy" were the only words he could muster when looking at his friend. Bobby had seen worse injuries while in the Marines. Back then, the poor soldiers had survived, but they were taken to the hospital and given the best care available.

He looked around at Dr. Chien's immaculate kitchen, with its light green cabinets, stone countertops, and stainless-steel appliances, wondering how he'd gotten here—how had his life brought him to that point? Had it all been one huge mistake?

Dr. Chien reappeared with a large black stiff leather bag. She opened it, took out a stethoscope, and placed it on Officer John's chest, telling Bobby that his heart still sounded good, all things considered. She took out a bottle of fluid, inserted a syringe, and gave Officer John a shot of whatever it was. Bobby knew not to say a word because this wasn't Dr. Chien's area of expertise—she was a pediatrician, after all—and he hoped more than anything that she'd be able to save Officer John.

He watched as she moved from task to task, getting a scalpel, making an incision, getting what looked like a fancy set of tweezers out, and plunging them into the opening in Officer John's back. She moved the tweezers around inside of Officer John's wound before breaking the silence with a "Gotcha!" and pulling out what Bobby assumed was the bullet. Next, she poured something on his wound and looked at Bobby. "He should be okay." She cut Officer John out of his shirt, got some towels, and cleaned up Officer John's back before dressing his wound.

"Let's take him upstairs," she said.

Bobby picked his friend up once again and took him up the wide, wooden stairs, with their white banister and occasional squeaky step. At the top of the stairs, she opened the door to the room in the middle.

"Let's get him out of these bloody clothes and put him to bed," she said. She left and returned with another blanket while Bobby removed Officer John's shoes, socks, and pants after laying him on the bed. They covered him with the sheet and two blankets, and Dr. Chien recommended that Bobby move his car around back.

When Bobby returned, Dr. Chien was waiting at the head of the dining room table. She stared at Bobby as he entered the room. He sat down in the chair closest to her. Before he could say anything, she ended the silence. "I put on a pot of water. I'm making us some tea. What happened?"

Bobby wasn't sure if it was a good idea to tell Dr. Chien what had happened. He trusted her, but he didn't want to put her in danger. "I'm not sure telling you is a good idea."

She looked at him. "But bringing him here was? Whatever it is, I'm already involved, so you might as well tell me what's going on."

Bobby sat for a moment before beginning with a warning, "Remember, you asked for it."

He told her about everything from the first shooting to the filming that had been on the news to the planning that had ultimately led to the killing of five—and almost six—people.

Dr. Chien sat there, listening without offering a sound in return. They were both so involved in the story, they didn't hear the teapot whistle to announce that the water was ready for tea.

Once Bobby had finished his story, Dr. Chien got up without saying a word and disappeared into the kitchen. Bobby sat in silence, listening as Dr. Chien rattled dishes. She had said nothing—no words, questions, accusations, threats, or anxious cries about why they'd brought her into their mess.

Dr. Chien returned from the kitchen with an antique, Polka Rose tea set for two, complete with biscuits. She placed the set on the table and served Bobby a cup of tea. "Earl Grey, okay?" she said as if the past hour and a half hadn't happened.

Bobby was nervous and confused until Dr. Chien sat down, took a sip of tea, and finally spoke. "When I was a little girl of about eight-years-old, I began to realize that we were different than the other families in the neighborhood and at school. Prior to that, I had been told by my mother to keep my eyes facing forward when I walked and not to pay attention to what was happening around me. She said a good rule of thumb was to look at the ground a few steps ahead of me, so I didn't trip while walking. I didn't know why, but I followed her instructions.

"On the first day of school that year, there was a blonde-haired girl named Heaven, I haven't said her name in ages, but I'll never forget it. She, for whatever reason, didn't like me, a fact she made very clear. On the playground, she made fun of my straight, black hair and slanted eyes, as she'd called them. She'd mock my eyes by pulling the corner of her eyes and making faces. Soon, her friends would join in.

"After recess was over, I told my teacher, who simply said that when you are different, you have to get used to people teasing you. I was so upset, but I decided that everything would be okay when I got home and told my mother.

"After school, I hurried home, and with tears in my eyes, told my mother what happened. She held me tightly and said that there were mean people in the world. She said they'd be mean to me because they were ugly inside, and when you're ugly inside, you act ugly outside. She said that the ugly people will try and hurt us, but we have to ignore them and keep on moving forward with our lives.

"There are beautiful people in the world, and those are the people that matter. Those are the people we talk to and make friends with. She told me to find some beautiful people to make friends with at school, and everything would be okay. Since then, I have seen a lot of ugly people in this city in all levels of school, police, at the hospital, and in all walks of life, but I have to say that some of the worst, the ugliest, are the police. Many of them abuse their position of power in ways that I never thought imaginable. If I see it then I know their leadership is aware of it, but they either don't care or they encourage it.

"As a physician I don't just see the effects of their abuse of power I have to attend to its results in the form of bruises and broken bones or worse, the gunshot wounds. I see it all, and it makes me incredibly angry. The worst part is there's no shielding our children from all of this ugliness. They are the casualties that I have to find a way to mend."

Bobby listened to her story. It was very similar to his own. He didn't realize that she'd experienced the same racism he had. He'd thought that the police brutality was limited to black people.

Dr. Chen continued, "it's so hard to ignore it, the racism and sexism, when it is so pervasive and ingrained in everyday life. I see kindhearted happy people turn into monsters when they are confronted with it when they aren't on guard. It changes people, wears them down until sometimes they turn into people, they themselves don't even recognize.

It has changed me." Dr. Chen's gaze had not moved from her tea, her gaze so intense the room disappeared, Bobby disappeared, there was nothing except darkness and her cup of tea.

"Are you sure the other men are all dead?" Dr. Chien asked.

Bobby was shocked out of his own reflection of pain by the matter-of-fact way she asked such a question, "Yes. The men I shot would've died instantly based on where my bullet hit them, and I checked the two crooked cops for the keys to their van when I was trying to get away, and their bodies were without life when I moved them around," Bobby replied.

She thought for a moment. "Bobby, what are you going to do next?"

It was a question he had not considered.

"Honestly, I have no idea. The only thing I've thought about since the shooting was getting John to safety. I was so worried about him that I hadn't considered what comes next."

They both sipped their Earl Grey and thought.

Bobby broke the momentary silence. "Our plan was for John to review the footage of the incident and get a copy to the press like we did the last time. That's not my area of expertise, so that will have to wait.

"The bigger problem is the crooked cops. You see, this was to be his initiation, so to speak, and he'll be the only one that survived. They'll no doubt know within very short order that Officer John is missing and assume that he had something to do with what went down. We should wait until he wakes up to figure out what to do next. I have no idea what we will tell the cops if they question us."

Dr. Chien nodded, not knowing either. She thought for a second, then looked at Bobby. "Maybe there's something I can do in the meantime. His absence is bound to cause suspicion and a search. I should call the school and the department to inform them that Officer John was in an accident and would need a couple of weeks off from work." She said she'd write him a doctor's note. She doubted anyone would put two and two together to realize the note was from her, hoping they'd assume it was another Dr. Chien.

"That's a good idea," Bobby said. "But what will you do if the crooked cops come here looking for him?"

Dr. Chien thought for a moment. "Lying is not my strong suit."

"Maybe that's when we start getting back to the truth?" Bobby continued, "tell them that he called you and said that he needed your help, he needed the help of someone he could trust. That's when you went to pick him up near the edge of the park, he was bleeding but didn't want to tell you what happened because he didn't want to get you involved or put you in danger. That after you successfully removed the bullet and got him to bed, he passed out and you never found out what happened. The one thing you knew for sure, what he was adamant about, was that you were not to take him to the hospital, so you assumed that he must have been involved in something top secret."

Dr. Chien stared into her tea as if searching for answers in a magic eight ball. "I guess it will have to do. One thing for sure, my fear and confusion will be authentic should they show up."

Bobby stood up. "I'll dispose of his bloody clothes here in case you need evidence of your work. I'll burn mine and clean up my car. It's lucky we have you on our side. If you weren't willing to help us, I don't know what I would've done."

She gave him a kind smile. "Bobby, what these officers are doing to us, and the rest of the community is criminal. They've been getting away with it for a long time. If you and John are willing to do something about it, then I'll help you. The anger and hatred I've dealt with at times was debilitating, and for a time I felt completely powerless. I may not be able to hold them accountable myself, using Bobby's words from his account of their actions, but I can help the two of you. You have my word, anything you need, I'm with you."

Bobby was relieved. "I should probably go. It's getting late. I have a lot to do before work tomorrow, and I can't be late. I can't give anyone reason to suspect my involvement in any of this." Bobby got up. Dr. Chien followed him upstairs, where he gathered all of Officer John's clothes.

Dr. Chien took them from him. "Let me, it needs to look like Officer John, and I did this all ourselves." Bobby took one long look at his friend before leaving.

As they descended the stairs Dr. Chien promised to let Bobby know as soon as Officer John woke so he could come over and they could all talk. She followed Bobby to the front door, gave him a warm hug, and said, "Never question what you're doing. The amount of pain these crooked cops have caused is immeasurable, and they must be stopped. If the courts won't do it, we, as citizens, have to. Maybe this is why you went into the military—not to protect the country from foreign threats, but to protect your community from the threats right here. Your father would be proud of you."

Chapter 26

Dr. Chien gathered Officer John's clothes along with her own and placed them in a plastic trash bag setting them outside the back door by the trash cans before heading to bed. The next morning, she contacted the police department and after explaining the situation was directed to HR where she was given a number to fax over her doctors note ordering Officer John's bedrest. She asked if she needed to send to contact the school to which the HR officer replied that it wasn't necessary and for her to let the doctor know that they had what they needed and politely thanked her for calling. It wasn't the first time someone had mistaken her for an office assistant or nurse, she no longer paid it any mind.

After hanging up she went to check on her patient and hung an IV. Officer John was still unresponsive but was alive and breathing well. Dr. Chien knew that all he needed was time, so she left him and continued her day as normal. A few hours later she was startled by a rather handsome man walking into her back yard while she tended to her garden, she was not expecting company.

"Hello," she recognized the man's face. "Chief Brice?" She asked, sure she recognized him from the television. "I almost didn't recognize you outside of your uniform. Are you here to see Officer John?"

"Asst. Chief Brice actually, I don't want to misrepresent myself," he said coyly recognizing when women found him attractive. It began in his late teenage years and never stopped. He naturally used it to his advantage. "Yes, I am. I am off duty but was obviously concerned about one of my men being injured. I went by his home but obviously he wasn't there, and this was the address on your doctor's note so I hoped I would find him here. You see patients here?" He asked in a non-threating way, but acknowledging that this was neither a clinic, hospital, nor even a doctor's office.

"Of course not, my days of practicing medicine are long over. I'm a friend of Officer John's and he called me asking for help. Rather unusual circumstance that he didn't want to talk about. I understand his line of work, so I helped him as best I could. He's upstairs resting."

"I see. Can I speak with him? I want to make sure that he has everything he needs and that he's ok."

Dr. Chien stood up from her garden. "You can certainly see him, but I'm afraid unless something's changed in the last few minutes, you won't be able to speak with him. He was in pain, so I gave him something to help him sleep. He won't be awake for hours, and rest is really what he needs right now."

A.C. Brice knew no matter what, he needed to see Officer John. He wasn't in uniform, in case he had to force his way in as he was not there on official business. "I'm here unofficially but wouldn't want you to question my identity even though you obviously recognize me." He pulled out his badge secure in its leather case and handed it to Dr. Chien. She looked at it more carefully than she wanted, she knew who he was and why he was there but played this game for his benefit.

"Thank you for your professionalism," she replied, as she handed the badge back. "Come this way, and please excuse my mess I wasn't expecting company."

A.C. Brice followed Dr. Chien through her immaculately clean house to Officer John's room. A. C. Brice stared at him for a moment before asking "what did you give him again?" Dr. Chien was prepared for inappropriate questions, she had been getting them all her life. "I'm sorry Chief Brice I cannot discuss Officer John's care with you that would be a violation of HIPPA. You can certainly visit, and I can give you some privacy but that's as much as I can do. A.C. Brice didn't bother correcting her assertion that he was chief he simply acknowledged her discretion, "Of course, if you don't mind, I would like a moment alone. It is difficult seeing one of my men injured."

Dr. Chien honored his request and left the two men alone. "I'll be downstairs, making us some tea. Please close the door when you leave." Dr. Chien descended the stairs worried what questions A. C. Brice would have for her once he was done testing Officer John's sleep.

A.C. Brice leaned into Officer John's ear. "John, can you hear me?" When there was no reply, he tried again. "John, you've got some fucking explaining to do." He said softly in his ear. Still no response. "Get your rest, you seem to need it, but know that we will talk when you're better." He studied Officer John's face for signs of any response and when there were none he left.

He descended the stairs and found Dr. Chien sitting on the couch with a magazine. "That was quick, I put some tea on if you'd like."

"No, thank you. I really must be going." A. C. Brice hoped that Officer John was smart enough not to tell Dr. Chien anything about the night in question. He had picked up on what she had said in the back yard about knowing about his line of work.

A. C. Brice assumed that Officer John had misled her to believe that he did more than just patrol the elementary school. She would be of no use to him. Just another woman impressed with a badge and a fancy story, he thought. "Please do let me know when he is better, this is my cell."

Dr. Chien took the card and offered what she was willing to do. "As soon as he is awake, I will let him know that you came by."

A.C. Brice gave her a nod. "That will be fine." As he walked towards the door followed closely by Dr. Chien he turned and as he exited the home had a few final words of advice for her. "Thank you for caring for him. It is best that you or he get in touch with me as soon as he is awake. There is a lot we need to discuss and the sooner we talk the better." He gave her another nod and walked down the stairs.

As soon as A.C. Brice car disappeared, leaving a cloud of dust, Dr. Chien dialed Bobby as she ascended the stairs to check on Officer John.

Before Bobby could complete his lengthy salutation, Dr. Chien interrupted him and began filling him in on A.C. Brice visit. Bobby listened without interruption. He detected some anxiousness in her voice even though she sounded surprisingly calm. He thought it best to let her say what she needed to say.

After he was fully briefed, he replied, "sounds like you did one heck of a job! I'm sure he came prepared for the worst. I would not be surprised if he were armed ready to kill if he wasn't assured that he and his men are safe. You clearly gave him what he needed without putting us in harm's way."

Bobby's logic was sound she thought. "That may be why he came in plain clothes. He didn't want his police car or uniform to be spotted in my neighborhood if we were found dead later on."

Dr. Chien thought for a moment. "We'll know for sure if he comes back. I told him that I would let Officer John know he came by when he was awake and alert."

Bobby asked the only question left unanswered. "Did you leave him alone for any period of time?" Dr. Chien was surprised by the question. "Yes, why?"

"He may have bugged your house, wherever he was you should assume it is not safe to talk freely in that room, just in case."

Dr. Chien hadn't considered that. "Hmmm, that's probably good advice. I'll keep that in mind. I'll let you know as soon as the patient is awake. I'll also keep an eye out for anymore surprise guests. No news is good news for the next couple of days."

Dr. Chien hung up the phone and walked into Officer John's room. She wasn't expecting to see anything but that didn't stop her eyes from looking around. She did not have a landline in this room so there was no phone to tap. With a heavy exhale she checked Officer John's bandages and exited the room that now made her slightly uncomfortable.

It was three days before Bobby finally received a text from Dr. Chien, saying simply, "He's awake."

Bobby got to Dr. Chien's house as quickly as he could. As he entered Dr. Chien's home, she began to fill him in. "He woke up a couple hours ago and is feeling strong. I suggest we move him to another room so that we can talk. I haven't said much to him in that room, I've been writing him notes and speaking for an audience that may or may not be there."

"Perfect," Bobby replied, as they headed up the stairs.

Officer John was in bed, eating soup, but stopped when Bobby walked into the room with his index finger pressed against his lips. He moved Officer John's tray and turned to Dr. Chien and did a walking motion with his fingers.

Dr. Chien nodded and continued her performance for whomever might be listening, "might be a good idea for you to see if you're strong enough to walk." Officer John slowly turned and with their help began to get out of bed. They escorted him down the hall to another bedroom.

"What happened?" Officer John asked.

"They turned on you. The minute you turned around and began walking back to the van, they shot all three of you in the back."

"Fuck!" Officer John exclaimed. "Did they get away?"

"No. I killed all three of those sons of bitches. I wasn't going to let them get away with what they'd done. I left everything there at the dock and brought you here. There hasn't been anything about it on the news."

Officer John stared at Bobby in disbelief. "You brought a gun? That wasn't part of the plan."

Bobby looked at his friend, confused. "I don't trust any of those crooked cops. I don't know what they're going to do next. Of course, I brought a gun. Marines are always prepared for whatever might go down. I made sure I was close enough to protect you, should something like this happen. I hoped it wouldn't, but I prepared for the worst."

"Well," Officer John said. "I'm grateful you were prepared, otherwise, I'd be dead on the dock with the others. I need to get to the station and find out what's going on."

Bobby thought the same thing, but it was Dr. Chien who asked the obvious question. "What do you do now?"

Officer John sat up in his new bed, looking weak and wincing slightly in pain. "We may have blown the opportunity to get in with the crooked cops. Based on what's happened I don't think so, but I'll find out."

"There's one other thing, we haven't sent out the footage I took. I don't know how to edit the footage. Also, I removed all of our equipment, the other pictures, and any old footage from your shed, I was worried they would find it if they went to your house. I figured it's easy enough to put back later. It shows, clear as day, what went down, so there is no way they can explain their way out of this."

Officer John thought for a moment, "We may have to hold onto that indefinitely, it's one thing for me to have survived the incident. It's another thing for the incident to have been recorded and I am not implicated or recorded at all. That isn't a coincidence that's evidence that I was involved. I'd be a dead man walking."

"I think the only reason I am still alive is there are questions left unanswered and I am the only one alive to answer them. Internal affairs will be all over this, possibly the FBI as well. I have to make contact with A.C. Brice asap. Figure out what he is thinking and what's going on with the investigation."

Dr. Chien interjected, "that's why we put everything on hold. I called your work and reported that you were involved in an accident, so neither the police nor the school are looking for you, but those crooked cops are definitely looking to find out what happened, which is Why A.C. Brice came here."

Officer John thought for a long while. "I'll tell them what happened from my perspective and at the same time corroborate your version of events," he said looking at Dr. Chien.

Bobby and Dr. Chien looked at each other and then at Officer John. Before they could say anything, Officer John answered, "I know it's dangerous but at this point we don't have a lot of options. I just have to be convincing because if they suspect anything, I'm as good as dead. It certainly helps that I was shot in the back too. Thank you both for the quick thinking, it saved my life.

"I've got to get home and make some calls. They've no doubt been to my house, so I need to give them my dog and pony show, asap, in order to eliminate suspicion. I'll have to keep a low profile before communicating with the two of you again, at least until I know what's what."

Bobby allowed the silence to hang for a few minutes before breaking it. "You're going to need my gun and bullets; in case they need proof that you shot them fighting for your life. Let's hope they buy it! I'm going to see if there's any word on the street about the incident, see if anyone saw or suspects me in any of this. It'll be pretty obvious if they do." Bobby turned to Dr. Chien. "I can't thank you enough."

She looked at the two men. "We're doing the right thing. Someone has to look out for the innocent. Someone has to hold these crooked cops accountable. I'm happy to do my part, whatever you need."

After helping Officer John into his car, Bobby left Dr. Chien's house as he'd arrived—on foot, through the back. He walked to the bus station, avoiding busy streets, and took the bus home. Bobby knew that no one would pay much attention to him there.

Chapter 27

Officer John wasn't looking forward to having to go up the stairs and into his house without help, but he was going to have to manage. He turned on his street and immediately recognized the car parked across the street from his house. It was one of the crooked cops, waiting for him to get home. They had, no doubt, been waiting for him ever since they'd discovered the deal had gone bust. He pulled into the driveway, opened the door, sat in the car, and waited. As he suspected, two men came over to the car to inform them they were waiting for him.

"Well, here I am," he said.

One of them replied, "You've got some explaining to do."

"*I've* got explaining to do? One of you motherfuckers has some explaining to do!" Officer John quickly replied.

"Watch it," one of them said.

"Are you gonna help me out of the goddamned car? In case you brainiac's can't tell, I've been shot!"

"Save your story for the boss," one of them said as he reached into the car, helped Officer John out, and escorted him to their vehicle. He didn't need to fake grunts when they moved him. His pain medication wasn't strong enough for their manhandling.

Once in the car with its blackened-out windows Officer John was handed a hood to put over his head, he complied without argument. After what seemed like approximately half an hour, the car stopped, and Officer John was escorted out of the car. With the hood still on and his vision completely blocked, he was escorted into a building and placed in a chair. His heart beat a mile per minute. The only thing he could think about was if he was going to die or not.

The hood suddenly removed, Officer John squinted at the flash of light that came in contrast to the darkness, taking a second for his eyes to adjust he saw a crooked cop whose name he couldn't recall but who he'd known from his past, standing before him. His arms were crossed, and he was staring at Officer John.

"You, okay?" he asked.

"I'd be lying if I said yes, but it's no thanks to your associates, they double-crossed us, shot us in the back the minute we did the exchange. It was a set-up from the word go. Who set up the deal? If this is what I have to look forward to, I'm thinking I need to go back to my uneventful life at school. No amount of money will help me if I'm dead."

"We're trying to figure out that one, too. We've done deals with them before without problem, so we're not sure what the fuck is going on. Something must've set them off, why don't you tell me exactly what happened?"

While he spoke, Officer John looked around. He was in some sort of warehouse that seemed fully operational but was abandoned for the moment with the exception of the men that surrounded him. Most wore uniforms but some did not. He recognized three of the fourteen men surrounding him.

"I know you, when I was doing patrol. We were both rookies, but you worked narcotics." The Crooked Cop responded, "I know you, John. I was surprised to hear that you of all people wanted to earn some cash doing some work on the side," He looked at Officer John with suspicion.

"Part of it is money, the other is just getting out of that house full of memories of a life I no longer have."

The crooked cop looked unconvinced, "Mitchell's my name."

"That's right, you helped me out back in the day, before I came clean and stopped using, seems like a lifetime ago."

"It was. So, what happened?"

"Like I said, we were doing the exchange, they showed us the inside of the briefcase, we gave them the money, and they asked why the order was so small this time. I didn't know anything different, so I looked at Officer Grant and he said that we ordered what we needed. Then one of the guys asked if we had another supplier, that we've never had an order this small before. Grant didn't seem to know what was going on or why. They were asking so many questions. He said there were some problems within the department that we were taking care of, slowed things down."

Mitchell interrupted the story with an exchange with one of the men in plain clothes that Officer John did not know. "Fuck, he should have kept his mouth shut. They can't know about our shit. We have to fix this."

The only reply was, "understood."

Mitchell refocused on Officer John, "and then?"

"So, they took the money and gave us the briefcase and we tried to leave when they shot us. I was hit but was conscious, so I returned fire. I wasn't going to wait around for help because I definitely couldn't explain what had happened, so I called out to Grant and Jones, but they didn't answer so I called my girlfriend for help. Made my way towards the street where she picked me up. That's really the last thing I remember until I woke up this morning at her place."

Officer John looked at Mitchell, "why would they shoot us?" He knew he was in no position to ask questions but that seemed like a fair one even in his position.

"That's what we are going to find out. What did you tell your girlfriend?"

"She knows that I'm an officer and that some of the work I do puts me in harm's way. I told her a long time ago not to ask too many questions for her own safety. I didn't tell her anything because she wouldn't ask."

Mitchell got up, walked around the desk, and sat directly in front of Officer John. "Why didn't you get the money and our drugs?"

Finally—the question Officer John had actually been prepared to answer. "I wasn't worrying about drugs or money. I was worried for my life. I needed medical attention and it wasn't like I could call for backup or go to a hospital. People know I'm a police officer. They'd have put two and two together, and that would've been the end of me. I'm alive because that doctor was home. If I had to wait for these fucks," Officer John motioned to the two crooked cops that had brought him there. "I'd be dead. The truth of the matter is that none of this fuck-up was my fault, so I'm sitting here wondering why I'm being asked all these questions. I've got a bunch of unanswered questions of my own, like why did they turn on us if you've worked with them before? Why did they try and fuck us over? And why didn't anyone see this coming?"

Officer John felt it was the right time to exercise a little aggression. He had every right to be angry, this was their deal. He was there to make a little money and got shot.

Mitchell got up, smiled, and walked back around the desk. "What makes you think we didn't?" he said as he sat down. "We know every fucking move before it happens, and most times, we set the shit into motion. We had some unfinished business with those pricks. They're just lucky they shot our boys before we shot them. That was the plan, but it didn't quite work out the way we'd planned. Grant should have just kept his mouth shut, done the deal, so Jones could have killed those bastards.

"We're pretty sure they are behind the murders of our guys, so we wanted to send a message. The good thing is you delivered the message. The bad thing is our guys got hit in the process. They needed to know that if you fuck with us, you'll pay."

Officer John all of a sudden had difficulty swallowing. "Would've been nice if someone told me," He replied. He looked at the blank faces of the men surrounding him and realized Mitchell was lying, they had no idea the deal was a setup and if not for Bobby they would look weak and incompetent to every dealer they worked with. He and Bobby had just saved their ass and they were afraid of what was going on, he thought, why else would they need fourteen men to question him.

He began to think that he might just make it out of there alive and in a better position than he could have ever imagined.

"Go home. We'll give you information on an as-needed basis," Mitchell said. "Get some rest. We have a lot of business that needs attending to.

"Nice job taking care of the garbage the other night. Those boys get away with our money and the drugs, and we look weak. That's a liability we cannot afford. We'll be in touch."

Officer John's escorts got up from their chairs. One of them pulled the hood from out of his back pocket. Almost imperceptible to anyone except John and his escort, Mitchell waved his index finger, and the hood was put away. Officer John was officially one of them, and safe… at least for the time being. They'd bought his story and created one of their own.

As Officer John was chauffeured back home, he realized how close a call this experience was, and he and Bobby had not been engaged in their quest for very long. He wondered if he was strong enough for the journey ahead.

What are we doing, he thought? *I'm too old for this.*

He looked at the two crooked cops in the front seats, one at least twenty years younger than him. The other maybe thirty. What was he doing running with these guys? Record and report had quickly turned into act and engage. *Am I ready for all of this, ready for what's to come?*

He glared at the driver in the rear-view mirror. Noticing that he did not look back, once. Officer John was struck by their arrogance. They considered him no threat at all because of his age. When they looked at him, they saw an old man. That's why they dismissed him as the source of the ambush at the dock. He might be an old man, but he might still have a few tricks in him.

In that moment of reflection his wife came to his mind again. Her smile, her kindness, her admiration always on display for the work Officer John did. Just as when she was alive, her presence helped him think and see things clearly. Their dismissing him will be their downfall. *Should this lead to my death,* he thought. *At least I will be reunited with my beloved.*

It wasn't until he was on his couch and his two escorts left that he finally let out a sigh of relief. He was exhausted, hungry, and in pain, but he was more tired than hungry. He took some Advil and went to bed. Saying goodnight to his beloved as he drifted to sleep.

In the morning, he reached out to Bobby and Dr. Chien with a three-word text.

"We are good."

Dr. Chien replied, "I'd like to see you two today if possible. Come by for dinner at six."

Officer John was relieved and energized in a way he hadn't been in years, despite being shot a few days ago. Although he wasn't returning to work for at least a week, he decided to go to see his kids as they left school. It had only been a few days, but he missed them.

He arrived about thirty minutes before the end of the school day and went to the office to chat with his friends and end the worry they no doubt felt about him. Everyone was happy to see him and to learn that he was okay. He explained that he'd had an accident at home, and he'd be off work for another few weeks per doctor's orders, but that he'd still come by to see the kids. He definitely wasn't ready to be on his feet all day, and if he was honest with himself, he'd already begun to feel the pain of the gunshot wound after only being on his feet for a little over an hour.

After chatting for a while, he decided to head out to his normal spot to see the kids off and exchange pleasantries with the parents when they picked up their little ones. He was really enjoying himself and all the gentle hugs he was getting until he saw little Arvin coming toward him.

Arvin had a look about him that Officer John knew all too well, he'd been hurt by his father—one of the crooked cops—again. Arvin walked past Officer John, keeping his gaze down, his sad, confused face numb because of the beatings he'd been subjected to, which had happened so many times for reasons he never understood. He said goodbye to Officer John as he walked by as if he hadn't been gone at all.

Officer John's blood began to boil. "This ends today," he told himself in no uncertain terms.

Chapter 28

Officer John and Bobby arrived at Dr. Chien's house at exactly 6:00pm. She greeted them at the door bringing with her the smell of home cooking.

"How are you feeling John? You're looking a lot better."

"I feel pretty good. I haven't been standing too much, which helps. I went to the school and saw my kids … that helped a lot."

They entered Dr. Chien's dining room. The table set with attractive China, polished silver, elegant napkins, and a tablecloth. The impressive presentation did not go unnoticed.

"Wow." Both Officer John and Bobby chorused.

Bobby continued, "are you having people over after we leave?"

Dr. Chien chuckled. "Should I pour you some Glenlivet or would you like wine? We are having pasta." Bobby, becoming more accustomed to his comate's rituals knew that saying no to either was not an option. "Glenlivet, I'll fill the water glasses."

Bobby followed Dr. Chien into the kitchen, pulled a pitcher of water from the refrigerator and began to fill the glasses on the table. "Is there something on your mind Dr. Chien?"

She was going to address what was on her mind, but not while she was cooking. "Let me get this prepared and us sitting before we get into that." Officer John and Bobby looked at each other with curiosity.

"Well, then I'll talk while you finish up," John said and began filling them in on what had happened the previous day with the crooked cops.

He left no detail out, including his concerns with his own involvement and his conclusions.

Dr. Chien finally spoke, "that's what I was concerned about, and why I asked you two over. I want to make sure that you were thinking your actions through. I'm not suggesting what you're doing is wrong, just that it is extremely dangerous, and we already had one very close call."

Officer John replied looking at Dr. Chien but was speaking to them both. "I'm concerned about myself as well." Dr. Chien interjected, "I'm not talking just about you." Officer John continued, "look at Bobby, he is every bit the soldier that he was a year ago when he was in the Marines. He acted quickly and decisively when I was shot so I'm not concerned about his abilities, I'm concerned about mine. But we don't have a lot of options. Me being the insider while Bobby does the heavy lifting is out best chance at making a difference. I'm willing to take the risk if the two of you are because let's face it, the cops and A.C.Brice already know about you Dr. Chien, we just need to make sure that they don't find out about our relationship with Bobby until we decide, and have a plan—"

Bobby interrupted. "Whatever you're cooking can you make sure it's not burning. It smells really good and that would be the real tragedy."

Dr. Chien disappeared back into the kitchen followed by Bobby as Officer John stared into his drink. They reemerged momentarily; hands full of dishes prepared by Dr. Chien. They prepared their plates with warm gazes and smiles but no words. Prior to taking their first bite Officer John raised his glass for a toast. "To good friends…"

Officer John picked up the conversation where he left off. "I know it's risky, but I have turned a blind eye to more than I would like to admit. I got so good at ignoring what was happening that I no longer saw it until Bobby forced me to see it. I reconciled in my mind that if I focused on my kids and their families, I was doing everything I could. That was the lie I convinced myself of. The truth is a lot more complicated but that was a lie, nonetheless. I know that years ago I could have begun liking for a way to confront the crooked cops. I could have talked to people, formed a coalition a long time ago and worked with internal affairs or the police union. If I wanted to, I could have done something, but the truth is I was afraid. I had too much to lose."

Bobby and Dr. Chien listened intently.

"I had my extended family and my wife, and I was too concerned with putting their lives at risk, so I ignored what was happening to my friends and neighbors." He looked up from his drink and into Bobbies eyes. I have often wondered if I could have prevented your father's death and the suffering of a lot of people in our community."

"Don't do that to yourself," Bobby responded gently.

Officer John's tone changed. "I don't punish myself for the past. I mention it only to clarify why I'm determined to continue what we started, regardless of the risks. I'm not going to let fear stop me this time. Plus, I have the best doctor in the state looking out for me and a true American hero by my side. We can't lose."

Bobby and Dr. Chien smiled.

"It's done then, let's put the topic to rest and enjoy this wonderful dinner. Dr. Chien, you have outdone yourself," Bobby replied. Officer John concurred.

"My pleasure," Dr. Chien answered, and the conversation shifted to a more pleasant topic.

Despite the good times presented during dinner, Officer John's mind went back to Arvin and his mother. It was getting too late to discuss with Bobby, so he decided it better to wait until tomorrow. The two men approached the front door with full bellies and light hearted chatter, followed by Dr. Chien who against her objections had a clean kitchen thanks to her guests who insistence on helping her clean before they left. The evening ended on a high note with warm hugs and thanks and although the topic would not come up again, they would continue to worry about Office John's safety.

Chapter 29

Officer John texted Bobby the following afternoon. Checking to make sure that he was home so that they could talk. Bobby was surprised to hear from his friend, but excited to hear what news he had to share. Bobby was finally fulfilling his purpose, helping his community, which had been terrorized by the crooked police department for as long as he could remember—he was ready for their next mission.

Bobby bombarded Officer John with questions from his first step into the small apartment. "What's going on? I wasn't expecting to hear from you today. Not that I mind at all. Did something happen? I was just thinking which one of those assholes are we going to nail to the wall next?" He went on talking as they entered Bobby's living room, and Bobby finally noticed his friend wasn't listening. Something was wrong. Bobby paused, sat on his couch, and waited for Officer John to speak.

Officer John looked at him and asked if he had any scotch or whiskey.

He didn't. He wasn't really a consumer of a lot of alcohol. He tended to buy significantly cheaper stuff or nothing at all. "I have some Sailor Jerry's if you want it," Bobby replied.

Officer John wasn't interested. He began recounting all the times he'd seen Arvin or his mother with bruises, and the many times he'd gently tried to get her to get some help.

Bobby interrupted his friend. "Which of these asshole crooked cops is a wife-beating child abuser?" He had one other question for Officer

John, and he tried to ask it in a non-judgmental but very direct way. "Why didn't *you* ever do anything about it?"

Officer John let out a sigh. "I approached his wife, Sarah, on multiple occasions at the school asking about her son's bruises, and if there was some aid I could provide when she made excuses. I gave her my personal cell, but she never called."

Officer John was silent as he thought about how, if this had happened in his youth, he might have been strong enough to take *Crooked Cop #3* on himself, beat the shit out of him, and let him know that if he touched either one of them again, he'd regret it.

"In my youth, maybe I'd have been stronger and done something." Even as he said it, he wasn't sure it was true. He'd never been what you'd call an imposing figure, and he wasn't particularly skilled in combat. He continued answering Bobby's questions, a bit of defeat in his voice. "I'm too old for many things, including giving this asshole the royal beat-down he deserves!"

"These guys are just bullies hiding behind a badge waiting for someone to stand up to them so they can arrest them. That's why they put the cuffs on first so you can't fight back. No real man takes pleasure hitting someone who cannot defend themselves. They are cowards." Bobby looked at his friend.

"I'm not too old," he said. "How well do you know this guy? Given the opportunity, I'm happy to talk to him." Bobby said in a way Officer John understood.

Thinking for a moment, Officer John confessed what he was thinking, "I'm not sure talking to him or roughing him up is going to make that big a difference. He's an addict and quite frankly will be that way till the day he dies. Thing is, I know him very well, I know that the department has had him get help many times and each time he goes back to the same habits after a few months. I know the union leadership protects him from having to face any real consequences for his actions, which make him even more of a threat.

"I never thought I'd say this but there's really only one way to deal with this guy."

Bobby interrupted so that Office John didn't have to say what he was thinking, "His drinking might be something we can use to our advantage."

Officer John thought, *yes, we can.*

"He works out regularly and is very fit, which could pose a challenge. He is a proud white supremacist and trains with them more often than not, so we need to be careful how and when we engage him, but alcohol is a definite weakness. We need to make whatever happens look like an accident, a fistfight would cause a ton of suspicion. Even in your physical condition Bobby, I'm not sure you'd win."

Bobby wasn't concerned about his physical abilities against some small-city cop, he'd dealt with bullies before in the military, and he knew, from experience, how to handle them.

What he was concerned about were the white supremacists in the city and what they would do to the Black community if they found one of their own attacked.

"Where does he hang out? Where's his favorite drinking spot?"

"Hooters on Jefferson Ave. He's there every other Thursday thru Sunday because they have cheap drinks and that's when he's off."

"Near the old mall?" Bobby asked.

"That's the one," Officer John replied.

"Let me think about this one," Bobby said. "I have an idea but need to do a little research. I'll call you when I have something, in the meantime try not to think about this a-hole. We'll deal with him soon enough."

Bobby followed Officer John to the door. "You're walking better, your strength back to 100% already?"

Officer John opened the door and looked back at Bobby. "Not even close but I'm too angry to think about it. Maybe anger, not laughter, is the best medicine."

Bobby put his hand on Officer John's shoulder. "We'll get him. Don't lose yourself to anger, trust me, it's a long road to come back from. Plus, we can do something about this so no reason to let it eat you up inside."

Officer John gave Bobby a nod and left with a feeling of hope.

Bobby had done security at the mall across from the Hooters several times since he started working for the security company.

For whatever reason, the company rotated the assignments of security guards pretty regularly. At first, Bobby thought they'd lost some contracts, but then he'd end up back at a location at which he'd worked months before. His coworkers told him it was a union requirement that everyone had an equal opportunity at jobs because some jobs were easier on the security guard than others. Bobby thought it ridiculous, but he *was* new and didn't have the same experience as the others. He had to pay union dues out of every check, so they were, at least, doing something with his money, he thought. The union didn't do a lot for him personally, if he were, to be honest, it was more of a liability at his company than an asset, but in this instance, rotating job sites worked in his favor.

There were several sites that his security company provided services that were closer than the mall, but because of the union requirements, Bobby had spent several months at the vacated mall. There were plans for tearing it down and building housing on the property, but that was over a year away, so they protected it from vandals and the homeless.

Bobby knew what he needed to do. He had everything he needed. He decided not to waste any time and got in his car heading to the mall to make sure that nothing had changed since he hadn't been there in at least a month.

Bobby exited onto Mercury Blvd and pulled onto the service road across from the abandoned mall. He dared not go into the parking lot because the security personnel working that day might recognize his car. He pulled out his small binoculars and confirmed that there weren't any changes to the structure and the patrol was nowhere in sight.

I have the where, now I need the when. With that thought he shifted into drive and headed to the security office.

Bobby entered the security office and was greeted by the admin at the front desk.

"Bobby, good to see you. Do you have an appointment with someone?"

"No, just came by for a copy of the schedule. I lost my copy and didn't want to miss anything. I was in the neighborhood and thought it would be nice to see everyone. So, figured I'd pop in."

Bobby knew that most everyone would be out by now, and there would only be a few people in the building.

"I'm sorry, hun, it's just me and the supervisors on duty. They're in a meeting, but I'm sure happy to see you."

Bobby was half listening as he entered his username and password into the computer and printed the entire schedule for the month, which included who would be on patrol at the mall. He grabbed the schedule from the printer and forced himself to listen to the chatty admin. She was responsible for answering all the phone calls, so he knew his opportunity to leave was just a phone call away.

Nodding and answering pointless questions with a smile, the phone finally rang. As she answered, he stood up and mouthed, "talk to you later, good seeing you."

She covered the phone with her hand. "Thanks for coming by and saying hello! Good seeing you, Bobby."

As soon as Bobby was in his car, he checked the schedule at work to see who was working the next few Thursdays. It was someone he knew, so he'd have to be careful that they never saw him. The guards took their jobs seriously because they had families to support and needed their low-wage jobs, so they constantly patrolled to keep the site under close supervision. It wasn't going to be easy. What would, however, work in his favor was that the mall was so large. It took a while to circle the entire perimeter.

Chapter 30

Bobby now had the where and when to execute his plan, but he needed to make sure of one detail that would make or break his plan and force him to start over from scratch. He headed back to the mall.

This time pulling into the Wendy's parking lot, he bought a sundae so he could park without drawing attention. As the ice cream melted, he watched the security patrol circle the lot a few times until he was confident that if he was in and out within ten minutes he would not be seen.

He got out of the car and walked across the street to the shipping and receiving area of the mall. There he saw what he needed, the entrance they used for restroom breaks was open. He went in and checked the service elevator that granted access to the roof. Oftentimes, the guards would take the elevator to the top and eat their dinner on breaks. It was actually the perfect spot because you could see half the lot from their spot.

After confirming nothing had changed, he made his way back to his car and headed for Officer John's. He texted to confirm he was home and arrived shortly after receiving confirmation. Bobby sat and reviewed his plan with Officer John and waited for any concerns Officer John had.

"Have you thought about doing this before? You came up with this in really short order."

"No, but often when I'm up there on the roof of the mall it runs through my mind. Since there is no reason for delay, I'll attempt to put my plan into motion on Thursday, just make sure you are home so I can call you after, as my alibi," Bobby responded.

Thursday finally came and Bobby had a nervous energy all day. It made his workday go faster which was a welcomed change. After work he made his way home where he took a nap, he wanted to be alert for his mission happening later that night. At seven o'clock fully refreshed and alert he headed to Hooters.

It had been a long time since he'd been in a place like Hooters but not much had changed. He scanned the restaurant for *Crooked Cop #3*. He hadn't arrived yet, which was good. He needed time to figure out how to execute his plan. Bobby searched for a single guy with whom to strike up a conversation. There were more than enough guys in the bar area, so he needed to find the right one, someone not too distracted by the beautiful women or the game on the television, someone dressed casually and approachable—a working man, just like him.

As Bobby made his way to the bar, he heard his name being called. He turned around. If it were the wrong friend calling him, his whole plan would be ruined. His barber, Fred, was standing near the bar, giving him a wave. *This is bad,* Bobby thought.

He walked over and extended a handshake while scanning the table. They already had the check. A ten-dollar bill was sitting in the tray.

Bobby's tension subsided a little. "Hey, man—what you doing here?" Bobby asked.

Fred motioned to the young lady with him who was still sitting. "Jasmine and I were just grabbing a bite before we head to the movies. What are you up to?"

Bobby shook Jasmine's hand and apologized for the interruption. As they engaged in small talk, in walked *Crooked Cop #3*. Bobby watched him take a seat near the dartboard, which was perfect. He returned his attention to Fred and Jasmine. "I don't want to keep you from your movie. It was nice meeting you, Jasmine. I think my friend is in the bar area. Were you all leaving? I can see if they're still over there, maybe we can play some pool?" Bobby gambled their movie wouldn't allow for it.

"We were just leaving, actually, but if your friend isn't here, we can wait a few," Fred said.

Bobby assured them it wasn't necessary. He put his hand on Fred's shoulder and took a step toward the door.

Fred reached for Jasmine as they headed for the door.

Bobby kept an eye on *Crooked Cop #3* as he moved to the bar and ordered a beer. He'd need to be patient.

He noticed there was a Virginia Tech game on the television, and he thought about his sister, wondering if she'd lost her voice yet. It was the third quarter, and Tech was up. She'd have been screaming for a good hour and a half by then.

Bobby scanned the bar for what would be his perfect guy, someone watching the Tech game. There, at the end of the bar, he saw a guy wearing a VT hat, and he began making his way toward him.

"They gonna pull it out?" Bobby asked his new friend.

"I hope so, but there's still a lot of game to play," the man replied.

Bobby continued the light banter by introducing himself. "I'm Bobby. Pretty sure my sister is at the game. She's an alumnus. I've been there a few times with her. She goes to every home game." They continued their banter as Bobby kept a keen eye on *Crooked Cop #3*. By the time the game was over, Tech had won. Bobby had a new best friend, and just as he'd hoped, *Crooked Cop #3* had more than a few drinks in him.

He asked his new friend—who also had a few in him—if he wanted to play darts as a way to get closer to *Crooked Cop #3*, and he began to lay his trap.

Bobby let the first couple rounds of darts pass before starting to whistle *Dixie*. "Funny how I whistle this racist song," he said. "You know, the song originated in the 1850s and quickly became popular for some reason. During the American Civil War, it was the unofficial national anthem of the Confederate States." Bobby kept an eye on *Crooked Cop #3* who was dressed in jeans and a plaid shirt.

Bobby continued, "It's weird that a black man would whistle a tune dating back to his enslavement, that basically celebrates it.

"*Oh, I wish I was in the land of cotton,*" Bobby sang. "*Old times there are not forgotten. Look away, look away, look away Dixieland.*"

As Bobby sang, his new friend seemed completely confused, but he smiled politely and kept playing his darts.

Bobby continued to lay his trap. "I don't know. I think I would've been killed on a plantation. No way I'm gonna let some white slave-owners work me like an animal for no wage, rape my woman, and kill my brothers and sisters. They'd have had to kill me first." Bobby watched to see if his target was taking the bait. Sure enough, he was as red as an apple.

Bobby watched and listened as *Crooked Cop #3* poured himself another beer from the pitcher and slammed it on the table causing it to splash and make a mess. When the waitress hurried over to clean it up, he waived her away and barked at her "leave it."

Bobby had just begun to wonder how much longer this charade would have to continue when his unasked question was answered: "People knew their place back then, if they stepped out of line, they paid for it." *Crooked Cop #3* said after having heard enough of Bobby's bullshit. There to escape and forget about people like Bobby but now Bobby's constant talking was interfering with his buzz. "Not like now where y'all think you're worth more than a hill of beans. I'd kill every one of you if I could. Only thing you know how to do is steal, take drugs, or cause trouble."

Bobby looked over at him and smiled. "I'd expect that response from a piece of shit like you," he said. Bobby pushed his darts into the board and said to his new friend. "I'm done. It smells over here." And he walked away, knowing *Crooked Cop #3* wasn't about to let his words go without a fight.

He paid his tab without waiting for the check but leaving twice as much as the bill should have been. He told the bartender, "This should cover it. I'm gonna get out of here before my friend over there starts some trouble." Bobby motioned at *Crooked Cop #3*, who was sitting alone, looking at him with fire in his eyes.

The bartender replied, "That's a good idea, son. He's a cop and not one you want to cross."

Bobby walked out of the bar, leaving his jacket on the chair next to the dartboard, went up the street, and called Officer John. When his friend answered, he said, "No matter what, don't hang up." He propped his phone against a light post and looked back to see if *Crooked Cop #3* was following him.

When he appeared outside the bar, Bobby jogged across the street slow enough for *Crooked Cop #3* to see him and follow. He ran faster than Bobby, gaining ground on him. When Bobby was sure he was coming for him, he ran as fast as he could toward the mall, keeping an eye out for security.

He went in through a door he knew security left open so they could easily get in and out when it got too cold. If one of the guards were there, he'd alert them that a crazy, drunken cop was after him. To his luck, no one there. He made his way to the service elevator and pushed the button feverishly.

Crooked Cop #3 came in through the same door and made a beeline for Bobby.

The doors opened. Bobby jumped in, pushed 'R', and held the door, waiting for his prey.

Crooked Cop #3 came in like a flash and took a swing at Bobby, who swung his right arm, diverting the punch.

Bobby grabbed the back of *Crooked Cop #3*'s jacket with his left hand and in one motion, had him on the ground as the doors closed.

The elevator began to ascend, and *Crooked Cop #3* flipped over onto his back and kicked Bobby's legs out from under him. He reached for Bobby, who was on the ground, waiting for his next move. When he got within reach, Bobby grabbed him, pulled him to the ground, and held him tightly to restrict his movement. As the two men struggled on the elevator floor, the doors opened to the roof.

Bobby released *Crooked Cop #3* and shoved him against the far wall of the elevator. Using him for leverage as if he were a starting block, Bobby launched himself into a sprint toward the edge of the building.

Crooked Cop #3 followed him out onto the roof in quick pursuit.

When Bobby got close to the edge, he stopped and turned to face *Crooked Cop #3*, who was running clumsily toward him. Bobby steadied himself and waited for his next move. When *Crooked Cop #3* was close enough to engage, he took another swing at Bobby, who ducked, grabbed the back of his jacket, and gave him a pull. With a forearm to his back, he sent *Crooked Cop #3* flying off the roof. Bobby called out the last words he hoped that vile person would ever hear. "Wife beating child abusers don't belong on the police force!"

Bobby stood near the edge of the mall's roof in the darkness, broken by the light of the moon, stars, and lights illuminating the parking lot below him. His view was good for several miles, but he didn't enjoy any of it. His only hesitation was to ensure that *Crooked Cop #3*, who now lay on the concrete three stories below, wasn't moving. Bobby held his stare for about five seconds before making his way to the elevator.

The doors opened on ground level, and he looked slowly around to check for security. He heard voices, but he didn't see anyone, so he went toward the exit.

"Someone fell from the roof!" came a voice from around the corner.

Bobby ran as fast as he could toward the street, hoping he wouldn't be seen. He made his way back to his phone, said to Officer John. "I'll be by soon."

He headed back toward the Hooters, wiping the sweat from his face before entering. Bobby put on a fake smile as he walked in and made his way to the bartender. "I forgot my jacket," he said. "Is my friend still here? I don't need any trouble from no cop."

The bartender seemed happy to see him. "He went out right after you did, I was afraid he might be going after you."

Bobby scowled, but then he resumed his charade and fake smile. "I thought he might follow, so as soon as I got out of the door, I made my way up Jefferson Avenue out of view. Guess I'm lucky he didn't see me." Bobby picked up his jacket. "If he comes back, don't let him know I came back."

The bartender smiled. "Of course not. He causes enough trouble in here as it is. He gets drunk on the regular and drives home. Crazy how guys like him drive drunk, and nothing happens, but some young kid does it once, and they're dead."

Bobby turned to leave, offering him some parting words. "Some guys are just lucky, I guess."

He walked all the way to Officer John's house. It was far, but Bobby didn't want his car spotted on any traffic cameras. When his friend answered the door, Bobby greeted him with two words, "It's done.

Chapter 31

Bobby stood in the doorway of Officer John's house, expecting his friend to let him in. Instead, he suggested they go for a walk in the neighborhood. Bobby was taken aback because he didn't think it a good idea for them to be seen together too much in public.

As they walked down the porch steps and turned onto the sidewalk, Officer John recounted the strange meeting he'd had that day with some of the crooked cops on the force. They'd been discussing the murder of cops on the force, how everyone was a suspect, and that whoever it was must either be an officer or getting help from an officer. He recounted that he'd had the funny feeling that he was watching a performance.

One of the crooked cops had 'went to the bathroom,' while another had 'asked for a beer.' He made air quotes with his fingers as he explained the unusual interactions to Bobby. Officer John also told him he suspected his house might be bugged, and they'd have to meet someplace else. They agreed to meet either at Bobby's apartment or Dr. Chien's house until further notice.

Bobby began recounting the night he had.

Officer John was relieved Bobby hadn't been hurt. "Sounds like your plan worked exactly as you designed. Nice work soldier."

Bobby nodded, but he was there for a purpose—he had business to discuss. Bobby was certain there'd be a pretty intense investigation before they labeled the death an accident. He'd no doubt be at the center, considering he'd been interacting with *Crooked Cop #3* and that Bobby was the reason he'd left the restaurant in the first place. Although he'd come back for his jacket, as they reconstructed the timeline, they'd no doubt see that Bobby would've had plenty of time to push the officer off the roof and get back to the restaurant to pick up his jacket. He explained that he was careful not to have entered into a fight with *Crooked Cop #3*, so there wouldn't be any bruising. He would always use the phone conversation as his alibi.

They'd technically been on the phone for the entirety of Bobby's alibi, and the phone records would validate it. There was just one detail left to work out, as Bobby stopped walking and turned to his friend.

"What reason would we have to talk on the phone for that long? We have been friends for a long time, but that particular conversation would stick out if there were ever any analysis of our conversations. The length of that particular call wouldn't escape the attention of a skilled lawyer and given the circumstances we have to assume that the best will work the case."

The two men began walking again. "We need a solid story to explain away the question that will certainly come up," Bobby continued.

Officer John knew Bobby was right. "Just because the crooked cops didn't shoot me dead, the night they'd questioned me, doesn't mean I'm in the clear. I'm still the new guy who became part of the gang at the same time all of this started happening, at worst they would think I'm involved somehow, at best they may think I'm bad luck, either way it's not good. They have plenty of reasons to be suspicious of me, if not yet, they will in time, and we are spending a lot of time together which will not go unnoticed in this racist group. We need to come up with a story, and quick otherwise we are both putting our lives in greater risk."

They'd walked for over an hour in the calmness of the night, ignoring the crescent moon and the millions of stars filling the night sky, partially lighting their path. "I've got an idea!" Bobby said. "We are going into business together, starting a company of some sort. Maybe a security company."

Officer John smiled. "Okay, I like it."

Bobby and Officer John talked through Bobby's idea, which started out as a cover story but quickly began to sound like a real business opportunity.

"I knew how unhappy the other security guards are at my job, and that the union representing us isn't making things materially better, what if we start a security company?" Bobby continued. "I figure we can do no worse than the company I work for a with minimal effort, we could do a lot better. The owners of the company are totally disengaged from the operation, leaving it to the union and the managers to figure everything out, it would be months maybe even a year before they realized there was new competition."

Officer John thought for a moment. "Combined we probably have a lot of contacts and a really good history to sell—me a police officer with a long career on the force with a clean reputation in a city with so many crooked cops, and you a decorated and honorably discharged marine with twelve years of service who was involved with many conflicts all over the world, it could work. I've heard you telling stories, if anyone can engage people and get their respect, you can."

Bobby smiled. "I think there was a compliment somewhere in there, we could call it Code of Honor Security. Whether it works out or not it is the perfect cover."

"I agree, we should discuss it at your house in case someone's listening at mine. Let's head back."

The two men spent hours discussing Code of Honor Security and getting their ideas ready to turn into a business plan in short order. Around 1:30 a.m., they called it a night and agreed to get together over the weekend to start fleshing out the details to bring the idea into reality.

As they walked to the door, Officer John couldn't contain his thoughts. "I'm really excited about this next chapter in my life, I've been at the school for so long, sort of in a rut. Don't get me wrong, I love it because of the kids, I would never want to lose the connection I have with them, but I've always felt like I could do more. Especially now that my wife is gone, I spend far too much time at home waiting to die, you my friend have given me more purpose and a reason to live." Their embrace was genuine and heartfelt.

Officer John arrived at home and went straight into the kitchen to gather up his whiskey. Most of it was cheap brands that didn't do much for the palate but got the job done when he wanted to escape the grief and depression that seemed to envelop his world more often than not these past days. He looked down at the open bottles and knew that he'd spent way too much time under their influence. He considered what his life would look like if he hadn't spent so much time after work, sitting on his couch and drinking his nights away. He was energized by his new business opportunity, and he knew that if it was going to be successful, he needed to keep a clear head, and that meant there was no room for cheap whiskey and feeling sorry for himself. One by one, he poured the contents into the sink, saving only the bottle of Glenlivet. *The next time I open this,* he thought, *it will be to celebrate.* There will be no more pity parties. He put it back into the cabinet and went to bed with a feeling of excitement he hadn't felt in years.

It all evaporated into the darkness of the night when Officer John's phone rang at what was an ungodly hour. He immediately thought of Bobby as he turned to look at the caller id, only to have his heart skip a beat when he saw that it was Chief Dolan.

He jumped to a sitting position on the side of the bed and stared at the caller id as the phone blared in the quiet of his bedroom. He couldn't not answer, no officer ever not answers the chief. The only thing he could do is take a deep breath to try and calm is completely frazzled nerves and pick up the phone.

"Hello, Chief, how are you?"

Officer John sat, hand shaking, and eyes closed as he braced for what his chief was about to say hoping that it wasn't about Bobby or some evidence that would immediately end everything they were trying to accomplish and potentially put him in jail for life or worse.

"Hi, John, sorry to no doubt wake you but I need your help pretty urgently." Officer John repeated in his mind, keep cool, keep cool, and answered his chief. "Sure, Chief, what do you need?"

"Well, we have another officer involved incident. We don't know all the details, but *Crooked Cop #3* is dead, and by the looks of things it looks like he committed suicide."

Officer John couldn't believe his ears, not because he didn't know but because his chief called him. His mind was racing. *Why is he calling me?*

"Oh my god, I can't believe it." It was the only appropriate response he could think of. "I'm sorry, Chief, how can I help?" He asked genuinely wanting to know why he got this call.

"Well, it's sad to say given the circumstance but I don't know *Crooked Cop #3's* family at all, I had to look at his file to know that he has a wife and son, and since A. C. Brice is at the scene working the case, I was hoping since his son goes to John Marshall Elementary, that maybe you know him and his mother?"

Finally, it all made sense to Officer John, and he could breathe again. He let out a much-needed breath of relief and responded.

"I do Chief." He knew what his chief was about to say, and he knew that he couldn't say no, but he didn't know how he was going to do what was about to be asked.

"John, as you can imagine this is hard enough for the family without some sort of a friendly face. I'm embarrassed to say that I don't know them at all, and quite frankly I don't know why. If I were a betting man, I would have thought that *Crooked Cop #3* was single because he never brought his family to the few department events he attended."

Officer John had his suspicions as to why he didn't. The better Sarah knew the other officers and their wives, the harder it would be for *Crooked Cop #3* to be able to get away with the abuse.

Chief Dolan continued, "I'd like you to accompany me when I tell them. I'm at the station looking over *Crooked Cop #3's* file, I can be at your place in twenty minutes."

Officer John thought about Sarah and Arvin. "No problem, Chief, I know them well and am happy to go with you. I'll be outside waiting for you."

After the call ended Officer John stood up and went to the bathroom intending to just take a quick look to make sure he was presentable but his reflection stopped him in his tracks, "how am I going to be able to look Sarah in the eye knowing what happened and that I am responsible?"

He didn't have time to think about it, he splashed some water on his face which was not yet needing a shave, luckily, got dressed in his uniform and headed down to the street. Standing waiting for the chief he wondered how Sarah would take the news, would she be relieved that her abusive husband was gone, or would she be stricken with grief despite the horrible man he was. His thoughts were interrupted by the site of the chief's car.

"Hi, Chief, I should tell you what I know about Sarah, his wife and Arvin, his son. Do you want me to do the talking, or do you just want me there for comfort?"

Chief Dolan knew that the responsibility was his and accepted it as part of the job. "No, the brief is fine." Officer John thought it best to bring up the abuse and his earlier conversations with Sarah now, as they might come up and did not want his Chief surprised. In spite of what he and Bobby had done, he had to let the Chief know everything he knew because to omit any pertinent details would bring suspicion on him.

"Well, Sarah is very private and shy. She doesn't speak a lot or make eye contact so when you deliver the news just know that is her norm. I believe she is that way because there were problems with their marriage. I'm not sure if you know but *Crooked Cop #3* was an abuser, not only of his wife but of their son, Arvin. I've spoken to her and him many times about getting help and to my knowledge they never did or if they did, I was never informed."

As Officer John spoke, he looked at the Chief trying to figure out if this information was a surprise or if he already knew, but the Chief didn't react at all. Officer John continued, "the last time I saw Arvin it was clear that someone had recently abused him, I assume it was his dad." He stopped talking and waited to see if his Chief had any questions.

"I assumed there was some reason they weren't engaged with the department, there is always a reason. When I deliver the news, I want you to be prepared to comfort Sarah if she needs it. It is difficult to know how people will react so I try and prepare myself for the unexpected and I'd advise you to do the same, if she reaches for a hug of support, or sits with her hands on her lap don't be afraid to extend compassion by offering a hug or extending a hand of support. I know you probably know these things, but I just want to make sure."

"Sure, Chief, no problem." The rest of the short ride the two men stayed in silence.

Chapter 32

Chief Dolan and Officer John pulled up in front of a modest home with a meticulously manicured yard and white picket fence, trying very hard to look perfect. *No doubt because of the awful things that happened inside,* Officer John thought.

Ringing the bell of the completely dark house, the only light was the porch light that illuminated the toys on the porch and a swing that looked comfortable and welcoming. A light illuminated inside indicating to Officer John that this was going to happen. He took a deep breath as Sarah opened the door in a cotton housecoat and matching slippers.

"Chief Dolan, Officer John," she said, having recognized them right away. "What are you doing here? It can't be good news. Come in."

They stepped inside the modest but cozy living room and began scanning the area out of habit. The carpet had clean spots suggesting something was cleaned off of it, the television was rather old which surprised Chief Dolan as *Crooked Cop #3* could certainly afford a better set.

Chief Dolan suggested that Sarah sit down, to which she complied. Chief sat down next to her on the couch, close enough that it would have been inappropriate outside current circumstances. Officer John sat in a worn to comfort chair next to the couch wanting to be close but also wanting to give the Chief space.

The Chief looked into Sarah's youthful eyes that belonged to a face that was older than its years.

"I'm sorry to have to tell you this, Sarah, *Crooked Cop #3* died in an accident tonight."

She looked at Chief Dolan and then Officer John.

"How did it happen?"

Chief Dolan continued, "it appears that he may have committed suicide, but the circumstances will require investigation. So, I obviously cannot say for certain. We found him at the base of the old Newmarket Mall. It doesn't *appear* as though he would have suffered. He would have died instantly from the fall. I'm sorry to have to tell you this."

As the Chief spoke, Officer John felt like he was going to throw up. He knew the truth and sitting having to listen to a wife being told that her husband and the father to her son was dead, he wasn't so sure that he and Bobby had done the right thing. He wondered to himself what gave him and Bobby the right to decide this man's fate. Looking at two people trying to deal with the results of his actions was almost too much for him to stomach. *What have I done?* He thought.

Chief Dolan sat, preparing for a reaction that he wasn't seeing. He waited for Sarah to breakdown into tears or to show some sort of emotion.

Officer John felt like it was proper to say something since Sarah had not reacted to what Chief Dolan had said other than to stare into space.

"I am so sorry for your loss, Sarah. We will work tirelessly to get you and your son any answers we can." He reached over an put his hand on top of hers as he took position next to Sarah on the floor taking one knee as if he were proposing marriage. The two men knew that it was time to stop talking and wait for her to process the information and give them some clue as to what kind of support she needed.

"I expected this would happen someday, and I wasn't sure how I'd feel," she finally responded. "My husband wasn't the kindest of men, quite honestly, he was a terrible husband for most of our marriage," she said staring into space.

"It wasn't soon after our wedding that I began to think I'd made a mistake marrying him. He quickly became a different man than the one

I'd fallen in love with. He was no longer patient and kind, I wondered if I'd fallen in love with a man that didn't really exist.

I thought that having a family with him would make him a better person, but that was foolish, and our son paid the price for my bad decision."

"Chief, why is it the victims of abuse have to confront their attackers alone, why didn't the department help us, me and my son?" She turned to Officer John. "The many times you asked me if I needed help, why was it my responsibility? I had to take care of our son, why didn't you act based on the information you obviously knew?"

All color instantly left Chief Dolan's face as this was not a question he expected or was prepared to answer. Officer John started turning red as he was now convinced that he and Bobby had done the right thing. He knew that if he had taken some action to separate Crooked Cop #3 from his family that there was no way of ensuring that he did not go after them as so many abusers do. They want to control their victims and no laws or court orders could stop them, especially when the abuser could hide behind his badge. Someone like *Crooked Cop #3* would have made Sarah and her son's life a living hell if Officer John hadn't done what he did, he was sure of it.

He couldn't however say any of that to Chief Dolan or Sarah, in her living room. He couldn't say, I saw the awful things your husband did to you and I took care of it in a way that will set you and your son up for the rest of your life because Officer John knew that the suicide would be blamed on work related stress and that they would be financially ok.

The only thing Officer John could do was to hang his head in shame, not for what he did but for the fact that he didn't do it sooner.

Sarah continued to speak softly and calmly while staring at her hands. "*Crooked Cop #3* was abusive to me and my son, as I'm sure you and most of the department are aware. You and other officers would see the condition my son was in. You would see the bruises on my face and ask me how I was doing? What was I supposed to say? I have no job or money other than what my husband would give me for food. Why didn't you or someone on the force do something? Why is it me, the victim who is already in a dire situation, responsible for holding an abusive law-breaking officer accountable for his actions and in doing so risking my life or my son's life confronting an abuser. How do I stand up to an officer on your force? Why weren't you here then instead of waiting until now to come to my door?"

Sarah was now giving Chief Dolan the reaction he had expected although not for the reason he thought. Tears streamed down her face as she alternated between Officer John and Chief Dolan looking in the eyes for answers, wearing a look of desperation.

Sarah spoke when Chief Dolan and Officer John did not because they had no answers for her questions. "I'm obviously not happy he died today, but I cannot help but feel me and my son's life will be better with him gone. If I were to be perfectly honest, I prayed for this day to come, for my awful husband to have some sort of accident so his abuse to us would end, he was very troubled man having suffered abuse as a child and watching his mother's abuse. His mother confided in me before her death. She asked for my patience with him, but he never spoke about it. I had hoped he would get help, but it never happened. He just became more and more controlling.

"I was never afraid of raising my son alone, children need so little outside of love and compassion, what I have always feared, what kept us in this house was the knowledge that if we ever left my husband would certainly come after us and kill me or both of us. More than anything, right now I feel relief. Do your investigation but don't concern yourself with updating me on the details, this is a welcome relief and a blessing. Maybe my husband has found some relief from whatever tormented him, whatever pushed him to treat me and his son as he did."

Chief Dolan didn't know how to react. He sat listening to what Sarah was saying and thinking about all the times he reached out to *Crooked Cop #3* and asked him if everything was ok at home. He tried to get him to talk about what was troubling him so that he could get *Crooked Cop #3* some help. Chief Dolan didn't know exactly what was going on, but he knew there were others on the force that suffered the same demons as *Crooked Cop #3*. He often asked himself, *how do I reach them?* What could he do if they did not ask for help?

As he sat, he thought about the men on his force, how much they had to deal with; so much hatred and bias, the expectation to be perfect in their service to the community, it was a lot of pressure they were under and some handled that pressure better than others. Then there was the constant pressure of the lazy, good for nothing, completely entitled black monkeys that challenged authority and caused problems. *It's overwhelming,* he thought to himself.

Chief Dolan turned his attention from his thoughts and back to Sarah and Officer John who now sat next to them on the couch with his arm around Sarah. She tried to compose herself while was wiping tears from her face.

"I am sorry I could not have done more for you," Chief Dolan said. It was his truth. "The police union does good work to ensure the families of fallen officers are taken care of. You're going to be ok. There are counselors within the department that are available to support you and your son, you do not have to go through this grief alone."

Without realizing it, and without ill intent Chief Dolan began giving Sarah the speech he gave to all spouses in this situation. It was information they would get in the next few days, but he delivered it in the hopes that it would ease their concerns about the immediate future. It was what he was trained to do. After he had gone through all the information, he took his scripted pause.

"I know it's a lot, do you have any questions Officer John, or I can answer? We want to be as helpful as we can in your time of need," he said as he reached in his pocket to retrieve his business card with his personal cell number. These cards were reserved for situations like this, as the general public did not get the Chief of Police's cell number.

Sarah took the card and accepted that the neither the Chief nor Officer John were going to answer her questions about her husband's behavior. In death, just as in life she would be alone trying to figure out how to deal with the abuse. *Counselors*, she thought. *The police union supplies counselors but not protection or consequence.* She learned long ago that the union was more concerned with their agenda than the wellbeing of spouses and children.

Chief Dolan slowly stood, looking at Officer John to make sure that he did the same and waited for Sarah to do the same. He gave her a supportive hug and left her with the same words he left all spouses in her situation.

"You're not alone, there will be friends from the force reaching out to you, let us help you." Officer John extended a comforting hand to Sarah which she bypassed and gave him a hug, she needed support and hoped his strength would somehow transfer to her.

Following the embraces, Chief Dolan turned towards the door, followed by Officer John and Sarah whose final words were to put the two men at more ease after she had lectured them.

"Thank you for your support. I do appreciate your show of compassion."

Chief Dolan walked towards the car not thinking about the valid questions Sarah had asked about accountability in his department and for officers that abused their wives and children, he thought about more bad press and the disposition of his officers.

Officer John followed his Chief staring at the back of his decorated uniform, signifying to everyone that he was a brave hero, but all Officer John saw was a coward. A supposed leader that didn't know, or ignored, the awful things his racist crooked cops were doing to the people they supposedly cared about. Whatever respect for the Chief he had disappeared, and all he saw now was a small racist man hiding behind a badge.

This made him more convinced than ever that he and Bobby were doing the right thing. People needed protection from the crooked cops on the force and Sarah was, like a lot of people, he thought, waiting for someone on the force to do something. As he walked, he became emboldened to continue the work that he and Bobby had started regardless of the danger that it posed to them. The people in the community like Sarah needed it and since no one else, including his chief that he now sat next to in the passenger seat of his car, was going to do anything, he and Bobby would.

Chief Dolan finally spoke as they approached Officer John's house. "Thank you, John for your help, and I don't want you to beat yourself up about what Sarah said. There is only so much we can do. It's important to understand that she is in grief and did not mean what she said, I'm sure you know that, but I just want to remind you."

Officer John got out of the car and looked back at his Chief. "Of course, Chief, let me know if there is anything else, I can do for you." Turning and walking up his steps Officer John was exhausted and energized. It was almost 4 o'clock in the morning and he had never felt more alive in his life, as he got back into bed he thought about his departed wife and how proud of him she would be that he took matters into his own hands to protect an innocent woman and child from an awful and deeply troubled man.

As he closed his eyes to go to sleep, he silently thanked Bobby for having the courage to take this cause on and ending the reign of terror *Crooked Cop #3* was causing everyone he came into contact with. Again, thanks to Bobby he would go to sleep with a feeling of accomplishment and contentment. He wished Sarah and her son Arvin peace now that *Crooked Cop #3* was gone, he hoped to see a positive change in Arvin and promised to lend him support going forward.

Chapter 33

It didn't take the detectives working the case of *Crooked Cop #3*'s death to end up at the Hooters and then to Bobby.

Whey they knocked on Bobby's door, he didn't need to act surprised or afraid because he was, and it was genuine.

The detectives were polite when they introduced themselves as Det. Robinson and Hines. They flashed their credentials and asked if they could come in as they were investigating the death of a fellow officer and believed he could supply information, assuring him it would only take a couple of minutes.

Bobby replied with the answer he'd rehearsed many times.

"To be honest, I'm not comfortable being alone with police officers. No offense to the two of you, who are, no doubt, honorable men, but people like me don't fare well with cops in this city."

The detectives looked at each other before one of them spoke. "We were informed that you had an interaction with an off-duty officer at the Hooters on Jefferson a couple of nights back, we're sorry to say but he was involved in a pretty bad accident shortly thereafter and we are trying to better understand his state of mind that night. We understand your apprehension but really this is less about you and more about the officer and understanding him, anything you can tell us would be a great help."

Bobby was silent, still standing in the doorway waiting for an invitation which he got after an awkward pause from Det. Hines. "If you prefer, we can do it at the station where you would not be alone."

It was exactly what Bobby had wanted, he smiled and nodded his head.

"I'd feel a lot more comfortable at the station." Bobby stepped out of the door between the two detectives. "Excuse me," he said as he turned to close and lock the door behind him. "Should I meet you there or ride with you? I've honestly never been in a police car so that would be an interesting experience."

The two detectives looked at each other puzzled, why was he wanting to get in their car if he was uncomfortable being alone with them? Shifting their gaze back to Bobby. "Well today is your lucky day; you can ride with us."

Bobby knew what he was saying wasn't making any sense, but he didn't care, his plan was working. He texted Office John as he walked with the officers. "There are two police officers taking me to the station to ask me questions about a police officer that was involved in some sort of accident. I didn't realize such a tragedy had happened. If you need to talk, let me know, I'll help any way I can."

Once in the squad car, Bobby continued his act in an attempt to cover his tracks. "That's horrible news, the accident I mean, the officer didn't die, did he? It's such a dangerous job that you do, I understand probably better than most. I have a friend on the force. I've known him for many years, and he didn't mention anything about an officer's death when I spoke to him, but I guess that's not the type of thing you discuss in casual conversation. As a marine, I understand the dangers such positions can present, never knowing what dangers the day will bring, did the officer have a family?"

Up to that point, the detectives hadn't acknowledged any of Bobby's chatter, even when he'd referred to his friend on the force, but once he'd paused, Det. Robinson acknowledged what he had said with a question. "You're active duty on leave?"

"No. I did my twelve years, and that was enough. Been working in security ever since."

"So, you're an ex-marine," Det. Robinson replied?

Bobby calmly but firmly replied, "There is no such thing as an ex-marine; once a marine, always a marine."

Det. Robinson didn't respond, however Det. Hines did, offering the kind of response deserved of a veteran of twelve years as he looked at his partner in disappointment.

"I think what Det. Robinson meant is that you are no longer active duty. I'm sure he meant no disrespect and appreciate your service, right?" He said in a somewhat stern tone.

"Yes, of course, I just wanted to understand your current status, I have the utmost respect for our brothers in the armed forces and veterans like yourself. My father was in the Army for many years as well."

"Thank you" Bobby replied. "Maybe it's better if I stop distracting you from your job. I do have to say I expected more from a squad car, more bells and whistles but it's comfortable."

Bobby sat back and looked at a text from Officer John. "If you can offer any assistance, it would be really helpful." Officer John knew that the less said, the better.

Det. Hines responded, "yeah, so we've been told. You know it gets the job done and that's really what's important. We're not looking to waste tax dollars on bells and whistles."

It was a silent uncomfortable ride for Bobby which seemed much longer than it was, so he was relieved when he arrived at the station.

Once inside, the detectives escorted Bobby down a series of hallways separate from the public areas and stopped at a door labeled "Interview Room 3." Det. Hines opened the door and motioned for Bobby to go in.

"Please have a seat," was his only instruction.

The room was sparse with just a table and four chairs."

This is just like on television," Bobby said. It was what he genuinely thought and not a part of any act he'd planned. He sat in the chair furthest from the door, which was a habit he developed after Basic Training. He wanted to be able to see who was coming and going wherever he was.

The detectives didn't respond, just smiling as they sat opposite Bobby whose heart started to race. He thought to himself, this is the moment you've been practicing, it's go-time.

Det. Hines began. "If you could start by just telling us what you remember about that night and specifically anything you remember about a conversation you had with this gentleman, he pulled a photograph from an envelope and showed it to Bobby. It was a picture of *Crooked Cop #3* in full dress uniform and beside it a picture without his uniform. If Bobby had to guess, it was recently pulled from the wall of officer pictures he noticed as he followed the detectives to the interview room.

Bobby looked at the picture for a moment.

"I do remember him, but he wasn't in his uniform. I guess he wouldn't wear it to a bar or be drinking when he is on duty, and he wasn't wearing these clothes the night I saw him."

Detective Robinson interrupted Bobby.

"Yes, that's correct, he was off duty and in plain clothes the night he died. The pictures aren't from that night, we just want to be sure that this is the person that you saw and spoke to. What do you remember from your interaction with him that night?"

"Wait, he died that night, I thought you said that he was in an accident? Oh my God, when, that's horrible." Bobby tried his best to seem sincere.

"Shortly after you had your conversation according to the bartender and witnesses at Hooters which is why we are trying to get an understanding of your interaction with him, like we said, get a better understanding of his state of mind. Whatever you can provide no matter how minute the detail, would be helpful," Det. Hines said, trying to sound nonthreatening.

Bobby sat back in his chair, grasped his chin as if he were in deep thought thinking to himself, don't over think it.

"Well, I was obviously drinking that night, but I do remember the interaction, mostly because it was unusual."

Bobby began his narrative. "I remember when I arrived, I saw Fred, my barber who was there with his girlfriend."

As he spoke, he stared at the mirrored wall wondering if there was someone on the other side. He worried that he might not be believable in his performance especially considering the detectives were no doubt used to dealing with all types and might see through his lies. His heart pounded as he looked at their faces for clues he did not see.

"I have their names but not their numbers. We're friendly but not that close. I do have the name of the Barber shop if you want it, anyway," Bobby continued. "I began to watch the Tech vs. Boston College game and began chatting with another fellow that was also watching the game. If you're a Tech fan, and you see another fan you have just made a friend so naturally, we watched the game together."

Bobby tried to control himself, his breathing and facial expressions, even where his eyes focused. He struggled to control bodily functions that he normally never thought about, finally thinking to himself stop freaking out. *Being aware of every movement not wanting to appear deceitful will make you appear deceitful, just remember you're just telling a story. Just say what actually happened, you got this.* His pep talk began to calm him.

"After it was over, we began playing darts and chatting"

"Do you remember how you began your interaction with the officer, can you tell us a bit about that?" Det. Robinson asked hoping that Bobby would say something of substance and not just a useless narrative.

Bobby sat up straight in the chair, he had tried to relax and had begun to slouch. He needed to remember to not oversell his comfort. He wasn't sure what to do with his body and arms and began to worry that the detectives, whose expressions hadn't changed since he began talking, weren't buying his story which up to this point was completely accurate.

He was talking for his life and although he was used to tense and even dangerous situations, he was not used to talking during them. He hoped that the words he was trying to say, were actually coming out of his mouth.

"If I recall correctly, I was having a conversation about a song, oddly enough. I believe it was *Sweet Home Alabama* or *Dixie* or some song like that, and was interrupted by the officer, who seemed bothered by what I was saying. I think he took offense to my interpretation of the lyrics. I left after that because the game was over and this guy, the officer, seemed to be getting upset. I like that place, but I don't go very often because guys occasionally drink too much and that can sometimes lead to people saying or doing things they regret. I wasn't looking for any trouble, so I thought it best to just leave—"

"What happened when you left Hooters?"

"Sorry," Bobby said. "Let me think." He paused trying to get the right words. "I called my friend, Officer John, he's the police officer that I mentioned I know. We were having a conversation about a business venture we're considering. I must've been on the phone with him for at least twenty minutes or so, I remember because I was almost halfway home when I realized I'd left my jacket at the Hooters, so I went back to get it. I was just in and out, but I was there long enough for the bartender to tell me that the guy, or the officer, was upset with me, and he was a cop and that I should try and avoid him because he had drunk a lot. It was pretty quick. I didn't really talk to anyone else."

Bobby looked at the two detectives. "Is this helping at all?"

"Yes," Det. Hines said. "Can you tell me about your interpretation of the song that got him upset?"

Bobby smiled. "Sure, I was just pointing out that it was an interesting song for a man like me to make a habit of singing, do you know the song, *Dixie*? It's basically about slavery. I think it's catchy but also very racist, so when I made a comment to my darts partner the officer got upset and made some off the wall comment about slavery being ok or something like that. It was that comment that let me know that he was drunk because clearly no one in this day and age would think that slavery was a good thing, and now knowing that he was a police officer, he definitely wouldn't have that opinion, right?"

The detectives who had been taking notes as Bobby recounted the night for them, looked up at Bobby not sure if his question was rhetorical or if he was actually asking them.

"Of course not," Det. Hines responded.

Bobby now sat in anxious silence trying to remain calm. The truth was running through his head like a horror movie demanding to be on the big screen. It was as loud as an airhorn blaring in his mind. Should he say something or keep his mouth shut? Did he already say the wrong thing and not realize it?

Stay calm. Just don't say anything more, he told himself, but his mouth had a mind of its own.

"Was he involved in some sort of auto accident or something? I know we were all drinking, but I certainly didn't drink enough to impair my driving. Still, just to be safe I didn't drive, it's just not worth the risk. Driving after even a few drinks for most people is foolish, I'd think an officer would know that, it's such a shame, he didn't look much older than me."

Det. Robinson looked at Bobby. "We didn't say that, why would you assume he was involved in some sort of traffic accident?"

Bobby didn't reply to the question at first but thought he should say something. "I didn't mean to assume, just that you said he had an accident I assumed it was an auto accident. I wish I could be more help, but I didn't see him after I left. What else can I do for you, detectives?"

Det. Robinson seemed less than convinced. "There is, thank you for asking, who is this Officer friend that you were speaking to again?" They had written the name down but wanted to keep Bobby talking, there were still so many unanswered questions and given enough time the guilty usually talk themselves into an arrest in their experience.

It was the question Bobby had been waiting for so he could stop talking about that night and shift focus. "Officer John Fitzgerald, he and I have been friends for years, since I was in elementary school. We were discussing a business venture, as I said before."

Det. Hines, in a move that seemed aggressive to Bobby because he thought he was supposed to be the "good cop" in the interaction, leaned forward in his chair and rested his arms on the table, looking directly into Bobby's eyes.

"Can you give us some of the details about this business venture?"

"Sure, we're considering starting a security company together. Having worked in the field, I've identified an opportunity to do it better than what I see currently being done. You know—a police officer and a marine—if you can't count on us, who can you count on?" Bobby replied.

The detectives stared at Bobby, looked at each other, and then at the mirrored wall to the mystery observers.

Bobby, not knowing what to do or say, sat on his hands and followed the officer's eyes. Was this the time to push for his release by making up some excuse to get out of there? They hadn't arrested him so he should have the right to leave at any time.

Thinking he was lucky that the only thing the detectives had done up to that point was ask him questions, he quickly dropped the thought from his mind. He couldn't forget the reality of the situation. He was a Black man guilty of a crime in a station full of crooked cops lying for his life.

He swallowed hard and spoke in a measured tone. "I can give you Officer John's number if you need it. I call him Officer John, always have, since I was in school. He was the officer assigned to the school to protect us."

"That won't be necessary, but if you could give us the phone number to the barber shop and name of your friend and his girlfriend…" and with that, the detectives thanked him for his statement.

"Are you planning on leaving the area any time in the near future?" one of them asked.

Bobby shook his head as he scribbled the names and numbers they requested. "No. I have work, and certainly no time for a vacation."

Det. Hines got up. "Thank you again, you can follow me." He escorted Bobby to the station entrance. "Let me get the keys to the patrol car so I can give you a ride back to your apartment." He was just turning to the counter when Bobby interrupted him.

"That's not necessary, it's a nice day, I'll just walk. Besides, I may visit a friend on the way home." As Bobby walked out the door, he looked back to see the detective pick up the phone, Bobby wondered if he was calling Officer John to corroborate the story.

Chapter 34

Bobby left the station not confident about his safety but with few options for action. As he walked home, he began to become overwhelmed by feelings of powerlessness and fear for his safety, feelings that he desperately tried to eliminate or control since childhood but never could fully.

Once again, he felt at the mercy of crooked cops and their control over his life. He looked back at the station, at the place that was the cause of all the bad feelings in his life. Surer than ever that he was doing the right thing, but how could he take on the department? He was completely outnumbered and bringing Dr. Chien into it, he wondered if that was the right thing to do given the danger. She was in full support of their efforts, that he was sure of, and she was committed to helping however she could, but he was reminded how dangerous what they were doing was and how close to the edge of a huge cliff they seemed to be standing.

Surrounded by crooked cops, having to interact with them and now he was brought in for questioning about what he had done, he wondered if he had been seen. Was it some sort of cat and mouse game they were playing giving him just enough rope with which to hang himself?

He began to hear his thoughts and feel warm with anger.

I'm out free, I wasn't arrested, and I've got Officer John, he thought. *They have no idea what's going on, we're ten paces ahead of them and they are running around lost trying to find us.*

He slowly lifted his head and his gaze shifted from looking at the ground ahead of him to the neighborhood and city ahead and around him. Suddenly, shifting his mind from that of prey to predator he shifted his awareness to his environment. He started becoming aware of his surroundings and the sounds of the neighborhood. His feelings of doubt began dissolving as his anger grew.

He shifted his thoughts to his father, to Johnny and his wife and son, and the many other people whom he knew were victims of the corrupt department. He was getting strength from the raging blood pumping from his heart through his body. He was regaining the focus that helped him excel in the Marines and without trying, subconsciously his shoulders shifted back, and he was two inches taller and to an onlooker, transformed once again into a formattable force.

He reminded himself that he was in control. He was the hunter of the crooked and unjust. The crooked cops were the criminals, and he wasn't the one that needed to be worried, it was them. He was the law that would hold them accountable. He was no scared little child. He was once again a Marine.

As he walked into his apartment, he took stock of the situation. He needed to let the officers do their work and discover the truth to the story he created. He called Officer John who answered on the first ring.

"Bobby, where are you, are you ok?" Bobby thought he needed to be measured in his responses not knowing what Officer John's surroundings were. "I'm fine, the detectives finished questioning me and I'm home now. We should talk soon, I tried to be as helpful as I could. I expect they'll reach out to you soon to corroborate my story and understand the nature of our business relationship, no need to worry, I'll see you soon."

Officer John appreciated Bobby's call and the need to make it brief, he was relieved to know that his friend was safe, and their plan was working.

Bobby woke up the next morning feeling good, following his normal routine with a pep in his step as he relieved the night security guard at his job.

"You hear about the crooked cop that jumped off the roof of the old mall we patrol, the one, off Mercury Blvd?"

"I didn't, but it's been a crazy last 24 hours for me. Can you believe they brought me in to ask some questions about it because I had a run in with him at the Hooters before it happened?" Bobby replied.

The security guard looked at Bobby. "You were at Hooters, I didn't know you went there. I hang out at that spot sometimes, never saw you. What night do you go, we could hang out there together?"

Bobby smiled as he responded. "Nah, it's not a regular thing for me, just went to watch the Virginia Tech game. My sister was talking my ear off about how big this one was against B.C., so I watched. You know I don't have time for all that or the money," he said as he laughed.

Bobby briefly recounted what happened, wanting to shape the narrative the way he wanted it to be shared. As he relayed the events the security guard listened in complete disbelief.

"You're lucky to be alive, man! They think you killed one of their own, you're toast whether you are innocent or not. You must have been scared sick."

Bobby didn't need to exaggerate. "I was, I didn't know what to do, so I just went along with whatever they said, hoping I didn't end up in a body bag. I didn't ever get the full story of what happened— you say he jumped?"

"That's what the night patrol told me. They aren't giving those details out to the public. I saw it on the news, and they didn't say what really happened. His wife was there, crying in the interview. They don't know what to make of it, calling it some sort of stress-related suicide or unfortunate accident but didn't say how he did it. Crazy, the stuff going on with these crooked cops, right? That's one hell of a way to end it all, once you're off the roof there's no turning back, you're dead! Either he jumped or he pissed off the wrong one and they decided they'd had enough of his BS and decided to take care of things themselves; I wouldn't be surprised if it were an inside job, they're all crooked, running drugs and causing all kinds of problems. Eventually that stuff comes around to bite you in the ass or in his case, throw you off the roof."

"Well," Bobby said. "Think about all the things these crooked cops do…you have to wonder how they can live with themselves, I guess maybe he couldn't take it anymore. All of that hate and anger builds up inside of you, it will give you cancer or worse, drive you crazy. Well, be safe out there." Bobby patted the security guard on the arm and turned to begin his patrol. "Let me go do this job," he said having accomplished his goal, he wanted to end the conversation.

He thought about *Crooked Cop #3's* family and the awful things Officer John had told him. They would no longer have to endure his abuse, and that brought him a sense of satisfaction.

One down many more to go, he thought.

Chapter 35

After their workdays were done, Bobby and Officer John began putting the final touches on the office they'd set up in Officer John's house for Code of Honor Security. It had been his late wife's sewing room but now lay in waste, so Officer John was happy to put it to good use.

It had been a comfortable space in its day, with its large sewing machine table with lift sitting just inside the door, next to it a large basket housing thick rolls of fabric in a rainbow of colors in the corner. There was also a large basket of yarn and crochet needles, spools of ribbons, and a half-complete quilt that would never be finished. It draped over a large, comfortable couch, centered in front of a large bay window overlooking a well-kept backyard. The space was a constant reminder of his departed wife that he needed to change if he was ever to start living again.

They moved things in silence with the care and reverence expected from men who had spent their lives in occupations steeped in tradition, including respect for the fallen.

Once Bobby and Officer John were done with the room, it was unrecognizable, with its two, large, mahogany desks and wall decorations honoring a distinguished military and police career.

Bobby's desk was covered with a cornucopia of sentimental items, including a V.T. lamp from his sister, a paperweight from Japan, and a letter opener and pen set from Djibouti Africa, his favorite T.D.Y. as a marine. He had a picture of his family prior to his father's passing, which he used to remind himself to cherish each day because no one knew when their time would be up.

Officer John's desk was similarly decorated, with his first accommodation as an officer, a pen set with his name engraved in a plate on the front, a photo of his departed wife a few days after they'd met, and a picture of him in front of his school on his first day of work.

They'd assembled a database of contacts and had three meetings scheduled for the following week with potential clients. As they sat finishing up the order for their business cards—which Officer John would drop off the next day on his way to the station—he sat looking at Bobby and the office they'd created and reveled in the excitement that came with new opportunities such as the one upon which they were about to embark.

Bobby suggested they go for a walk to get lunch. Once on the street, Bobby spoke of a concern he had.

"We cannot let the business get in the way of our work. We are the real protectors of our community. What's our next step?"

Officer John nodded in agreement.

"I'm going to the station to connect with one of my crooked cop friends to see if I can get in on a job. They aren't going to stop their crooked dealings, so we can't stop either. Plus, we need to move the camera—no one's going to conduct any more illegal activity on that street, so the recordings are useless. I don't want them coming back to me. It's been on my mind, but I haven't wanted to go back so soon."

Bobby, ever focused, looked straight ahead and offered his next moves. "Okay. I'll confirm our appointments on Monday after work and let you know if there are any changes. I'll also try to get in touch with a few more of my contacts over the weekend."

"I'll do the same," Officer John replied. "I'm worried about involving Dr. Chien in too much of what we're doing."

Bobby thought for a moment. "She's a strong lady, and besides, at this point, I don't think we can afford to continue without someone with medical knowledge. I'm comfortable with my abilities, but that doesn't mean I'll never get hurt, and you've barely recovered from getting shot. We need her as much as we need each other. Maybe we should discuss it with her at dinner tonight?"

Dr. Chien was busy in her kitchen when the two men rang her doorbell. She greeted them with warm hugs and led them into the kitchen. "Glenlivet, I assume? How's my patient?"

Officer John assured her that he was feeling much better thanks to her. She'd been to see him many times over the weeks since his unexpected visit to her house the night of the shooting. Dr. Chien had appreciated practicing medicine again, although she would have preferred to do so under different circumstances. She'd retired three years prior and felt as if her life was lacking. Even though she'd kept busy volunteering at the local hospital, she wasn't a practicing physician. At heart, she was a caregiver, and she'd been without a patient until Officer John was brought to her door. Now, taking care of his injuries and looking after her defenders of the public—for this is how she thought of Bobby and Officer John—gave her what she'd been missing in her life.

Bobby poured three fingers of whiskey into their glasses over the large, round ice cubes, and Dr. Chien turned toward them, showing off a dish of ratatouille she'd taken from the oven.

"What's the latest?" she asked.

Dr. Chien listened with excitement as her dinner guests explained their new business venture over dinner. Dr. Chien's home had not been so full of laughter, energy, and excitement since her daughter had gone away to college. Her home had been one of emotion—both happy and sad—as life tended to be. Myia had been four when Dr. Chien and her husband bought the property, having fallen in love with the house at first sight. It sat on a large lot, surrounded by a white fence. It even had a tree swing in the backyard, hanging from a tall yellow-poplar. The yard was dotted with all sorts of beautiful trees, including a few apple trees. When the family had settled into the house, it at once felt like home. Myia had run up the stairs to pick out her room while Dr. Chien and her husband slowly toured the home, looking for a reason as to why the house had been on the market for so long when it seemed ideal for them.

After not seeing any faults, they made an offer slightly below asking, keeping their fingers crossed that because it had been on the market for so long, the sellers would accept it. In spite of the fact that it was in move-in condition, they needed to renovate the kitchen to make it larger because Dr. Chien loved to cook. They also needed to install central air; summers got too hot and humid in southern Virginia to not have central air.

When the offer was accepted, it was like a dream come true.

Upon moving in, Dr. Chien made it a point to meet the neighbors, checking to see if there were any children that might befriend her daughter. She didn't want Myia to go through the teasing and bullying she'd experienced in school, so making friends and getting to know the parents was priority number one. She met numerous young families in the neighborhood, and they were all friendly, welcoming, and eager to meet the people that had bought the vacant home.

Shortly after moving in, it was as if they'd been there for years. Their furniture from the large townhouse they'd been renting had fit perfectly into the new house. With the extra space, they were able to hang more pictures and bring family heirlooms out of storage. Dr. Chien was active at Myia's school, organizing fundraisers and doing talks about nutrition and overall health at a health fair she started. The other parents loved having a doctor so active at the school and close by when their kids got sick. Soon, Dr. Chien found herself the pediatrician for nearly every family at the school. She even made the occasional house call, which was unheard of and greatly appreciated. Not everyone in the school was financially well-off, and Dr. Chien was happy to waive co-pays and other out-of-pocket expenses for families she knew needed financial help. As her practice grew, she hired more help and made sure that she kept a good work-life balance; she wanted to be a good wife and mother.

Dr. Chien thought to herself just how wonderful the years in the house had been, and how grateful she was for the life she'd lived, and the new energy Bobby and Officer John had brought to it. As she laughed and listened to Bobby and Officer John talk and joke, she was reminded of happier times when her husband was alive, and her precious Myia was home. Myia had recently graduated from William & Mary and was living in Maryland with her boyfriend, whom Dr. Chien adored. She hoped that they'd marry and have kids soon. She visited them often, which made coming home to the empty house full of memories that much harder. Dr. Chien had many friends from her many years of living and working in the area, but she was reminded of how much she missed having her family there.

She came back to the conversation and the present moment, and they filled her in on their business plans. They told her how they'd set up their office and applied for a business loan that they expected to hear about any day now. They spoke about the three sales meetings they were preparing for the next week and how they knew a lot of guys that would jump at the chance to leave their dead-end jobs for the opportunity to be minority partners in the new business. Officer John and Bobby would always keep equal majority stakes in the company no matter how large it grew, and they had a vision for huge growth. With so many security companies in the city taking advantage of a large number of unemployed and low-paying jobs, they'd be able to draw top-notch talent to provide professional, customer-focused service.

Former military and ex-police officers that really cared about the community and making it safe would be their preferred partners. They already had a list of twenty-plus names and numbers they'd call upon as they closed new business.

"We'll still have time to do our most important work," Bobby said with a serious look on his face. "We won't let up until all of these crooked cops are all in jail, have left our city, or are dead—it'll be their choice."

"It gives me great comfort to know that the latest crooked cop will no longer abuse his child or wife. No, we will not stop," Officer John replied.

Dr. Chien shared her thoughts on the subject before they put it to rest.

"I truly believe you're doing the right thing, and I'm happy to help any way I can. Racism in the south has only gotten worse, more covert. Politicians take money from special interest groups and enact laws that hurt everyone except big business. Then, they turn around and attack us—minorities, the elderly, the poor—as if it's somehow our fault. We have guns everywhere, and they're empowering people who are full of anger and rage, fed to them by politicians and the news, and used to commit unbelievable acts of violence. All the while, those in power and the wealthy laugh all the way to the bank. We won't solve this problem, but we can try to stop the police brutality from destroying what was a community just beginning to heal."

They all knew her words were true. For a moment, they sat in silent reverence to the words she had spoken.

When the clock struck ten, they were at the door saying their goodbyes and agreeing to connect the following week to celebrate the signing of their first customer.

Chapter 36

Bobby and Officer John sat in the lobby of the management company for two large retail spaces in Newport News and Hampton. They knew that in order for their business to become a reality, they'd need customers like that to give them legitimacy. The bank also required documentation or contracts with customers in order to approve the loan. The men were confident but nervous when the receptionist escorted them into the conference room, which had glass walls, a handsome cherry wood table large enough for ten, cushioned black chairs, and a large television set. One of the walls had writing on it. Bobby suspected they used it instead of a whiteboard. He was impressed by the idea as it was something he hadn't seen before.

Three people stood and extended their hands to greet them as they entered the room. Sandy, the director of operations, a woman in a business suit who appeared to be in her early thirties, with attractively styled hair and brown skin. Doug, the chief operating officer, a man in his late fifties with grey hair and a handsomely weathered face, wore a power suit with a bold-print tie. He had a firm handshake which Bobby took note. Finally, there was Antoine, the chief financial officer, a man that could have been anywhere from the early-thirties to late-forties. He had a shaved head, goatee, and dark brown skin. They sat around the table as Bobby began the presentation, "security work can be boring and uneventful for hours and that's what makes it challenging, maintaining the discipline to actually do the work and not just sit in a corner and nap or play cards. It seems like the type of work that anyone can do and that's why most companies do a poor job of it, they tend to hire unskilled laborers that fall into the trap of that boredom.

"The result is insufficient reporting, vandalism, and increased insurance premiums. Well Code of Honor plans to change all of that, I am retired Marine Sergeant Major Bobby Harris, and this is Officer John Fitzgerald, and we believe that if you use skilled labor, men and women trained to understand that during those times of boredom, exists the highest levels of risk, and that understanding helps to eliminate that trap.

"That's why our entire team consists of former military and local law enforcement trained to be at the top of their game when others are slacking off."

Officer John chimed in referencing the presentation on the screen, as rehearsed.

"If you look at a sample of vandalism and theft that occurred last year, many of these sites had security assigned, so what happened, where were the guards when these crimes were committed."

"With our service level guarantees, incidents like this are much less likely to occur."

The presentation advanced as Officer John continued to talk but Bobby's attention was on their audience of three who were nodding and taking notes on their copies of the presentation, which he took as a good sign.

"When arriving at the scene of a disturbance with security as an officer on patrol, I was often struck by the lack of information and documentation the officers had, regardless of how long they had been on their shift, and that is how we will be different," Officer John continued.

They finished the presentation and discussion—which lasted almost ninety minutes—with Bobby acknowledging. "There's a risk contracting with a new, unfamiliar company, so if you're willing to sign a one-year contract, we'll provide the first month's services free of charge with termination language, so you'll be under no obligation until after the first month."

The business leaders all smiled, knowing that taking the opportunity would add almost forty-thousand dollars to their operating budget, and if it didn't work out, they could easily find another security company or contract with their current provider, which was on a month-to-month contract. The chief operating officer thanked them for coming in and assured Bobby and Officer John that they'd be in touch later that week with a decision.

Bobby and Officer John left, feeling like they'd done a good job, and they felt good about their prospects, but celebrating a successful meeting wasn't on the agenda for that day. They had to put those feelings quickly to rest because they had other work to do. They needed to scan the south end for the right place to plant another camera. The crooked cops were constantly causing trouble, so they had to be ever-vigilant to keep them in check.

They cruised Jefferson Avenue and found the perfect spot near King Lincoln Park. It bothered Officer John that these crooked cops were trying to ruin a place that he and his wife had enjoyed so much.

Officer John reminisced about the fun times they'd at the Fall Festival of Folklife, enjoying amazing food while walking around, checking out the crafts, and enjoying the live music. These happy memories washed over him like a flood as Bobby spoke about surveillance cameras and catching crooked cops in the act. He thought about the last time he and his beloved wife had been to the park. It was the fourth of July, the year before she'd passed. They'd arrived right at 7:00 p.m. when the festivities had started. They'd brought a picnic basket, chairs, and blankets, as it tended to get cool near the water at night. There were so many of the families that Officer John had met and gotten to know over the years, seeing them through from when they'd first brought their little ones to the school to their last day before going off to Middle School, so much bigger than when they'd arrived. Officer John and his wife would spend the first few hours chatting with students past and present and their parents loving every minute of it until they'd bundle up and settle in to watch the fireworks.

After the fireworks, they'd remained snuggled up and waiting for the crowd to disperse so they could easily exit the park and head home. He loved that park and the memories he'd had, enjoying the wonderful events the city had put on there, and now, the crooked cops in the community were trying to ruin it.

"I have to say," Officer John began. "This is one of the nicest parks in the area, and it pisses me off that those crooked cops are trying to bring their drugs down here. I was just thinking about all the times I'd spent with my wife before she passed," Officer John said. "Did you go to any of the events they had?"

Bobby recounted the many times he'd gone to the park as a young adult with his family because it was an inexpensive way to spend the afternoon. They'd gotten together with friends and family and had barbeques and family reunions there.

"This is such a special place with some really good people. There are military families settling here from all over the country. Some of them even stay permanently, no doubt lured by the amazing seafood, thanks to the Chesapeake Bay."

"It makes me so angry when I think about how those crooked cops cause most of the problems in the area," Officer John continued. "They incite anger and distrust between people that really have no reason to dislike or distrust one another."

Officer John knew that what Bobby had said was the truth. It was becoming more and more difficult for Officer John to put on his uniform and feel anything other than disgust. He respected so many of his colleagues around the country. They did their jobs with honor and distinction, putting their lives on the line every day to protect and serve the great people in their communities. Somehow, knowing that did not change the fact that when he put on his uniform, all he could think about were the crooked cops that had sullied the meaning of the uniform, taking advantage of their positions of power, and doing unspeakable acts of violence to people that did not deserve or understand any of it. To Officer John, knowing what was happening in his police department would never allow him to feel pride when he put on his uniform, those days had long passed.

Officer John rejoined Bobby's conversation, acknowledging that they'd meet the next morning around six and head to the park to set the video recorder up. After they'd merged on to I64 heading north, Bobby shifted his thoughts to their business and posed a question to his friend.

"Once we get our first client, I was thinking that I'd quit my job and work on the business full-time. What are you thinking?"

He verbalized what he'd been thinking the past couple of days.

"I was thinking one of us should, and when we get a second client, we both could. I know we'll have the loan to carry us until we start collecting on our invoices, but that could be a few months. I'd feel better if we both weren't exclusively working for the business, and I think it's important that you do because it'll send a message to the people who hire us that we're serious. What do you think about that?"

Bobby agreed that his plan was a solid one. He added that he had been reviewing their list of potential partners, and it was impressive. There were several police officers that actually did their jobs well, more than a dozen young veterans with whom Bobby had become friends since leaving the Marines, and a few security officers with whom Bobby had worked with over the years. He'd prioritized them in order of most likely to least likely to accept.

"I don't think we're going to have a lot of luck with active-duty police officers initially—we just can't compete with their compensation package as a small business," Bobby said.

Officer John agreed, adding, "they'll jump at the chance once we begin to grow and can show a healthy return."

Officer John dropped Bobby off, promising to be at his place promptly at 6:00 a.m. in the morning. He was looking forward to getting to bed. He'd gotten up early—it was approaching his bedtime, and he hadn't eaten yet. Officer John was thinking about feasting on the leftovers in the refrigerator before going to bed when he turned onto his street and saw the patrol cars parked in front of his house. There were two of them, so there were anywhere from two to four officers waiting for him. He hoped they were his crooked cops and not something he hadn't anticipated.

His stomach churned, and he lost his appetite. What could they want? He hoped it was A.C. Brice and his crooked cops, meeting him to discuss a job so he wouldn't have to seek one out on his own. He hadn't received any money for the botched job he'd done for them, and he could use that to his advantage.

He pulled into his driveway and stepped out of the car, paying close attention to the three crooked cops standing on his porch, smoking. His uneasiness decreased when he noticed A.C. Brice, standing on his porch. Things might turn out to be all right.

Chapter 37

"Hello, gentlemen. To what do I owe this pleasure?" Officer John stepped out of his car and greeted the crooked cops.

A.C. Brice answered, "We need to talk."

Officer John approached with an even but slow pace, scanning the men for weapons. All three had their pistols holstered on their sides, which was normal and not what he was looking for. He looked for blunt instruments. If they were going to harm him, it wouldn't be with a bullet, he thought, certainly not in his neighborhood at his own house. Nothing went unnoticed in his neighborhood, in fact, there were neighbors directly across the street, sitting on a porch swing, enjoying the cool night air. Officer John looked for nightsticks, fortunately, he didn't see any.

"Come on in, gentlemen," he offered as he opened the front door. "I'm about to heat some leftovers for dinner. I wasn't expecting company, but I can order something in if you're hungry." Officer John tried to keep calm though his heart was racing.

"We're not here for dinner," A.C. Brice said, closing the door behind them. "I'll get right to it. I understand that you've gone into business with some monkey."

Officer John was stunned. Before he could respond, A.C. Brice continued, "We don't share our business with no monkeys. Why didn't you come to us?"

Officer John stared at Brice in disbelief. "I didn't think anyone would be interested. It was his idea, besides. I've known him for a long time, and he has the right background."

"Right background? What's that supposed to mean? You in the monkey market so you need a monkey? Is that the background you're looking for?" A.C. Brice said.

Officer John continued to explain himself. "He was in the Marines, so it fits the business model of the police and the military joining forces to supply security. It seemed like a unique angle we could take advantage of. Besides, I need the money." It was a lie, but they wouldn't know it wasn't true and it followed the narrative he had been feeding them. "I didn't make any money form the last job I did, which almost got me killed, so I figured I'd give it a try."

He turned and walked toward the kitchen. "I'm starving, so if you don't mind, I'm going to get my dinner started." The truth was that Officer John couldn't eat then, even if he tried. His stomach was in knots, but he tried to play it as cool as possible.

The crooked cops followed him into the kitchen and continued their questioning. "How do you know this monkey so well? How'd you meet him?"

Officer John knew he couldn't be too specific—he couldn't let on exactly who Bobby was and why they'd grown so close. "He's one of the kids from my school. I keep up with a lot of them that stay local, so many of them leave for jobs or school. Why the million questions? I told you, I needed some extra money," he said, repeating the lie. "So, why aren't you trying to help with that instead of getting on my case for trying to make some?" Officer John tried to seem annoyed but not too aggressive. He knew he had to ride a fine line if he was going to get out of the conversation with his connections intact. He couldn't alienate the crooked cops, or he and Bobby wouldn't be able to continue their work.

One of the crooked cops said, "What type of work are you trying to get into?"

Officer John answered, "We'll be providing security services to—"

"We don't care about that," one of the crooked cops interrupted. "We wanna know how far you're willing to go. We have some jobs, but we're not sure you can handle them."

Officer John knew this might be his opportunity to get further in, so he turned to look directly into A.C. Brice's eyes. "I earned my stripes when I took a bullet and still had enough strength to take care of your mess. If it weren't for me, your money and your drugs would've been taken. You think these two could have done the same?" He motioned at the two crooked cops, eying him intently. "I'm ready to go, like I said."

"We'll see. Meet us at my home—I believe you have the address. We'll fill you in on the details then. Be there at eight." The men turned to leave. "Don't be late and enjoy your dinner," A.C. Brice responded,

Officer John didn't move until he heard his front door close. He walked slowly to the living room to make sure they were actually leaving. For the first time since he got home, he was able to breathe.

Officer John grabbed a jacket and walked toward the liquor store a few blocks away. He needed to call Bobby, but he still wasn't fully convinced that his house hadn't been bugged.

When Bobby answered, he relayed his encounter with the crooked cops.

"We need to move the surveillance equipment, my house is a revolving door these days and we can't risk them discovering what's in my shed, do you have a place we could set up the monitors and the rest of their equipment?"

Bobby thought aloud. "My apartment isn't small, but I don't trust it there either."

Officer John concurred. "You're definitely too close to what's happening and may still be on the detective's radar, perhaps a storage space?"

"What if we set things up at Dr. Chien's, temporarily, until we have a permanent place?" Bobby suggested. "I'm sure she won't mind. We can ask her tomorrow. Nothing really ties her to either of us"

Officer John agreed. The two ended their conversation as Officer John entered a liquor store. He realized he didn't really want to buy liquor, he'd decided it best to not drink alone anymore, it was one thing to enjoy a drink with his friends, it was quite another to drink when he was upset or sad. Silently he vowed to not let Bobby down by not being at his best, instead he grabbed a bag of chips and a soda and headed back home. The smell of smoke welcomed his as he rushing into the kitchen to see that his leftover clam chowder had burned to a crisp.

What am I doing, he thought? Happy he hadn't burned the whole house down, he realized he really wasn't hungry at all.

He put away the junk food he hadn't wanted in the first place, ran water in the scalded pot, cracked open a window, and headed to bed.

Lying in bed for what he figured was thirty minutes, he couldn't immediately fall asleep even though he was exhausted. He had a lot on his mind. He and Bobby had started down two paths that could not seemingly be successfully traveled at the same time. He wondered how they'd navigate holding the crooked cops accountable for their crimes and successfully launch their business at the same time. One mistake could ruin any chance of getting customers for their business or worse, getting them killed. He also worried that neither of them had studied business in school or had extensive experience in that area. It would be hard enough to navigate the company's launch without the distraction of the late nights and dangerous encounters that most assuredly lay ahead, dealing with the injustice in the department. He wondered if they had taken on too much, adding insult to injury, they'd brought Dr. Chien into their cause when it was still in such a volatile state, how could he have been so cavalier, she wasn't a soldier or officer? What were they thinking? Was this all a big mistake?

As he lay in bed thinking and torturing himself, he was taken back to a time when his beloved wife was still with him, and as they'd lay in bed at the end of a day like this one, he would discuss his thoughts with her. She was the perfect sounding board, helping him to ease his mind when needed, encouraging him not to not worry so much. More often than not simply stating that if his heart was in the right place and he focused on one step at a time and didn't get too ahead of himself, he'd be just fine. He wondered if she'd approve of what he was doing. She always had supported his career in spite of its dangers because he was doing it for the good of the community and their children. With the number of school shootings happening over the years, his job had become more dangerous as people's obsession with guns seemed more like an epidemic. Schools had once been relatively safe, but now guns were everywhere, and children made easy targets for the sick and evil. None of the elected officials were willing to disrupt a reliable source of campaign contributions, so they downplayed the problem. Through it all was his wonderful wife, listening and understanding his concerns. She was, in so many ways, the perfect wife. He wondered if he'd let her know just how much he loved her often enough. At that moment, he felt a calmness came over him as if she were there comforting him, and like so many nights before, her presence comforted him, finally allowed him to fall asleep.

Chapter 38

Bobby woke up to a message from Officer John saying he was on his way, so Bobby got ready quickly and headed out to the street to make sure he was outside waiting, when he arrived. Within minutes, they were on their way to plant their surveillance cameras.

Once inside the car, Bobby followed up on what happened last night.

"Do you think our working together will cause a problem? If they perceive me as a threat or a distraction it might be a problem."

Officer John thought about what his wife would say, his self-advising from last night. "Let's not get ahead of ourselves. It might be a problem at some point and if it is, we'll address it then but right now it actually helps, continues the narrative that I need money."

Officer John shared what he was worried about. "We have a hard road ahead of us, and a zero margin for error, I'm concerned about managing it all. I'm not worried about the risk when it's just us but the more people we involve, the more we spread that risk. I'm worried we will not be able to manage it all, that it will prove too difficult."

Bobby thought for a minute before speaking from the heart. "Black folk like me have had a hard road since birth, and it won't end till we're six feet under. It comes with being African-American unfortunately, it's not right, but it is what it is.

"When we're kids, we worry about why adults treat us differently than our friends and why some kids don't like us because of the color of our skin. As teenagers, we worry about being singled out when a group of us are messing around and just being silly, the way kids do sometimes. We're always to blame, even if there are ten white kids and one black kid. We wonder why some people love us when we play sports and score points and then hate us when we're on the streets and out of uniform. We worry about getting jobs after college or the military when we're really good at what we do, but every interview is being done by a white person, and the answer is no. I say this to make the point, that life is hard sometimes, but if you take one step at a time and as you said, don't get too ahead of yourself, you'll be just fine. I honestly haven't been this excited about my future since I made the decision to join the Marines. We're doing the right thing and are on the right path; you watch, things will continue to go our way."

Officer John nodded in agreement, but in his heart, he wasn't as certain as he led on. In that movement, he seemed to understand something he had never before thought about or considered, Bobby and Dr. Chien had experiences and struggles that he would never have because he'd been born with a skin tone that gave him the benefit of the doubt, that signaled to people that he spoke from a place of knowledge when they had no proof to that fact, a skin tone that mattered in the world.

They pulled up to a good spot on Jefferson and followed the same routine as the last time. They'd planted their cameras and were back in the car on the way to Dr. Chien's house less than five minutes later. Bobby was starting to get hungry and was looking forward to breakfasting at Dr. Chien's.

The men arrived and were greeted by the smell of biscuits and bacon. As they entered the kitchen, their eyes took in a traditional Southern feast of homemade biscuits fresh out of the oven, a pot of gravy on the stove, grits with a few pats of butter melting on top, and a bowl of steaming scrambled eggs that had, no doubt, just come off the stove.

Dr. Chien smiled as they entered the kitchen.

"Just in time, do you mind setting the table?"

Bobby without prompting washed his hands and began taking what was already in serving bowls to the table. Officer John shook his head as he took the good plates to the table.

"My wife would never have used these plates for breakfast unless there was a formal celebration."

Checking everything before sitting, Dr. Chien admired the table they had set. "Fit for a spread in Southern Living Magazine, let's eat before it gets cold."

Officer John filled his mouth with the southern food, insistent on filling his empty stomach while making his request to Dr. Chien.

"I had a visit from A.C. Brice last night, there is no way we can run the monitoring out of my house, the risk is too great. I'm the new guy so I think they are still vetting me, I got the feeling they were at my house for a reason, either to bug it or to check me out, wither way that equipment in the shed is a problem. I don't suppose we could set up here," looking at her as he added a piece of bacon to his already full mouth.

"I'd be happy to have you set up shop here, I have a room upstairs that I rarely go into, have at it. It would also be nice to have the company."

"It will be temporary, we will hopefully grow Code of Honor Security to the point where we need an office, right now that is set up in my house, now all we need are some clients."

After breakfast was over, Officer John helped with the cleanup as Bobby nervously checked his voicemail to see if they had heard from the management company, the 3rd time he had checked since he arrived.

After cleanup was done, Officer John emerged from the kitchen.

"We better start moving the surveillance equipment now, I am not going to be able to calm my nerves until it is here safe and out of A.C. Brice's reach."

Getting up, they thanked Dr. Chien for breakfast and promised to be back shortly. As soon as they were out the door, Dr. Chien made her way to their new base of operation to remove any items that might get in their way.

Officer John and Bobby were making good progress carefully packing the sensitive equipment when the phone rang.

Officer John put it on Bluetooth preyed aloud, "please do not be another problem,"

"Hello?" he said, answering with a measured but friendly greeting. The voice on the phone was a welcome one.

"Hi John, its Sandy, did I catch you at a good time?"

Officer John waved at Bobby excitedly. "Yes, Sandy, now works, how can I help you?"

"I just wanted to call you and let you know that Doug, Bob, and I were very impressed with your proposal and are happy to sign a one-year contract under the terms outlined in their meeting."

Officer John could hardly contain himself. "That's great news. I'll let Bobby know and we will have the contract dropped off and pick it up after you have reviewed it. Our template is rather simple but feel free to make any updates you deem necessary and let us know when it's ready for us to pick it up, looking forward to working with you."

As he hung up the phone, almost as if he didn't believe what just happened was possible.

"They're ready to sign a contract, we have our first client!"

Bobby pumped his fist in the air. "I knew it, when you do good things, good things happen."

Dr. Chien was equally happy for them.

"Now the work really begins, as soon as that contract is fully executed, we have thirty days before their current vendor is out, which is amazing but not a lot of time to secure the loan and get things in place for our first day."

"We got this!" Bobby cheered.

They ended the conversation and hung up as Officer John looked at his watch, he had to meet A.C. Brice at eight that night. "We need to get a move on, that bit of good news puts everything on a much tighter timeline."

Bobby tried to put him at ease.

"I will work with my lawyer friend draw-up the management company's contract, I can hand-deliver it tomorrow, don't worry about it, you focus on your meeting with A.C. Brice. Let's get busy moving the equipment to Dr. Chien's, she can help me set it up while you handle your business. After this all comes together, we have to celebrate!"

Officer John looked at Bobby with a look of concern. "We have a lot to do and not a lot of time to do it."

Bobby's reply was indisputable. "We have to eat. I'm going to take you and Dr. Chien out to dinner Friday night after we're done with work. I'm sure your job with A.C. Brice and those crooked cops will go off without a hitch."

"Hopefully!" Officer John responded.

Chapter 39

Officer John was nervous when he arrived at A.C. Brice's house, he'd received instruction that their meeting location had changed so he was worried something might be up. Officer John pulled into the driveway of a home that someone in A.C. Brice's paygrade shouldn't be able to afford. Word among the guys on the force was that A.C. Brice's parents had been wealthy in their day, and when they'd passed, he'd inherited the entire estate, which was true, but maybe it wasn't enough for him to support his five children, his wife's expensive tastes, the large home they stayed in, and their fancy cars.

When Officer John entered the home after A.C. Brice's very polite son answered the door, he was taken aback at the home of the man he very much despised. There were pictures of a very happy family man everywhere. He may not have cared about the community he was destroying, but he seemingly cared very much about his family. There were pictures of kids playing baseball and softball, the entire family in red in what appeared to be the photo on the Christmas card he'd received.

Officer John wondered, was nothing in this life simple anymore? How did you know the bad guys from the good guys when they hid behind pictures of smiling families and children? How could he and Bobby work to put A.C. Brice in jail when it may result in the downfall of a happy family with five children at varying stages of life?

Officer John reminded himself that he wasn't in the wrong, A.C. Brice was, he had everything most people only dream of, and he still did these awful things. He wondered, when did society become so screwed up that parents were the bad people?

Officer John followed who was most probably A.C. Brice's eldest son, given that he was just as tall as him and had the build of either a high school or college athlete. He asked the young man, "What grade are you in? Do you play baseball?"

The response came via a calm, confident voice. "I used to, but now I play soccer. It's my real passion. I have a scholarship to UVA and will be a first-year student in the fall. Dad's in the study, right through there, have a good evening."

He watched the young man walk down the hallway, and he couldn't help but wonder if he'd cheated himself out of having a son of whom he could be proud.

Officer John entered the study to find five crooked cops and A.C. Brice, standing by a fire.

A.C. Brice greeted Officer John with a firm handshake. "Glad you could make it, and thanks for being on time. I've briefed everyone, and they know what to do, I unfortunately had something come up so they'll brief you John, if you'll excuse me, you will all be fine without me."

Officer John's uneasiness increased tenfold, A.C. Brice was nicer and more polite than he'd ever been before. He wondered if the police force had turned this seemingly wonderful father into a complete jerk and de facto criminal or did he bring that mentality with him. Had he also joined the force with hopes of serving the community only to become corrupted by his superiors? It's hard to know who is the cart and who is the horse when everyone seems corrupt, Officer John thought to himself.

The A.C. Brice that seemed like a complete stranger to Officer John turned and headed towards the door without another word to anyone. After he left, one of the crooked cops informed Officer John that he'd be riding with him, and he should leave his car where he'd parked it.

Without delay, he six men were in their cars cruising toward the Hampton Road Bridge Tunnel on I64 but exited just before reaching the tunnel. They approached several police cars with their lights flashing, about a half mile off the exit, leaving Officer John wondering what was going on and what he'd gotten himself into. As the cars approached the officers, they were waved through the blockade. Officer John was getting more nervous by the minute, he had no details of the job, no means of escape, and no way yet to get help if things went south.

Bobby was standing by, waiting in his car for notice that help was needed, but realistically, if something did happen, Bobby feared he wouldn't be able to get to the location in time.

Officer John asked the driver of the vehicle. "So, what's the plan? I'm hoping it doesn't end with me getting shot again."

The driver replied through a smile. "Don't worry. This will be the easiest money you'll ever make."

The cars pulled into a warehouse, there waiting for them were three white men with a rough look about them, built like brick walls, standing next to two black Cadillacs, and holding AR15's.

Officer John nervously said to the driver. "This doesn't look so easy."

His only reply was, "Trust me." And they pulled up opposite the men, leaving about ten feet between the cars.

Officer John trusted no one, and his fear and anxiety were out of control as he scanned the area for a way to get out of harm's way if something went awry, but he had no time to figure anything out before they got out of the car.

The driver went around to the trunk, pulled out two large duffle bags, walked over to one of the men standing next to the Cadillac, and presented the bags. "Count it if you want, but we have no reason to short you, it's two million."

The man replied in a deep voice with an accent that wasn't Southern. "Then you don't need to count your pills, so we can exchange and just leave."

The men chuckled, made their exchange, returned to their respective vehicles, and began to count. One of the crooked cops instructed Officer John to keep watch by the entrance of the warehouse. Officer John quickly complied, taking a position half in the shadows of night and half in the light shining from the warehouse.

He wasn't sure what to do, cursing to himself as he wondered how Bobby would be able to do anything with them in the hanger. For sure, he wouldn't be able to record anything, and Officer John knew his time for action had all but run out. With no other ideas and seemingly out of time, he slowly pulled out his phone, sent Bobby the license plates of the two cars, and dropped a pin so Bobby would know his location, along with the message.

"$2 mil for drugs, 2 black Cadis. Talk later."

After sending the text, Officer John quickly deleted it from his phone; he knew Bobby wouldn't reply.

Bobby received the text and out of habit checked one more time the readiness of his two SIG Sauer P226s and shifted his car into drive, heading for the location Officer John had sent him. As Bobby got closer to Officer John's pin, he realized that he knew where the men were.

He turned off his headlights and exited the freeway. He could see the police cars ahead and decided it was better to park out of site and walk to where Officer John was. He pulled up approximately a thousand feet from the officers and walked to as close to the warehouse as he dared without risking getting discovered and took out his binoculars. Bobby saw Officer John standing at the entrance of the warehouse, pacing, he instantly felt relieved that his friend was okay. His relief was soon replaced by the excitement coming from knowing that he was about to put himself squarely in the center of the action.

Bobby waited patiently, watching Officer John pace back and forth until finally, he went back inside. It was what Bobby had been waiting for. He got up and made his way back to his car and sat with his motor running, watching the rearview mirror, waiting for the Cadillacs to appear. A moment later, they came into view, driving at a relatively high rate of speed, which was what Bobby had hoped for. He assumed they'd head toward I64, and he began driving in that direction, slowly enough that the Cadillacs would overtake him before he reached the freeway.

The Cadillacs zoomed past Bobby, who adjusted his speed so that he could follow them without being detected. The freeway would be busy enough for him to blend in but not enough for him to lose his targets.

Bobby followed the cars for about ten minutes until they pulled off the freeway and into the parking lot of the Hampton Coliseum, a circular concert venue to which Bobby had been many times. He pulled into an entrance opposite the Cadillacs, slowly got out of his car, and began to walk around the building. He stopped when he saw cars parked next to a Mercedes S560. There were four men there. If Bobby were to succeed, he had to be quick and precise.

He stood in the shadows and pointed his weapon, measuring the accuracy needed to take each man out. With a slow inhale and an exhale, he fired four quick shots. His silencer releasing a muffled alert moments before three of the men hit the ground, which alerted the fourth that didn't get hit.

In the darkened shadows of the Hampton Coliseum, Bobby stood, waiting for his fourth victim to make a move. The men he'd shot weren't moving, and the fourth had jumped behind the Cadillac and was out of view. Bobby had to decide what to do, and he had to decide fast. He couldn't stand there for long.

Just as he'd contemplated his next move, he heard a car door close. He had a decision to make, shoot the car and possibly alert someone within earshot or wait for his criminal's next move. No sooner had he completed this thought, the Mercedes turned and quickly accelerated away from Bobby. He waited a few seconds until the vehicle was far enough away that if it turned around, He would be able to get to a safe place and protect himself.

He moved toward the two remaining cars, his gun held firm, and approached the men bleeding on the ground. Bobby quickly checked inside the cars and then popped the trunks. Inside one was a large duffel bag, Bobby grabbed it, ran for his car, jumped in and headed toward the exit. Before he reached the freeway, he pulled over to remove the cover from his license plates.

Heart pounding, adrenaline pumping, he opened the duffel bag and looked at what he was sure was a million dollars.

Chapter 40

Bobby sat looking at the duffel bag full of money, more than he imagined he would earn in his lifetime, but he was more concerned about Officer John than the money. He could not reach out for fear that Officer John wasn't alone. He told himself to just be patient and wait for the message they agreed would be sent when he got home safe.

Bobby shifted his attention back to the money, he dared do nothing with it until they had a plan, but he couldn't take his eyes off of it. "I need to occupy my mind" he said to himself and put the duffel bag in his closet and turned on the television and numbly began to watch the news. Finally, after a full episode of Andy Griffith he received the text, he was waiting for, Officer John was ok, and he could go to bed, but a restful sleep was out of the question with so much money in his closet.

The next day as agreed, after a full day of work Bobby, Officer John, and Dr. Chien sat at a table at one of their favorite restaurants, 99 Main. They were in good spirits and ready to celebrate Code of Honor Security's success as well as the small business loan that had been quickly approved by the local credit union upon seeing the signed contract.

Bobby of course, had some news that he was itching to share with his friends, but he wanted to wait until the right time.

Dr. Chien was excited about their news and offered the men congratulations for what she was sure would be the beginning of a great business venture for them. When they received their entre, Bobby asked the waiter to give them some privacy.

Officer John looked at his friend and shook his head. "What are you up to?"

"How much easier would our business venture be if we didn't have to worry about money?" Bobby replied, smiling.

Dr. Chien and Officer John looked confused.

"I thought you got the loan," she said.

"We did, but I'm not talking about the loan. I'm wondering how awesome it would be if…say…a million dollars fell into our laps?"

Officer John's face went flush. "Bobby, please don't tell me you did what I'm praying to God you didn't do."

Bobby recounted his story to Officer John and Dr. Chien. As he spoke, Officer John's face turned beet red. He interrupted Bobby's story, just as he was getting to the point where he'd looked into the duffel bag and saw the money.

In a stern whisper he scolded Bobby. "You've gone too far, you have no idea who those men are, what connections they have, or what their friends will do. How could you do something like that without discussing it with me first? That's not our money to spend!"

Bobby replied still smiling. "It's not their money either, it's all illegal and they have no idea what happened, and they can't exactly call the police."

Dr. Chien having been quiet up to that point in order to get the full story, interjected to get one bit of clarification. "Was there actually a million dollars in the duffel bag or was that an expression?"

Bobby looked at her and smiled. "I'm not sure exactly, but it should be a million dollars."

Dr. Chien's face changed from a frown of inquisition to a smile and shook her head. "Nice work Bobby!"

Officer John, not sharing her enthusiasm, looked at her past his flared nostrils and brow that was starting to bead with sweat even though it was quite comfortable in the restaurant. "We need to get out of here and talk," he said.

In the private comfort of Dr. Chien's Lexus ES 350, Bobby explained his logic. "Don't you see? Whoever those guys were doesn't matter. The one that got away will report what happened, and it will naturally be assumed that it was the crooked cops that did it, and they'll have to deal with the consequences."

Officer John wasn't buying it.

"What makes you think they won't suspect me, plus we didn't start this so we could steal money from crooked cops and try to live in luxury. I'm in this because we need to protect the community, not so we can become just as crooked as those cops."

Bobby paused, hoping his friend would calm down, took a deep breath and continued as calmly as he could.

"We've had this conversation before, and I think we all agree that someone has to hold these crooked cops accountable, now we have the added responsibility of our new business, which is just starting out, how are we supposed to balance it all?

"With the money, we could set up recording devices all over the city if we wanted to and keep ourselves out of harm's way. As I see it, we don't have time to patrol our client's property, recruit new partners, collaborate with the crooked cops, help them do their dirty work, figure out how we're going to hold them accountable, and eat, breathe, and sleep. Dr. Chien, what do you think?"

Officer John answered before she had the opportunity to. "Why are you bringing her into this?"

Dr. Chien, who had been quiet for most of the exchange, finally spoke.

"Bringing me into this? Do you mean bringing me into this particular discussion or the quest for police accountability? I believe it was your getting shot that brought me into this. I've been in this since the moment Bobby brought you to my door close to death and asked for my help taking care of you. I've been in this since I agreed to nurse you back to health, and I got further into this when I lied to the police about your injuries and agreed to provide you a room for your surveillance and base of operation.

"Quite frankly, I take offense to the question. None of this will work without the three of us working together. While the two of you are out there doing your work, your lives are in real danger. This doesn't work without me sitting at home, waiting to patch up whatever injuries you bring back. Bobby's right," she spoke with emphasis but didn't raise her voice. "Your loan will go fast if you're not working and patrolling for your company, and the two of you don't have time to do that and patrol the police. It's a miracle this has happened. You should be thanking Bobby, not scolding him like a child. Exactly how long do you think you can balance all of this responsibility without slipping up?

"You need to be sharp when working with these people, you're in deep. They rely on you to carry out their dirty work, and you need to do it without them figuring out what you're really up to? We've been lucky up to this point, but one day, our luck will run out if we aren't always one step ahead of them but if you're tired from a long shift at work you can't possibly be at your best."

Dr. Chien shifted her focus to Bobby, in the rear-view mirror, he met her eyes with an eye roll and a shrug of his shoulders as he started to speak.

"I saw the men leave the warehouse, and you weren't with them, so those cops couldn't possibly suspect you, how could they, you were with them? The men in the Cadillacs met the ones in the Mercedes—what connection could you possibly have with them? You're new to all of this. The other crooked cops are the ones with experience—don't forget that's one of your assets, you're the naïve cop from the elementary school. They won't think you're smart enough to pull any of this off. In the Marines, we used every advantage we had to subdue our enemies. Taking their money is a good way to throw a wrench into their plans."

They'd arrived at Dr. Chien's house and were sitting in the car when Bobby finished, and Officer John finally spoke.

"I have to think about this," he said. "I don't think we can act until I can figure out what the results of your actions will be."

Bobby looked at Dr. Chien who was looking at Officer up and down. "Of course, I think we understand that part of ensuring the money is safe for use is whether or not those involved approach you about it."

Officer John let out a sigh. "Let's focus on the company for a while and let the crooked cops be while I try to figure all of this out, let's try to get some sleep. Goodnight, you two." With that, he got into his car and headed home, not sure if he, Bobby, and Dr. Chien were on the same page anymore.

Dr. Chien offered Bobby some tea as Bobby assured her that Officer John would come around. "We have a lot going on, and this money will relieve a lot of the business's financial pressure, which will give us the perfect cover to do our real work. You didn't see what I saw at the hanger, with Officer John standing there, fully exposed while these crooked cops did their dirty work. You were right earlier when you said that we couldn't afford any slip ups, and we have way too much going on right now. Money doesn't solve anything except money problems, and we might be fortunate to eliminate those problems before they start."

Dr. Chien listened as she made the two of them sandwiches, loading slices of ham, lettuce, cucumber, tomato, and green peppers onto slices of white bread.

Bobby pulled two plates down from the cupboard that were far too nice for the sandwiches, but he knew Dr. Chien wasn't in the habit of saving her nice things for special occasions. She used them regularly and enjoyed them.

They sat down to enjoy their sandwiches in welcome silence.

Chapter 41

As Bobby and Dr. Chien enjoyed their sandwiches Officer John drove home in a state of fear and anger. In his heart, he knew what Dr. Chien had said was true, that money problems would make what they were trying to do impossible, but he couldn't get past the fact that Bobby had stolen the crooked cops' money. He saw a patrol car up ahead, its lights flashing, and a Black man standing, facing a wall, his hands cuffed behind his back. His first thought wasn't about the officer's safety, but about the black man who'd probably been pulled over for being black while driving.

He was not in uniform so he couldn't interfere, but he decided to pull over and watch to make sure that the situation did not get out of hand. Watching he wondered what was the reason for the stop, had this man actually done anything wrong? Which cop was it, he couldn't see and didn't have any surveillance gear with him? He couldn't get any closer, fearing the other officer might notice he had an audience and what could he say as justification for stopping and watching.

The officer took the driver out of the car and had him place his hands on the trunk and assume the position that would ensure the officers safety. Another officer stepped into view and watched the suspect while his car was searched. Officer John's stomach was turning, why was one cuffed against the wall and the other being frisked? He wondered what had happened before he arrived?

Sitting in the car watching the scene, he suddenly didn't understand his own confusion. Having never considered the reality of what happens every day from the citizen's perspective before, he was not feeling good about what he saw. The officers had a right to search the car if they believed there was illegal activity happening but was there justification for every stop, for this stop? Depending on who these officers were, they could be up to no good or just protecting the community and doing their job. He just wasn't sure anymore.

He thought about crooked cops in the department, almost too many to count, and prayed that these were not two of them. Given what he and Bobby had put into motion, he knew that every crooked cop on the force would use a situation like this to take out their frustrations on the black suspects. Everyday challenges they believed were somehow the fault of Black people and what he and Bobby were doing would make the problem worse in the short term but better in the long. He sat watching, worried about the suspects' ability to be treated fairly. Should he get out of the car?

Officer John watched as the two officers spoke to the suspect at the back of the car. The suspect against the wall was talking to them as well. They seemed calm so that was good, he thought. He prayed that the suspects cooperated. Now the officer was putting the other man in handcuffs, was this warranted Officer John wondered, he had not seen any resisting or non-compliance on the part of either of the men? If something happens, he wondered, what could he do? He thought about the work he, Bobby, and Dr. Chien had begun, and he knew he couldn't interfere regardless of what happened. Did he really want to watch this if he is not in any position to react?

As his thoughts developed a mind of their own one of the officers walked back to the police cruiser and came clearly into view under a streetlight. Officer John did know this officer, thankfully he was one of the good ones, he thought.

Officer John felt a sense of relief just as the other officer kicked the suspect's feet out from underneath him. The other suspect turned to object as the officer drew his weapon and issued an order Officer John couldn't hear. He realized the officer he knew was turning off his body camera that had recently been instituted as part of a pilot program. Officer John had heard about them but didn't know how they worked but had heard that they could be turned off which he thought defeated the whole purpose, he knew in that instant that this was not going to end well.

One of the crooked cops removed his knight-stick and immediately started beating the suspect that was now on the ground with his hands cuffed behind his back. The officer he knew quickly went to intervene, pulling his partner away from the man screaming in pain on the ground just as people appeared from a building and began to shout at the officers.

Officer John had his hand on the door ready to open it if things didn't de-escalate quickly.

The two officers spoke at the side of the car for what seemed like an eternity but was a few seconds then they turned and picked up the suspect and put him and the other in the back of the patrol car.

Officer John was getting a sick feeling in his stomach, how could he sit and watch police brutality and not interfere? He wondered how the department had gotten to this point without him doing anything to stop it? Hiding at his school like a coward.

Officer John watched as the suspects sat in the back of the patrol car while the two officers spoke outside as another patrol car with siren blaring and lights flashing pulled up. As he watched the scene unfolded before him, his thoughts shifting to his departed wife.

He thought about how proud she was of him. How she spoke about him and the department and the good work they did. She was friends with many of the crooked cop's wives and involved in many of the department's activities. Would she have supported them if she knew the truth, would she have supported him?

He was overcome with disappointment with himself for not doing anything all those years. It was a feeling he'd never experienced before Bobby showed up at his door that faithful day and forced him to see and acknowledge the truth. Bobby forced him to remove the veil that blocked all the undesirable truths from his view and to pick a side and act. Bobby's courage and leadership was contagious, and it gave Officer John the strength to do something and here he was confronted with the truth after questioning Bobby's actions. Questioning whether Bobby's intentions were pure when in fact none of this was as black and white as it seemed except the crooked cops and their illegal activities that were going unpunished. He didn't need to see anymore, this wasn't the solution, watching like some sort of spectator at a perverted show. He was done being a useless spectator, he was acting, and Bobby and Dr. Chien deserved better from him. He wanted to be the man his wife thought he was. He wanted to be a man worthy of all the years of love and devotion she gave him. They would use the crooked cop's own money to fund their downfall.

Officer John started his car and took off with purpose, heading back to Dr. Chien's house. He knocked on the door wondering what he would say other than that he was sorry.

Dr. Chien opened the door but did not react to his presence.

"The kitchen is closed." She turned, leaving the door open behind her as she informed Officer John.

"I deserve that," Officer John responded.

They settled at the table, Officer John noting the two China plates holding the remains of their sandwiches.

"I didn't get far before I was reminded why we started this in the first place," Officer John said. "I have the privilege of being born with white skin, and I take the benefits that affords me for granted. The veil has been lifted so to speak and I'm fooling myself if I think that there are easy answers ahead. We are in uncharted territory, and we will have to do the best we can, making the rules as we go. But one thing is for certain, we have to keep the surveillance up."

Officer John begrudgingly told them of the horror he had just seen and the shame he felt. "You were right, if we're working all the time, we won't be very effective at our real work. Everything we do going forward is to support our real goal, to hold these crooked cops accountable and one day end their stranglehold over the department. We have cameras recording right now and I can't imagine how long it will take to process the footage and create a plan for any illegal acts committed—we can't do that if we have to be out patrolling our clients' properties. We'll have to hire people to patrol and deliver on our contract right away, or there won't be a Code of Honor Security for long."

Dr. Chien and Bobby just shoot their heads knowing that what Officer John had seen was an all too frequent occurrence.

"Do you have any idea who they were harassing?" Officer John shook his head as it hung in shame. "I didn't stay long enough to find out, I had to get out of there, if I stayed, I wouldn't have just watched I would have gotten out of the car and that would have killed our plan. We can't get caught up in reacting we have to be strategic. That crazy incident however tragic isn't our fight, it can't be. Anonymity is a protection we can never lose.

"We have to wait long enough to see if any of the events of the other night come back to me or if there's an immediate backlash. It would never have occurred to me that you would have had anything to do with the incident at the Hampton Coliseum. Let's hope A.C. Brice and the rest assume it was someone else too. Thinking about it I have a pretty tight alibi."

Chapter 42

Bobby and Officer John met at Dr. Chien's, but this time, they had different work to do. They needed partners for Code of Honor to be successful which meant combing through phone books, business cards, and organizers looking for friends and former colleagues that they would want to partner with.

As Officer John went through a career of contacts, he was struck by the number of officers he would never want to work with again, luckily there were a handful that fit the mold of exactly what they were looking for, hardworking, honest, with cool heads and an appreciation of the trust the community bestowed upon them.

Bobby wondered aloud, "going through all these names I could only come up with 5 people that I think would be an asset to the company, are my criteria too stringent, how many did you come up with?"

Officer John concurred, "I have 7 and I'm much older than you, but it's a start." They both made introductory calls to their contacts, after greetings and small talk to catch up, they had a business proposition that they wanted to discuss with them.

Bobby busied himself while officer John finished the last of his call, comparing notes after he was done. "All of my people are interested, I have meetings over the next three days, how about you?"

"Same here, I guess we picked the right people after all. I never realized how many people I know are seemingly unhappy with their lives. Simply going through the motions, never getting to a place of happiness. I guess settling with a level of contentment that isn't really fulfilling. Thinking about it, I guess we were the same way."

Bobby thought for a moment, contentment would have been a welcome state of being given his life. All the conflict, ager, and confusion plagued by fear, caused by the people he now spent most of his time thinking and talking about.

"Is contentment so bad?"

Officer John looked at Bobby and thought about what Bobby's life experiences had been and how different they were from his own, yielding the point, recognizing the privilege of his life, one without childhood trauma and loss. "I guess not."

When they broke for lunch, they turned their attention to the money still in the large duffel bag Bobby had brought to Dr. Chien's house because he didn't think it safe at his place. They ate their sandwiches, looking at the large sum of cash that now presented an opportunity and a problem.

"Maybe if we periodically deposit a few thousand through the merchant window at the bank, we have the business account." They both looked at Bobby and shrugged in agreement.

Dr. Chien also had a suggestion. "I could take on a few patients, my business was often conducted with cash payments, nothing too large but it's another avenue."

Bobby stated the obvious, "I guess it doesn't really matter how long it takes, it's a really weird problem to have ... right?" They all chuckled.

After lunch Bobby read the latest correspondence from Sandy the director from the management company, "we are cutting things close, we have a little over a month to get everything in order before we need to have boots on the ground patrolling the shopping center. Pretty exciting and scary at the same time, I've got a ton to do, they are really excited about the transition."

Officer John reviewed recordings while Bobby headed out to meet two of his marine buddies who were ready to talk about the business opportunity.

Bobby arrived at the small coffee shop and was greeted by a quick but genuine embraced by the two men who were part of his unit what seemed like a lifetime ago. Blade, whose real name was Jonathan, was fond of knives and antique swords back in the day had gained a few pounds since his honorable discharge but he still had a physical presence that rivaled most men. Still sporting his tight fade from his Marine days his goatee was the only sign he was no longer serving.

Trip, whose real name was Joe Grayson III, looked like he had just completed basic yesterday, his muscular frame made its presence known through the well-tailored clothes he wore. His grandfather, a rich African man that had started a construction company that he left to his son, the 2nd. His father did not approve of his son's military career because of concerns about his son's safety, showered the unit with everything he imagined they would need provided it could fit in a modest sized box.

Blade had settled in city not far from Bobby and had a job in an insurance office that he hated; Trip had moved within a short drive of his parent's house in an affluent area in Oyster Point. Still trying to figure out his next move he spent a significant amount of time a one of his father's job sites working in the family business, but he wanted something that would be his, knowing that his siblings were well positioned to run the family business one day.

After settling at a table and catching up on life and reminiscing and joking about their time in the Marines, Bobby decided it was time to get down to business.

"With a business partner, I am starting a security company, Code of Honor Security and I want you two to join us. Our idea is to not start with employees but to start with partners, part owners in the business that will treat the work like an owner would.

"After working as a security guard ever since I got back home it's easy to see the industry is ripe for the taking. We've got our first client and we start patrolling next month. If we do well, they have more sites that we can patrol, the up side down the line will be huge if we start the right way and do a stellar job, the growth opportunities are huge.

The salary is two-thousand dollars a month to start and as we grow and build our business and hire employees, the money will get bigger."

The questions were few as both Blade and Trip were looking for an opportunity like this, Trip offered one a solution to an implicit question he didn't ask. "I have a friend that I think you know too that could write up the contracts, otherwise I'm in."

Bobby smiles understanding the question that was not asked, "we have a lawyer that's a good friend that we use for contracts, I'll bring them next time for you two to review and sign, answering in the affirmative that everything would be in writing and not just promised."

Bobby left the first meeting feeling really good about where things stood, he had a scheduled time for Trip and Blade to meet Officer John and he had the people he needed to walk patrol their first day. There was a lot more work that needed to be done to provide twenty-four-hour security and prepared for the growth that he was sure would follow but he was happy with this initial success. Finding two people with the right background that he trusted completely, that weren't into drugs or too much alcohol that bought into what he was trying to do was a really good feeling. He was optimistic about what lie ahead.

Bobby was half way home when he realizing that they had no uniform shirts to wear, no flashlights, note pads, computers, or even ink pens, no of the equipment needed to actually get the job done in a professional manner. No knowing if Officer John had considered these items, he changed course and headed back to Dr. Chien's house.

Bobby entered the room in which Officer John was waiting. "How did it go?" he asked without looking away from the screen.

"It went really well, and they're in, but we need uniforms and gear A.S.A.P. if we want our guys to not only look professional but have the tools, they need to do the job on their first days. Before I made any purchases, I wanted to make sure that you hadn't already."

Officer John looked at Bobby with a sarcastic look on his face. "The only thing I've done unfortunately is look at videos of officers on patrol."

Bobby knew that was true. "I'm on it, no worries. I have some meetings for us tomorrow, did you schedule anything?" He asked as he looked in their book, as Officer John responded. "It's all in there as we agreed."

They reviewed the list of appointments for the next day as Bobby updated Officer John about the conversations he had just had.

"Sounds like things are coming along nicely, nice work." Officer John said with encouragement.

"Yeah," Bobby replied. "But it got me thinking, we aren't going to be able to deposit the money into our business account for very long before our partners want to know where it's coming from, and not having good answers will create distrust. We are going to have to come clean at some point and hope they are with us.

"Which brings me to my next thought, if we get the right people to work with us, I think we can bring them up to speed on everything we are doing, get their support with surveillance of more than just our client's property, they could help with these crooked cops. Think about how much we could do with a group of soldiers all keeping an eye on these cops and recording their activities. We could make a much larger impact."

Officer John was listening to Bobby, he had stopped his work and had turned his attention to what Bobby was proposing.

"Let's focus on one thing at a time and not get too far ahead of ourselves. I'm not sure where all this will lead, but I do know that if we move too fast, we increase the likelihood of a misstep. I think we have benefitted from the fact that it is only the three of us, we get too many people involved too quickly and we run the risk of losing control."

Bobby agreed but wanted to clarify his point. "Do you think it's a good strategy long term? An army of good guys making it their life's work to hold the police department accountable for their actions. It's something that should be in place already but instead we have the police policing themselves which we can agree has not worked out very well up to this point."

Officer John thought for a minute, what Bobby was proposing could get out of control if not done properly.

"I agree but I don't want to create a gang, operating outside the law, engaging in illegal activity. I really like the idea of having our company recording the illegal behavior of the cops but not getting involved to the level you and I are. It's a good long-term goal, now if you don't mind you apparently have some shopping to do, and I have to get back to my video recordings."

"I can't argue that," Bobby responded as he headed out the door with his copy of their calendar book under his arm. "I'll work on getting us what we need and meet you tomorrow for our first meeting. Don't work on that stuff too late."

Dr. Chien responded as she entered the room, giving Bobby a hug as he headed towards the stairs. "Don't worry, I won't let him stay there all night!"

Officer John laughed. "I'm used to having women tell me what to do, I was married for more years than I can count. Plus, I've gone through the last two days of video, and I'm ready to take a pretty incriminating video to the press when the time is right."

Bobby stopped on the stair and considered whether he wanted to look at the video. Looking at Officer John for a moment, he thought it better to leave that to him, he had his own work to do and didn't need to get worked up over what the crooked cops were up to.

It seemed like an everyday occurrence, someone on the street, in the neighborhood, or more recently, on the news, was talking about a member of the community or someone somewhere in America being the victims of police brutality.

Initially, he thought it good that this was coming to light because people needed to see what was happening so things could change but having seen what he had over the past month, he was beginning to lose faith that change would ever come. This was not just a case of a few racist cops; this was a network of criminals working with the police. Having just scratched the surface, he wondered how big this actually was?

He knew that the KKK and white supremacists had infiltrated local police departments and state and local offices, seemingly this was their strategy after the Civil Rights Movement of the sixties and seventies, moving from lynching and mob justice to formal positions of power to exert their will over people legally.

He wondered why had it taken so long for people to demand the police department take accountability? Done something before it was so out of control, he worried if this was too much for the three of them and too late to change things. Was racism and discrimination a permanent part of American legal and governmental systems that there was no going back?

Standing there, looking at Officer John hard at work reviewing recordings and trying to hold police officers accountable for their behavior, he was convinced they were not alone and that there were more people out there wanting change but most likely didn't know what to do.

They could be on to something big, still looking at Officer John who now had Dr. Chien looking over his shoulder at the video, every revolution starts with a small dedicated few, the only question in his mind now was how long it would take before they made an actual impact and became more than just a nuisance, but a catalyst for change?

Bobby thought about his days in the marines, there was a trust that needed to exist within a unit, company, and branch. He had to be able to trust the person standing next to him, knowing that they were in the fight of their lives, together. Bobby had to wonder if he would have looked the other way had someone in his unit broken the law in a significant way. It was a question for which he had no answer, so he dared not question why the crooked cops did what they do but he did have to question their leadership.

They set the tone, they decided what was allowed and what wasn't. Leadership told young officers and soldiers what was formally and informally acceptable. He knew, in his heart, that the issue wasn't an easy one, and that America's race problem would only be solved when everyone tired of voting in leaders unwilling to tackle the issue. To blame anyone in his city for the current state of race relations was foolish, he needed to focus on stopping it from continuing to grow more out of control and exposing the corruption to the masses so the good people could see and demand change.

They may not be ready to form their army yet but looking at the two of them he was sure it would happen in due time, he said to himself as he continued his descent down the stairs and towards the front door. "All in good time Bobby!"

Chapter 43

It had been two days since Officer John had sent their latest tapes to his friend at the local news station. Bobby, Officer John, and Dr. Chien conferenced-in on a call to talk about the images they were seeing on television, the same images Officer John had sent to his friend.

Like earlier tapes, this one was shown on the local news, but they hoped the national news would pick the story up shortly thereafter. Their plan seemed to be working just as they'd hoped.

"Chief Dolan wouldn't be able to skirt the issue forever," Bobby said. "Catching one officer on tape was an unfortunate incident, catching another was strange, but you keep adding officers and eventually, you have a problem that needs to be addressed."

They watched Chief Dolan answer the same questions as last time, wondering how many incidents it would take. Officer John had a different concern.

"If we are successful in getting Chief Dolan out, we will no doubt have an even bigger problem if A.C. Brice takes over, he is worse than Chief," John said.

Bobby enthusiastically responded. "Then we'll take him down too!"

Officer John thought about A. C. Brice, a man who had, to his knowledge, no reason to hate anyone. He was a handsome athlete in his younger days, was from a middle upper-class family, had attended college and had a good job. Why would someone like him be a racist, he wondered?

It was surely taught to him by his parents, there really was no other logical conclusion. Racism, he thought, was something that was passed down from generation to generation and it was a shame a man that had so much, either bestowed upon him by his parents' good genes or given to him over the course of his life, wasted his time and energy hating people he had no reason to other than where their ancestors were from or the color of their skin.

When the news coverage had reached its end, Bobby had a proposition for them.

"We need to celebrate small victories like these, just like we celebrated Code of Honor Security's accomplishments. What we're doing is dangerous and important, and every success is a major accomplishment, considering we're putting our lives on the line."

They agreed.

Dr. Chien added, "Maybe I'll occasionally cook us celebratory dinners. It was really nice having you two over the other night. I didn't realize how much I've missed cooking for the people I care about."

Officer John expressed his gratitude as well. "It's nice having a home-cooked meal. It's been a long time for me, and I can't think of a better way to celebrate."

Dr. Chien acknowledged. "I guess we have our first tradition, and I'd say it's a good one. Let's go out for dinner to celebrate this time, I need to get out of the house. I'll pick you up at seven, Bobby, if you don't mind meeting at John's place?"

After enjoying an appetizer and lighthearted chatter at their favorite restaurant, Bobby turned the conversation to work. "We have a meeting tomorrow with a group of possible partners. If we're lucky, they'll accept the offer, so, staffing-wise, for the new account, we will be set."

"Who's our next meeting with?" Officer John asked.

"I think we need to hire a secretary to keep all of this straight. We have a ton of stuff going on, and we can't afford to miss appointments. I have a few folks that I can trust. I can see if they're looking for good-paying jobs if that's okay?" Bobby had directed the question to Officer John, who nodded his approval.

Officer John felt pride in his new business venture and the opportunity to help those in the community, not only dealing with crooked cops but also with employment opportunities, it was more than he could have ever hoped for in his life.

He lamented about a time not so long ago where this feeling of accomplishment was neither probable nor possible, so he spent most of his time at home alone with no real purpose other than work. Now, he sat looking at his two friends and partners, thinking about how his life could've easily gone in a completely different direction after his wife had died.

Bobby sat in contentment as well. He had found his calling and was becoming at peace with his life, something he never thought he would achieve after his father had been killed. Although he was certainly not the only young, Black kid to have lost his father at the hands of a crooked cop, it was something that could have sent him down a path of blind anger, drugs, crime, or even worse, suicide.

Bobby looked at his two friends and thought about his family. He knew that without their support, he wouldn't have accomplished so much in his relatively short life. His mother's determination to keep the family together had pushed them not to let one horrible incident ruin their lives. She was sure they'd all achieve something meaningful with their lives, and her vision was seemingly becoming a reality.

He thought about the sense of purpose he had in his life and about his siblings, who were both doing well, his mother who was as well. He realized that in this moment, he was happy, and it was a long time coming.

All the years of pushing himself and the things he had missed out on as a kid were not in vain because he was living his life calling, he was protecting others and it felt good.

Bobby took a sip from his glass. His eyes wandered around the restaurant, his gaze fixing on a somewhat familiar face that he immediately couldn't place but looking past the wrinkled face and grey hair that was not young but vibrant in age, the face that was smiling and laughing with a group of men and women much younger than they, a face that when he finally recognized robbed him of all the happiness he'd been feeling. In a split second, he went from genuinely happy and content to incredibly angry with a massive headache. He was instantly afraid and wanting to hide and also empowered and wanting to act. His out-of-control emotions brought with them sweat, a pounding heartbeat, and a feeling he was about to vomit.

Sitting there at the opposite side of the restaurant was *Crooked Cop #1*, the one that had killed his father.

Chapter 44

Officer John noticed the change in Bobby demeanor, asking what was wrong as he followed Bobby's eyes to *Crooked Cop #1*. "Oh God, we need to leave" he demanded but Bobby wasn't hearing him. He requested the waitress in a louder than appropriate tone and requested the check as she hurried to their table in embarrassed and confused by the sudden change in attitude of the table that was so jovial just a moment ago.

She disappeared into the back as Officer John focused on Bobby and not *Crooked Cop #1*, "Bobby, she'll be right back, Dr. Chien maybe you should go get the car at the valet." She didn't move but Bobby and Officer John didn't notice, they were focused on each other.

Back in an instant with the check, which Officer John began to pay with cash, she asked in a nervous tone" is there was something wrong?"

Officer John assured her. "No, my friend isn't feeling well, it's certainly nothing to do with you or the restaurant." His response did little to put her at ease as she turned and left.

Officer John calmly tried to reassure Bobby so they could leave the restaurant. "Keep calm, breath Bobby, we don't want to cause a scene or do something we might regret later," was the only thing he could think to say hoping to keep his friend in his chair.

He was afraid of what Bobby might do and he knew he couldn't stop him if he acted suddenly. His only hope was to keep repeating his words and hope that Bobby didn't follow through with whatever he was thinking.

He couldn't imagine what was going through Bobby's mind, and he wasn't going to stay there to find out. He needed to get him out of the restaurant and fast but was sure that forcing him up and out would cause the scene he didn't want; he was beside himself waiting for Bobby to give some kind of a response. The two men were so focused on Bobby and *Crooked Cop #1* that neither had noticed the reaction Dr. Chien was having.

She followed Bobby's eyes to *Crooked Cop #1* and her stomach began to turn as well when she realized who he was. She glared at him, thinking about the last time she'd seen him, and her blood began to boil. She went back to a beautiful, country roadside in Surry, Virginia, Colonial Trail Road. She'd never forget how happy she'd felt riding in her little convertible that day, her hair tucked under a scarf and wearing large, black sunglasses, she felt like a starlet escaping from the city to take in the beauty of the Virginia countryside.

She pulled to a stop at what would be the last stop sign for a while and noticed the young officer parked near the sign. On some level, she registered his handsome features, but paid him no attention and continued on her journey to nowhere, on a road she frequently traveled when she needed to feel free. She remembered the feeling of surprise when she saw the officer's lights flashing in her rearview mirror.

She remembered how handsome she thought he was when he walked up to the side of her car and began with a polite introduction, his muscular frame so much broader than her husband's. His strong hands were made more attractive by his manicured nails and a slim, gold band around his finger, similar to her husband's. His uniform hugged his body in a way that seemed effortless.

Dr. Chien answered his questions, removing her sunglasses and fluttering her eyelashes. When he asked her to step out of the car, she thought about how happy she was that she'd worn that particular outfit. It was her favorite, with its tiny blue and white checks and short skirt that stopped just above her knees. She loved wearing it for her husband because he often commented on how attractive she looked in it.

When the officer removed his glasses to reveal piercing brown eyes, Dr. Chien couldn't help but smile.

She thought nothing of the young officer as he directed her to the passenger's side of the car. He moved as if he were floating.

Dr. Chien followed his every instruction as she always had with people of authority. Her smile became uncomfortable when he moved closer to her and inquired about her husband. "I'm on my way to see him now," she said. "He's expecting me. Did I do something wrong, officer?" were the last words she said before he grabbed her and kissed her. She was no match for his strength, but she tried to fight him off, nevertheless.

There was no stopping him. He grabbed her and tugged at her as he pulled up her skirt. She didn't know what she should do. She called out for help, pleading for him to stop as he forced himself into her. She thought about her husband and how angry he would be with her for flirting with the officer. How could she have been so stupid to have led him on, putting herself into this situation? Her mind wasn't on the pain or the crooked cop raping her—it was squarely on everything she'd done wrong since she'd first pulled over and the embarrassment she felt about her actions.

When he was done, she stood there, leaning against the car, staring at him, asking why.

He replied, "You've been asking for it from the moment I pulled you over."

She blamed herself for many years because she'd been attracted to him, and she was married. It took many years for her to forgive herself for being attracted to another man because that was different than wanting to have sex with him. She'd long ago reconciled any conflicting feeling she had about the incident, knowing she'd done absolutely nothing wrong, that she'd been raped because that's what the evil, crooked cop had wanted, and it had nothing to do with her. Rape was about power, and he'd wanted to exert his over her.

As she looked at him, all these years later, she wasn't afraid, she was angry. She had changed a lot since that faithful day and was no longer a timid shy wife, she understood her power and promised herself that he was going to pay for what he had done to her.

Chapter 45

Within minutes, the three of them were in Dr. Chien's car without incident. Dr. Chien thought about how she might put an end to whatever evil *Crooked Cop #1* was up to. She knew he wasn't back in the city to do anything good. Dr. Chien thought about the sense of relief she'd felt when he'd left many years back, and she'd finally felt safe again. Even with her husband next to her in bed, she felt uneasy at times, but those feelings left when the cause of them left. Now, he was back, and she was convinced that he was up to no good. She knew how she would put an end to this chapter of her life, all she had to do was to be patient and put her plan into action at just the right moment.

As Dr. Chien planned her next move, Officer John enquired as to how Bobby was doing. "Are you okay, Bobby?" he asked.

Bobby answered, "I wasn't prepared to see him tonight. Everything was going so well. How does that piece of shit always know when to come into my life and ruin everything?"

Officer John remained silent for a moment making sure that he was thoughtful in the words he said, "That can't be easy, but hopefully, he isn't here for long, and we can stay on our path."

"I think he *is* our next step on the path." Bobby said, nonchalantly.

Officer John responded gently, "I don't think that's a good idea. The moment either of us gets near him, there'll be a cloud of suspicion. Maybe we could have gotten to him prior to our making our partnership public, but now, no way. Besides, this was never about revenge. It's about justice. Whatever crimes he did were so long ago, I can't imagine he's doing much now other than trying to get through another year. He's no longer on the force but he is still very close with A.C. Brice and many of the officers on the force."

"There's probably a reason for that, what we've seen is this is not only about racism and a few bad cops, there is a lot going on and I'm sure he is involved. Otherwise, why would he be here?" Officer John thought for a moment, "ok, let me try and figure out what's going on before we even consider any action. Like we've said before, we have to be careful, we cannot afford to act without thinking things through. Can you give me some time, I promise I'll get some answers!"

Bobby and Officer John continued their discussion while Dr. Chien focused on her next move. She thought about the pediatric syringes she had. B.D. syringes were available with short needles. Something with a thirty-two gauge, ultrafine would be the best. He most likely wouldn't feel the needle, but he might feel the injection, so she'd have to be quick, deliberate, and calm. She would have to look through her supply, she thought she had what she needed, I'll prepare the syringe when I get home and not waste any time. Keep it on hand at all times to be sure when the opportunity presents, I'll be ready. This will be the last time I see that monster and not do anything, I'll put an end to his reign of terror once and for all.

Bobby and Officer John followed Dr. Chien into her house, sat in the living room, and continued their discussion.

Dr. Chien interrupted to ask if they wanted tea or a drink, but neither of them did, too focused on convincing the other of their point of view and trying not to get angry over the other's stubbornness.

She excused herself and went back to the part of her house that had served as her physician's office for many years. Although she was no longer a practicing M.D., she kept the space as immaculate as when she was seeing patients. She went to her research area, removed a sample of bacterial meningitis, and carefully prepared the syringe for *Crooked Cop #1*. He wouldn't die immediately, but it would, ultimately, be fatal. He wasn't likely to see a doctor right away, thinking he had a cold or the flu, and that would be the death of him. He'd suffer, not nearly as long as his victims, but he would suffer.

She placed the syringe in a transport tube resembling a glasses case, it wouldn't cause suspicion if she were careful when she made her move.

Dr. Chien returned to the living room where Bobby and Officer John were teary-eyed and silent. She knew they were dealing with Bobby's demons. Another time, she'd have been there to comfort him and try to reason with both of them, but she had nothing left; she was exhausted by her thoughts.

"I'm truly sorry, Bobby," she said. "I can't imagine how you must feel. Please, stay the night in one of the guest rooms. I'm going to retire for the night, I'm exhausted. It might be a better idea to talk in the morning when emotions aren't so high?" She extended her arms to give him a sincere, warm hug and was off to bed. "Goodnight, John," were her parting words.

She ascended the staircase with what seemed like the weight of the world on her shoulders. Dr. Chien realized how bad a friend she was being and how her thoughts of revenge and justice were at odds in her mind. That Crooked Cop had done so many horrible things, yet she still could not fully convince herself that what she was planning was the right thing to do.

Once in her room, she looked through her collection of clutch purses. She needed one that would go with many outfits so that she could prepare the lining to hold her syringe case. None of them seemed quite right. She decided on a simple Crossbody Clutch Bag made of pebbled calves' leather with a chain shoulder strap. Its flap top and snap closure would be easy to open and close, and its inside pocket would be the perfect place to hide the syringe.

She put her clutch on the dresser and took a long look at herself. Could she actually do what she'd planned? Dr. Chien was too tired to think about it, but she was prepared. She removed her clothes, letting them drop to the floor before sliding between the baby blue satin sheets without putting on her nightgown or removing her makeup. She closed her eyes and waited for sleep to take her, but tears formed in its place.

Dr. Chien couldn't get the images, feelings, and pain of *Crooked Cop #1* raping her out of her mind.

Dr. Chien was overcome with the memories of how distant and cruel she'd been to her patient, loving husband, who had desperately tried to get her to explain the change in her mood and behavior. Almost a full year after her rape, with constant trips to the therapist, she was finally able to be intimate with him again. Their relationship had strained to the breaking point when she'd finally told him she'd been seeing a therapist about an issue with one of her patients that she couldn't handle. It was a partial lie that he'd believed because the change had been so sudden. She hadn't ever been dishonest with him, but she couldn't ever tell him what had happened on that beautiful country road or why she'd abruptly sold her convertible, a car he knew she loved. Dr. Chien needed to expel every piece of that afternoon, but unfortunately, she couldn't get rid of the memories.

She apologized to her dearly departed husband for the thousandth time. With the apology came the strength to carry out her plan as well as the sleep she so desperately needed.

Downstairs, Bobby and Officer John we so wrapped up in what they were feeling they did not notice Dr. Chien's unusual behavior. Officer John sat next to Bobby. "I think Dr. Chien's advice is spot on, we cannot accomplish anything tonight, let's just get some rest and talk tomorrow.

Chapter 46

The next morning, Dr. Chien awoke to the smell of fresh coffee, the same blend to which she awoke every morning. She looked out the window at the trees in her yard and the birds busy with their morning routines. No matter how many times she woke up to the same view and smell, she always took a moment to appreciate it.

She went downstairs to see Bobby and Officer John, looking as if they hadn't gotten much sleep. Both of them were in desperate need of a shave. "We helped ourselves to coffee," Officer John said.

Dr. Chien smiled and poured herself a cup. "How are you feeling Bobby, must have been quite a shock last night, did you get any sleep?"

Bobby placed his coffee down on the table keeping his gaze in the blackness of his coffee.

"I wasn't expecting to have our celebration end so abruptly. After the first shock of seeing him, I realized we have too much positive momentum for me to let him ruin my life a second time." He looked at Officer John. "I agreed, we need to get more information but not get distracted, he's not worth it."

Bobby got up and took the coffee cups into the kitchen and returned to the dining room. "We've got a lot to do today and no time to waste on the past."

"What's on the docket for the two of you today? I suspect you have a lot to do before your first day of service on Monday."

Bobby answered, "We have too much to do. We'll see you later." With that, they were off, as Dr. Chien had hoped, she had some things she needed to attend to as well.

Dr. Chien knew that *Crooked Cop #1* belonged to a civic and social club back before he'd left the area, and she needed to know whether he was still a member. Their parties and fundraisers would be her opportunity to execute her plan. She scoured her closet for just the right outfit, one that would fit into that crowd. She chose a yellow flower-patterned, open-backed, Vivienne Westwood business skirt suit that had been tailored to fit her like a glove. She hadn't worn it in a long time, it was the type of outfit she was likely to wear when she was with her husband. She chose a pair of velvet blue, Manolo Blahnik shoes with heels higher than she usually wore nowadays but had been a staple in her past. She looked herself over, descended the stairs, and went out of the house with purpose.

She pulled into the valet parking area of the club and headed straight for the membership office. Sitting in the office's comfortable and luxurious chairs she reminisced about the times she, her husband, and her daughter spent at the club. It was the perfect social outlet for young families with its many classes and activities for children of all ages which allowed the parents the opportunity to connect with friends, play tennis or just enjoy being social with the club members. It was also a vital part of her marking her practice and getting new patients. It was such an important part of her past, but she didn't miss it at all. Her thoughts were interrupted by the membership director welcoming her back.

"We are so happy to have you back after so long, and I am sorry to hear about your husband," the man said, having ushered her into his office and taking a seat across from her. He was young and smartly dressed in a tailored suit of his own with meticulously gelled hair and a neatly trimmed mustache, to Dr. Chien he looked exactly as she would have expected for his position.

Handing back her identification, he offered her a "special accommodation in light of her situation, "I could just update your membership as if you had never left, just at our current rates of course," smiling and nodding, "You'll notice that a lot has changed since you were last here. We've made quite a few upgrades, including adding to the tennis facilities and remodeling the dining and bar area. Can I print you and updated contract for you to review and sign, again you won't need to pay any initial dues, just your monthlies," he said with a confident smile?

Dr. Chien also wore a polite smile. "Yes, that would be fine, I hope to reconnect with some old friends I've lost touch with, such as the Hares, the Millers, and *Crooked Cop #1*—are they still members? I'm hoping to get back on with my life as I'm sure my departed husband would've wanted." She paused and waited for his response.

"Oh, wonderful," he turned to his computer and began typing feverishly, hoping to find the friends that would secure another member and get him a step closer to his monthly goal. "Yes, they're all active members, according to this, and with the upgraded facilities, you'll no doubt have ample opportunity to reconnect at one of our many social events. The calendar is online—can print you a copy with the contract?"

Dr. Chien had what she needed. "No, thank you. I'm pretty savvy with a computer." She took the contract and didn't pretend to review it, signing it quickly and returning it with a warm smile. "Thank you for making this so quick and easy," she said as she stood and extended her hand. "If there's nothing else?" He happily stood and took her hand, patting himself on the back for his shrewd dealings.

Dr. Chien walked through the familiar yet different areas of the club, remembering again all the time she and her husband had spent there, having fun with friends, and with each other. Looking out of a window overlooking the expanded grounds and the tennis area with many young people playing and taking lessons she thought about her daughter and their somewhat distant relationship. Her daughter was especially fond of this place, no doubt her sanctuary when home became undesirable. It was the perfect place to escape to, surround herself with friends knowing that her parents would never refuse her going because, it was the one place they didn't have to worry about her. It was perfect at that time in her life she thought as her mind came back to the present reality, it will be the perfect place again.

As Bobby and Officer John planned the client meetings and recruiting that would ensure their business's success, Dr. Chien reconnected with the club's members. She spent a few afternoons at the club during the first week of her reinstated membership, talking and laughing with friends, both old and new. She signed up for tennis lessons with the club pro.

"Just to brush up on her game," she'd explained, but she wanted to get in with a circle of people that would frequent the club for a purpose.

After seven days of careful planning and blending in, she was ready to spend some time with the people she really cared about, so when Bobby and Officer John proposed dinner to catch up, she was happy to oblige.

They all sat down and ordered cocktails, after which Bobby spoke with excitement "I never thought I would be my own boss, it feels good, but I had no idea how much work it is.

The guys are doing an excellent job with their documentation and reports, they are being very thorough which is just the level of service we need. If I were to compare them to my last company, we are knocking it out of the park. Everyone is so motivated to do the right thing to make the company successful because we all rewarded for good work."

Officer John and Dr. Chien felt his enthusiasm as he spoke. Dr. Chien offered her insight.

"It reminds me of my father speaking about his experience working in China. Everyone wanted the company to succeed so they worked very hard and took pride in their work. Sounds like you are experiencing the same level of commitment, but I think it's because your team benefits additionally, financially, from good work. I don't say that in a bad way, I think that's what's missing in most companies. The pressure to increase profits pushes leaders to make bad decisions like not give raises and bonuses but those decisions lead to a reduction in loyalty and pride in one's work."

Bobby nodded. "My last company paid just over minimum wage and my take home pay was just slightly above my expenses at the end of the month and I am single, I couldn't image trying to raise a family on what I make and the work I did was the companies charter. It wasn't as if I was in a support role, I was out in the field generating revenue and I still did not feel appreciated.

It all goes back to leadership, whether it's the owner or legislators, someone has to look out for workers and that starts with wages. The minimum wage is just too low."

Officer John interjected, "you forgot to mention the best part, the client has other sites they want us to patrol. It's all working according to plan."

Officer John could hardly contain his excitement when speaking about the feedback and future growth with their partners. It was music to their ears as they were all thinking about the money to be made.

Their tone settled just as their entrees arrived. "We've been talking non-stop" Officer John noted, "what's going on with you? I feel like we haven't spoken in a month, and it's been a little more than a week."

Dr. Chien smiled. "Same old story with me, although I did rejoin the social club, my husband and I had been members of for many years. I felt as if it was time for me to get out of that old house and start living again. The two of you inspired me, actually. I feel like I have a few more chapters in my life story, too."

Bobby raised his glass and proposed a toast. "To the next chapters of our lives!"

After a long dinner, dessert and coffee, and some port, they were at the valet stand, waiting for their cars. "We haven't forgotten our mission," Bobby said. "We'd like to come by in a couple of days to plan for our next step if that's okay" he said looking at Dr. Chien.

"Bobby, you don't need to ask. Just let me know when you're coming. We're in this together." And with warm embraces and went off in separate directions.

Chapter 47

Dr. Chien was halfway home when she changed course and headed for the club. It was a Thursday night, so there'd be a good number of people there at least until ten o'clock, when the club closed. She thought through her plan again, as she had done many times before, as she pulled up to the valet, grabbed her clutch, and took a deep breath as she entered the foyer. Immediately seeing someone she knew, she waving at the tennis buddy and pointed to the bar and then at her friend.

She slowly entered the bar area, taking the time to scope out the members and guests, paying close attention to the men with the hope of seeing *Crooked Cop #1* among them. After getting her cosmopolitan, she joined her friend.

"How is it possible that you look so put together every time I see you?" the friend asked. "I have to admit I'm jealous."

They joined a group of women, two of which she knew. There were quick introductions and then the normal small talk until one of them looked at Dr. Chien and said, "I understand you're a widow as well. I hope you'll be coming to the dance this Saturday. There'll be tons of couples there, and I need as many single women there as possible. There'll be too many single men for me to handle alone."

They all laughed.

Dr. Chien thought the dance might be the perfect opportunity to execute her plan, she would have to be patient because she could not draw attention to the fact that she was pursuing him. As one of the single members of the club any man she paid attention to would be noticed by her new friends.

She did not complete the thought fully when *Crooked Cop #1* walked by the bar in the direction of the restrooms. Seeing him again was like a bolt of lightning to her system. This could be the night if he would cooperate. If he were here long enough for her to make her move.

She shifted her attention between the chatter and laughter of her friends and the hall leading to the bathroom. It seemed like an eternity since he had disappeared from sight, where was he she asked herself. Should she go looking for him? Just as she contemplated her next move, he reappeared heading back to a group of men in the other room.

She needed to position herself to get a better view of him. Reaching towards the shoulder of one of the ladies in the group who occupied the perfect position, she leaned in repositioning herself as she whispered in her ear. "You've got to tell me who made this dress you're wearing. I have to have it." She said smiling, but not really listening to the reply.

Dr. Chien watched *Crooked Cop #1's* group intensely but covertly. She ordered another round of drinks for her group even before they weren't finished with the drinks they had. "We don't have to get up early, let's have a party of it" she said as they all laughed.

She needed to keep her group in tack and couldn't risk anyone leaving which could start an end to their evening and her plan.

Crooked Cop #1 was drinking at a rapid pace just as everyone else in the group. They were all getting louder with their speech and laughter and that's exactly what Dr. Chien needed, for them to stay long enough for another trip to the restroom. Men never went to the restroom in groups which was an advantage for her. She could never execute her plan if they were women.

As her drinks arrived, she handed her current drink to the waiter. "This is no longer getting the job done," she joked. Not wanting the alcohol to affect her judgement she could not drink too much.

It had been almost twenty minutes since *Crooked Cop #1* had last gone to the restroom. Both groups had ordered light snacks and had gotten another round of drinks when Crooked Cop #1 stood up from the lounge he was now sitting. Dr. Chien steadied herself, was it time she thought?

It seemed so as he started walking her direction towards the restroom. She put her drink on the table as he walked by her forcing herself to not make eye contact.

He disappeared again down the hall as she put her plan into motion. "Excuse me," she said. "I have to make a call," making it clear she was not going to the ladies' room, she didn't want company. She turned and went down the hall towards the restrooms. Dr. Chien pulled her phone out of her clutch and pretended to make a call as she positioned herself between the men's and women's restrooms. Luckily, they were across the hall from each other so she could remain at her post without causing alarm. As she stood there with opened clutch and her hand resting on the syringe pretending to be on a call, her stomach began to tighten as nervous energy took hold of her. She wondered if this was how *Crooked Cop #1* had felt when he'd approached her on that awful afternoon.

She used that thought to challenge her uncomfortable feelings, reignite her focus, and steady herself as she assumed Crooked Cop #1 would be exiting soon so she placed the phone in the clutch and retrieved the small syringe using her cell phone to cover it. She stood facing the wall, pretending to look at the phone making sure the syringe was in a comfortable position because she would only get one shot at delivering its contents. Her heart beating rapidly, she fought to keep thoughts of doubt out of her mind, thinking instead about that horrible afternoon and the grief it had brought into her life, the lies and deception it had introduced into her marriage, the distance it had created between her and her loving husband and wonderful daughter; doubt was replaced with rage.

Crooked Cop #1 exited the restroom, and she turned sharply into him, purposely bumping his abdomen to distract from the spall prick in his leg where she delivered the serum that would surely mean his death.

The he stumbled a few steps back, focused on the striking woman who had bumped into him. He reached toward her and smiled. "Well, excuse me. I didn't see you there. Have we met?"

Dr. Chien stepped away from his grasp, apologizing profusely, she quickly walked into the ladies' room. *Crooked Cop #1* stood for a moment pondering whether to follow the woman into the ladies' room, thinking to himself, *I may be old, but I still have desires.* Voices coming down the hall reminded him of where he was, and that this was not the place for those type of shenanigans. Letting go of his desires, he continued down the hallway noticing the slight pain in his left leg and abdomen but chose to ignore them because he was not wanting to call it a night just yet, he continued on rejoining his friends.

Dr. Chien sat in a stall, fighting back tears, not for what she'd done to *Crooked Cop #1*, but for her life, husband, and daughter. Tears slowly descended her cheeks as she thought about the impact the evil man had on her life and the power the memory from that afternoon still had over her.

She looked at the syringe in her shaking hand. Dr. Chien needed to steady herself and get back to her friends. She used toilet paper to dry her tears and carefully put the empty syringe and phone back into her clutch. She needed to leave but wasn't sure she could without running into Crooked Cop #1 again. She decided that if he were still outside, she'd apologize again but keep walking away from him to get to her friends as quickly as possible.

Dr. Chien splashed some water on her face and patted her face dry. She looked at her makeup, reapplied her lipstick, and composed herself and exited the restroom behind two women ready to make new friends if needed, her potential allies if Crooked Cop #1 was waiting for her. She was relieved to see that he wasn't in the hall and slowed her pace so that she could ensure that he was not near her friends, she did not want to engage him by mistake.

As she walked toward her friends, she concocted an excuse to leave. "Ladies," she said. "Something just came up. I'll see you at the dance Saturday?" She turned and headed for the door, ignoring their questions, asking if everything was okay.

One of her friends called. "Don't miss the fun!"

She glanced over her shoulder as she walked away and said, "Don't worry. Wouldn't miss it for the world."

Dr. Chien waited at the valet, keeping an eye on the door to the club. She released a huge sigh of relief when she saw her car pull up, she jumped in not really looking at the bill she gave the valet as a tip and was off, speeding home. Once there, she went into her house and laid on her bed.

It was done!

Chapter 48

Bobby was home, looking over the schedule for the following week, thinking about the sales meeting he and Officer John had on Monday, but his mind kept going back to Crooked Cop #1. The impact he'd had on Bobby and his family's lives was immeasurable. If his father hadn't been killed by him, would his mother have been absent so often and missed so much of their lives working and taking care of others instead of her own family? He'd had so many nights filled with tears, trying to deal with an anger for which he was not equipped. What would his life have been like without the years of pain he endured trying to be the best, be stronger, run faster; looking down at his weathered calloused muscular hands he wondered. There was nothing he could do about the past, but he was not about to let Crooked Cop #1 take control of his life a second time.

He picked up his phone and called Officer John. "We need to talk, nothing is happening" was all he said but Officer John knew what he wanted to discuss because it had been a week since he promised to try and gather information and he hadn't reported anything as of yet, so he didn't need Bobby to say anything more. "Let's meet at Dr. Chien's tomorrow afternoon, I'll check to see when she's free. Maybe we can all have lunch?"

Bobby didn't want to be rude, but he also didn't want to be distracted by food and general conversation; he had a purpose for their meeting. "That's fine, but my reason for getting together isn't exactly lunch conversation, let me know what she says."

Dr. Chien was happy to have received a text from Officer John proposing lunch the next day—at Bobby's request—to discuss Crooked Cop #1 no doubt, and although she wanted more time alone, she suggested that they meet for dinner tonight. She had yet to get out of bed that morning, instead, her large bed had become her dining area and refuge covered with photo albums and pictures. She'd been using them for comfort between casual conversations with her daughter, needing to be reminded of the good in her life, of all the positives that had transpired in spite of the tragedy *Crooked Cop #1's* actions had inflicted upon her.

Her daughter grew up knowing her parents cared about her, she had a long life with her husband, and now in retirement was content up until Bobby and Officer John came and offered her an opportunity to again take care of her community. Indeed, she had overcome his attack in every way and knowing her friends were coming over and Crooked Cop #1 was on his way to death she was done sulking and got out of bed.

Bobby glanced at the text confirming the meeting, it was just what he needed, to eliminate the only distraction to planning out how to get close enough to Crooked Cop #1 to kill him, make him feel as bad as all his victims and their families had felt? How might he collect all the hurt, anger, and struggle felt by his victims to deliver it into the soul of the evil man that had caused it?

Bobby arrived at Dr. Chien's house bearing flowers which brought a smile to her face, "Thank you, did I do something to deserve these, please let me know and I will do it again." He followed her into the kitchen where Officer John was standing pouring him a drink. Bobby hugged his friends joking, "you two are going to turn me into a drunk."

Dr. Chien wanted updates on the business, so they bored her with the details as she completed dinner and Bobby set the table putting the flowers in the center. As they settled into their meal Dr. Chien suggested they get to it because she was needing to put Bobby at ease but not sure if she wanted to tell them what she had done.

"Nothing has happened since the restaurant, so I'd really like to know what's going on" he said looking at Officer John.

"Well, I know for sure that he is not back on official business but apparently, he is very much involved with A.C. Brice and the rest with their drugs and guns. He's working up in Northern VA, apparently has been for years, but came down here when he got word of what is happening. He is staying with A.C. Brice, probably because he wasn't some assurances that he has a handle on things. This does not bode well for us because he is no doubt going to try and find out who is behind all the videos and deaths. This is not the time to act out of spite or anger because everyone is on edge, Dad is home and he is mad, so to speak."

Bobby put down his fork and looked into space thinking. "The problem is if he leaves, we will not have an opportunity to get him, we need to act before it's too late because we have no idea how long he will be in the city."

Officer John felt the need to remind Bobby. "We're not doing this because of Crooked Cop #1, we're doing this to change things, to make everyone safe, and bring these cops to justice. If we make this about revenge, then we risk becoming just like them." Dr. Chien listened thinking that it almost sounded like Officer John was talking directly to her like he knew what she had done. He continued, "What good is killing this one man if we lose the ability to change the department?"

Bobby knew that Officer John was right. "It's hard, you don't understand. It was one thing to live with the fact that he killed my father and was out there free somewhere without ever paying for his crime, but now he's here planning someone else's death for all we know, and we aren't doing anything about it."

Officer John wanted to assure them again. "Listen, we have no reason to assume that they are going to leave me out of their next deal. We still have cameras recording that no one has discovered, and we have a business that is just starting to blossom, I know it's harder than either of us will ever know Bobby but making the wrong move and going after *Crooked Cop #1* could ruin all the great things we are just starting. It's not going to be easy, but you have got to let him go and focus on the business and let me continue to get information."

Dr. Chien listened and was tempted to say what she had done but there was a possibility that it wouldn't work, and he would actually go to the doctor before the injection had a chance to run its course. She didn't know if Crooked Cop #1 was the type of person that ran to the doctor with every little cough or if his doctor was the type of doctor that didn't assume minor symptoms were nothing to worry about. There were so many unknowns that if the injection did not kill him, she would have to try again or make a different plan.

She knew that if she told Bobby he would have a sense of false hope and she knew what that was like, and it was something she was not going to do. She finally offered her advice to Bobby who was sitting looking into his plate for answers, putting her hand on his, "I think Officer John is right, and being patient is the right course of action. It's certainly not the easy route and we are here for you if you need us and you have your family, don't think that you have to go through this alone."

He looked at her and smiled. "You two are right," taking a deep breath and pushing his whiskey aside. "I definitely don't need that right now, I need to think clearly because as you said, I have a lot of work tomorrow and I don't need a hangover."

Officer John followed suite. "Maybe, I don't either," as he pushed his glass away.

Chapter 49

Less than twenty-four hours after being stuck by Dr. Chien's syringe, Crooked Cop #1 started showing signs of a cold, which quickly escalated, as Dr. Chien had predicted. Being the stubborn man, he was, he took cold medicine and rested rather than go to the doctor. That stubbornness ultimately sealed his fate. Not three days later, he was found dead in his bed.

News of *Crooked Cop #1's* death spread quickly. Officer John heard about it while saying goodbye to his kids at the end of an uneventful school day. One of the parents approached him to give him the news, "I'm so sorry to hear about *Crooked Cop #1* passing away this morning; did you know him?"

Officer John was shocked. He at once thought of Bobby, wondering if he'd has anything to do with it. "What?" he responded. "How, I hadn't heard, do you know what happened?" He hoped Bobby's name wouldn't come up.

"Apparently, he'd been ill with the flu or something and passed away in his sleep. There have been so many tragedies in the police department this year, it's really sad, I understand he was a good man."

Officer John had already left the conversation mentally, trying to surmise what might've happened. How might Bobby take the news? He hoped Bobby would feel vindicated and a sense of closure without having to put himself or others in harm's way. He also felt relieved, tinged with a sense of urgency to tell Bobby and Dr. Chien about it.

He rejoined his conversation with the parent. "Sorry—can you excuse me? I need to check on a friend who'll be quite upset by this news."

Officer John called Bobby and Dr. Chien and told them they needed to talk. He didn't want them to find out without him being there, also wanting to make sure that if Bobby had been involved, he'd left no trace of his actions behind.

Dr. Chien suggested they meet at her house, she suspected she knew what was going on and was in a place where she could discuss what happened and not get emotional. She'd already forgiven herself for what she'd done and didn't care about the judgment of others. Like everything in her life, if she was comfortable with her decision, it didn't matter what others thought.

She put down the phone and cleaned up a bit. When she was done, she ordered some fried chicken from Mimi's Café. She needed comfort food and wasn't in the mood to be healthy and she didn't have time to cook. She knew the boys wouldn't complain.

Dr. Chien took a long shower, thinking about how she might tell her confidants about how she'd made an evil man accountable for his horrible acts. What she wasn't sure of was if she wanted to tell them why, or if they might see her differently because of it. She wondered what men thought of women that were raped and what they might think but would never say. She trusted Officer John and Bobby with her life, they'd grown closer than she'd ever imagined. She went back over the last almost three months since Bobby had shown up at her door, completely lost and unsure of what to do with their injured friend, it seemed like a lifetime ago.

She got out of the shower and took a long look at herself in the mirror, frosted with steam, she wiped away just enough to see her eyes. They'd seen so much in her lifetime—maybe too much she thought as it struck her that they appeared permanently tired from her long, complicated life. Her eyes began to tear and with those tears came the courage to tell them the whole truth and be vulnerable with her friends for the first time.

Officer John and Bobby arrived at Dr. Chien's and as was their custom, she poured Glenlivet into lowball glasses with one large ice cube when she heard them pull up. She informed them she'd ordered dinner, as they sat in her living room, shifting their attention to Officer John so he could let them know what was on his mind.

"*Crooked Cop #1* is dead," he said. "He died last night from a cold or pneumonia or something. It was strange that it happened so suddenly, and I wanted you both to hear it from me and not someone else."

Bobby's mouth dropped open. He seemed shocked, relieved, and angry all at the same time.

Officer John continued. "I also wanted to make sure that you didn't have anything to do with it, that you didn't poison him or something. I know you had every reason to, so I'm not judging, I just wanted to make sure that you covered your tracks if you did."

Still in shock, Bobby replied, "No. I wish I had, but it seems karma beat me to the punch."

Dr. Chien sat, listening to the exchange, wondering if she should interject, she waited for a pause before supplying the missing details. "It wasn't karma; it was me." Dr. Chien explained her painful past to her friends. It was something she never thought she'd share with anyone. Leaving no details out, she confided in them the difficulty the rape had on her life, how she'd felt when she'd seen him again, and her plan to end his life. When she was done, she added one emphatic statement, "that evil man needed to pay for what he did to me and so many others. I knew that it would pose a significant risk for the two of you to do something, and I could get to him more easily and do what needed to be done, so I did."

"How?" Bobby asked.

"Does it matter?" Dr. Chien responded. "I'm trained in medicine, I used something that would raise questions but not suspicion. We don't have to worry, even if they do an autopsy."

The doorbell rang. Officer John jumped in his seat, startled by the sound.

Dr. Chien got up. "That's the dinner delivery, no doubt. I'll be right back."

As Dr. Chien disappeared into the hallway, Bobby looked around the living room, at its meticulous blend of design and comfort, with its patterned blue wallpaper and mixture of light and dark blue furniture. Two love seats and one armchair, a printed large rug with a mix of colors. Mostly burgundy and reds but enough blue to tie everything in the room together it was very meticulous. The fireplace and its heavy, cherry wood mantle mirrored the strength and delicateness of the room as it mirrored the woman who lived there, both masculine and feminine, nurturing and dangerous. He was reminded of the female soldiers he'd met in the Marines, both feminine and strong, depending on what was needed for the circumstance, and he realized he had a new admiration for Dr. Chien. She was clearer to him now than ever before.

Officer John stared into space deep in thought, processing what Dr. Chien had told him and thinking about his own beloved wife. He wondered if his wife would be capable of coming back from such a horrible attack. She'd been caring, kind, soft, and in his mind, delicate as a piece of China. He had protected her from danger his whole married life, be it him standing strategically between her and potential harm, speaking up when he felt someone's tone was too aggressive, or securing their home before they'd retired for the evening. He loved being her protector and, in a way, thought she was how women should be, but at that moment, after hearing Dr. Chien's account of strength and bravery, he wondered if he'd had it all wrong.

Dr. Chien returned, walking through the room toward the dining room, as she did Officer John looked at her in a different light than before. They sat and began to enjoy their "bad" dinner.

Dr. Chien looked at Bobby and said, "Are you okay? I know you've carried a lot of anger and resentment toward Crooked Cop #1. Now that he's gone, having suffered while poison raged through his body…he deserved to suffer, but that won't necessarily end your pain. Vengeance doesn't always have the imagined effect. I've learned that many times over the years."

Bobby looked up to see his two friends' eyes fixed on him. "I'm not sure what to feel. I'm relieved there's less evil in the world because he's gone and that he won't be able to hurt anyone else like he hurt us, but I'm also numb.'

They continued to eat. When they were done, Officer John gathered their dishes and took them to the kitchen.

Dr. Chien looked at Bobby with compassion. "You can stay here tonight if you don't want to be alone."

Bobby nodded in agreement. "I need to tell Michael and Nancy before they see it on the news or hear about it from a stranger or friend."

He sat at the table, thinking back to his childhood and the many struggles he and his family had experienced after their father was gone. He talked to his compadres about the emotional strain and the many nights he'd cried himself to sleep. He talked about the changes he'd seen in his mother, and how she'd been absent because she had to work, even though his father's life insurance policy ensured they wouldn't be put out onto the street. He talked about knowing that his little brother would miss out on so many father-son moments he'd been lucky enough to share with his father.

Dr. Chien and Officer John asked no questions, instead they just listened to their friend. When he was at a point where he'd said all, he needed to say, the three of them retired to bed. It was the first time in a long time in a long time that Bobby easily fell asleep and slept through the night, *Crooked Cop #1* was dead and no longer a threat to him. There were other racists, other crooked cops, but the source of a lifetime of fear and anxiety for him was finally gone and no longer a threat.

Bobby woke up early and headed home, wanting to be in a comfortable place when he called Michael and Nancy to share the news.

Chapter 50

Bobby sat across from his sister, exhausted and emotionally spent after a day of intense emotion and tears at her home in Williamsburg. She wondered aloud, asking the question that had plagued her since she was a child. "Why did *Crooked Cop #1* have to kill our father?"

It was a question about which Bobby had thought a lot. For the first time, he articulated an answer. "If not out father, it would've been someone else's."

She looked at him in disbelief. "What do you mean?"

Bobby couldn't believe the clarity within his mind. After becoming vigilant in his quest for justice and resolving the reason his father had been murdered, he said something he'd never said out loud before, "Slavery never went away for some people; it just changed. The obsession for money and power never left the white slave owners. They created that system to make themselves rich at the expense of everyone else. Poor whites—everyone, in fact—suffered as a result of slavery except for rich, white landowners. Jobs were taken away from the people in the south and given to a group of people forced to come thousands of miles to work—how could that help anyone?"

Nancy thought for a moment and replied, "I guess I get that, but what does that have to do with our father's death?"

Bobby continued his stream of consciousness explanation, "When white slave owners gave the job of supervising blacks to the poor whites and they created monsters of them, convincing them the blacks were the cause of all of their problems and grief and that they couldn't go back to where they came from, some mysterious and unknown place poor whites had probably never heard of, so they were burdened with dehumanizing and controlling them.

"When the system, after such a long time, ended, they had to find another way of making money, so they helped it evolved into what we have today, undereducated whites taught to believe that immigrants and Black people are the source of their problems. The rich have found new ways to control them, creating new jobs like our for-profit prison and healthcare systems. The government understates the number of jobs created for the sole purpose of denying people their basic rights. They also twist our history and manipulate the education system, so people in the South are unable to learn the skills necessary to move into better socioeconomic positions. They're just as trapped as we are."

Bobby seemed to give himself comfort and reassurance as he spoke, as if the last almost six months wasn't a series of mindless acts of rage but a war against the system of injustice in America. Just as his country had trained him to go to foreign lands as a marine and defend American ideals of democracy, he had, on his own, taken that training, and was using it to defend Americans against threats against democracy inside its borders.

"The only way our system changes are for enough white people to decide its wrong and force a change. The rich whites in power know this, it's the biggest threat to their business of oppression for profit. It's bigger than environmental destruction, a shrinking middle-class change, or the modernization of the rest of the world that will pass America in almost every facet of life," Bobby continued. "What they don't understand or don't care about is that this system is what's holding America back and why other countries' citizens are happier and more prosperous than us because they don't waste resources trying to keep an unsustainable system of oppression going. We'll never become as great a nation as we can without dealing with our system of slavery and oppression, it just can't happen."

As Bobby spoke what he knew to be true, a weight lifted off his shoulders, and he realized it wasn't his job to change the system. It was, however, his job to be a mirror for the millions of people in the country, to show them this system of oppression and the harm it caused, and they would hopefully decide it was a waste of resources. They could feel sorry for the Black man or woman that had been beaten, abused, or even killed, but that alone wouldn't compel them to make a change. They needed to see the system for what was, a huge waste of resources designed to make a few white men very wealthy.

Bobby thought he, Officer John, and Dr. Chien were at war with a system of oppression. They weren't the first, and they wouldn't be the last.

Chapter 51

There were mixed emotions as news of *Crooked Cop #1*'s death swept across the city. Many residents were shocked or grief-stricken by the sudden, unfortunate death of the beloved, honorable officer who'd served the community for so long and who had been taken suddenly by an unfortunate run-in with some sort of bacteria that had quickly taken his life. Other residents knew the type of man Crooked Cop #1 was and kept on about their lives as if nothing newsworthy had happened, but the residents he'd terrorized for much of his life silently celebrated the death of the awful man upon which many of them had wished death on many occasions.

As the cause of his death seemed mysterious to those tasked with explaining it, the theories around his death became more outrageous. One reporter suggested the water was to blame, though there was little reason for such a claim. The city responded quickly, checking the water supply to make sure his death hadn't been caused by some strange contamination. Within hours of the report, grocery stores in the neighborhood were giving away free bottled water to residents to ensure their safety.

It was quickly decided this needn't happen in all neighborhoods, only the ones he'd frequented. Less than forty-eight hours after the first report, it was determined the water was safe, and his death was the result of an encounter with some sort of bacteria, possibly while he was traveling. The city was safe, and the mysterious death solved. To the surprise of those who knew how evil the crooked cop was, a petition began to circulate, gathering support for a statue to be erected in front of police headquarters. It was the petition that led to Bobby's phone ringing one Sunday afternoon.

"Hello?" Bobby said, answering cautiously because he didn't recognize the number.

"Hello, my name is Susan, and I'm calling from Public Service Broadcast to invite you to a round table discussion about the initiative to get a statue erected in front of the county police station to honor Crooked Cop #1 for his many years on the force. He recently passed, if you weren't aware, and there is a growing movement to have funds allocated to honor the life of a highly decorated officer and leader how spent his whole life in law enforcement, most of it right here in Hampton Roads. We're getting a group together to debate the merits of this honor, and we'd like to invite you to participate."

Bobby listened in utter shock and anger. The man that had ruined his childhood was getting a fucking statue? Hell, no.

"Yes," he said. "I'll participate in your panel. When and where?"

"Wonderful," she said. "The panel discussion will be at the station on the twenty-second at seven, so we're asking panel participants to be at the station at five-thirty at the latest for set-up and preparation. Do you have a pen to take down our address?" Susan asked in a happy voice to which Bobby took offense. She must've known the history between Bobby and Crooked Cop #1, but she still approached the conversation as if she were asking him to be on some sort of game show.

"I have a pen and paper," Bobby responded flatly. He hoped his annoyance wouldn't travel across the phone line. Bobby took the address down and hung up without closing salutation.

He stared at the piece of paper with the address on it.

A statue.

A statue for the man who had killed his father.

He wondered how people could have such differing opinions about a person. How could there be people out there who knew how he'd terrorized black people, and at the same time, there were others who thought he deserved a statue. How could one group of people be so blind to the suffering of others?

Maybe they didn't care. Maybe all the white people in the city were racist a-holes who didn't care about the suffering of others. Maybe he was just doing what they couldn't, using his position as a cop to terrorize and kill black people, and they wanted to reward his great work as the murderer of the undesirables.

Bobby sat, fuming as he looked at the paper, trying to rationalize the conversation that had just taken place. They didn't know. They couldn't know. Maybe this would be his opportunity to talk about his and other black people's experiences with Crooked Cop #1 so that everyone would know the truth. At the same time, he'd expose all the crooked cops for who they were. This could be his opportunity to force the crooked cops out of the shadows, and they'd finally have to answer for the awful things they'd done. Their lawyers wouldn't be there to twist the truth and manipulate situations so that obvious instances of police brutality became questionable situations that put cops in the position of having to make quick decisions. He'd be on TV, telling the entire city the horrible things those evil men were doing. This would be his opportunity.

He got up, grabbed his jacket and headed out the door. On the way, thought about what Officer John and Dr. Chien's faces would look like when he told them the news.

Chapter 52

Bobby couldn't wait to get in front of a desk and organize his thoughts, in his mind, as he drove to Dr. Chien's house, he thought of different examples he would bring up to make his point. This wouldn't just be about *Crooked Cop #1* he reaffirmed in his mind, I'm gonna nail them all. As he entered the room that had become their office, Dr. Chien and Officer John were buried in work and greeted him without looking up.

"Guess what," he exclaimed. They both stopped what they were doing.

"What?"

"The city council is considering building a statue to honor Crooked Cop #1 and obviously there is a bit of controversy around it."

They looked at each other not understanding why Bobby was excited by this news but didn't interrupt him.

"Because this is such a divided issue the local station is having a discussion about the topic and invited me to join!"

They again looked at each other, waiting for the good news. Bobby sensing that they didn't get the opportunity he had further explained.

"I'm going to be able to get on television and tell the whole city and anyone that can see the broadcast exactly what these crooked cops are up to, expose them for the criminal racists they are."

Dr. Chien replied first while looking at Officer John. "Bobby, I think your conviction will definitely make some people who may be in support of the statue reconsider but I'm not sure expecting more than that is realistic. No matter how eloquent your points, some people are going to believe what they want whether it's based-on fact or not."

Bobby smiled. "I know but think about the people in the city suffering because the crooked cops had been left unchecked, often breaking the law without repercussion. They will see that other people are on their side, there's also a lot of people that I bet have no idea what leads people to distrust law-enforcement, they will understand why."

"It's hard in a city this big for everyone to have visibility to the awful things the ministers of justice at all levels do, they've never witnessed it for themselves, but this discussion will at the very least open their eyes to what they may never experience. It's not an end but a beginning, I know I'm not going to be able to solve the problem but it's another opportunity to expose the truth."

Officer John spoke after listening to Bobby's thoughts. "If that's your reason for going on the show, to bring awareness, I think your appearance on the program might achieve that and maybe even put this statue nonsense to rest."

Dr. Chien continued where Officer John left off, in a measured tone. "But I hope you don't expect much more than that, racism runs deep and not to be a sour puss, but the program may just be a formality to discuss a decision that has already been made.

"I think you telling your story and perspective is the right thing to do but let that be the goal, to give yourself an opportunity to speak you mind and not to change others because you have no control over them."

Bobby half agreed. "I'm sure that once these people hear about Crooked Cop #1's past they will not only put an end to the statue or any other honors for such an awful man, they may also question the Chief and A.C. Brice about my allegations."

Dr. Chien and Officer John hoping he'd reach the people on the panel, but they feared his words would have no effect. They listened and nodded their heads and smiled encouraging smiles, hoping he'd be well-received and understood. They had, however, seen a lot in their lives, and they knew that similar words had no impact, but people were full of surprises, so they gave Bobby support and encouragement, hoping the panel wouldn't let him down. They hoped the panel would see Bobby for who he was, a man who'd had his life permanently and horribly altered by the crooked cop for whom they were pondering building a statue.

When the day of the discussion arrived, Bobby was eager to get to the station. Upon arrival he was directed to a VIP area for parking and directed by a friendly security guard. "Are you hear at the request of the producer?"

Bobby was feeling good about his VIP status. "Yes, I am a panelist, Bobby Harris."

The security guard reviewed his list on a very official looking clipboard with lots of papers attached, "yes, Mr. Harris, go right thru those doors marked studio and Susan will assist you."

Once inside Bobby was greeted by a friendly, familiar voice. "Hi, Bobby Harris? I spoke to you on the phone, I'm Susan."

Bobby nodded and smiled. "Yes. Thank you for having me on the panel. I've never been on television before."

She smiled and guided him through the maze of activity backstage. "Let's get you ready for your big debut, then."

Bobby followed her slight hand as it guided him. She couldn't have been more than twenty-two, he thought. She was petite, with brown hair tied back in a loose ponytail, a headset with a microphone, and a clipboard. Her attractive face was noticeable even though they were partially hidden by large, brown framed glasses. He wondered if she was important but decided she probably wasn't since she was ushering people around.

She led him into a room where a lot of people were standing around, looking at note cards, and talking to one another. Susan spoke as they entered the room. "Hello, everyone. Our last panelist has arrived, so if you all can wrap things up and follow me, we can make our way to the green room for light refreshments and final instructions. Thank you."

Everyone shuffled toward Susan, and she led them to another area about the same size as the first. Inside was a table with pastries and donuts, coffee, and sodas.

"Please, help yourselves," Susan said. "Our producer will be here shortly to brief everyone. If you need anything, just holler for me. My name is Susan." She exited the room, leaving Bobby with strangers he decided to avoid for the moment so as to not get distracted. Though he wasn't hungry at all, he made his way toward the pastries, selected one along with a Coke, and settled into a corner, pretending to enjoy himself as he tried not to make eye contact with anyone.

The awkward tension in the room began to build, and Bobby wondered if he was going to have to eat another pastry when Susan reappeared. "We're ready to take the stage."

With a sigh of relief, the panel followed her to the stage. On it was a curved table with six seats and one more comfortable-looking seat between the table and the small audience of people, probably for the host. There were four cameras located around the studio that seemed larger on the inside than on the outside. In front of each seat was a nameplate, and Bobby took his seat.

A young man came quickly over to Bobby, attached a microphone to his shirt, and asked him to speak normally, so they could adjust his microphone.

Through the bright lights, Bobby focused on the audience. They seemed to have come in just before the panel because they were still shuffling around to find their seats and shaking hands as if to introduce themselves to their neighbors. He counts thirty people in the audience and made a note of the twelve African-Americans in the crowd.

Bobby's attention shifted as a man approached the panel and introduced himself as the producer. "We'll introduce each of you to the audience, and you may just smile and nod—no need to say anything other than hello if you like. We'll then introduce the host, and we'll introduce the audience to the topic for discussion, the proposed statue honoring Crooked Cop #1. After that, we'll have a series of questions to facilitate the discussion. If you wish to speak, just push the button to alert the moderator, and he'll acknowledge you. Please refrain from speaking until you're acknowledged because we want all points to be clear and on camera. We want to keep things cordial, so please refrain from directing comments to any one person on the panel, but just saying your point of view."

"We're live in ninety seconds, everyone," he finished receded into the shadows.

All at once, the cameras began to move, and the moderator—an older man in his late fifties or sixties—introduced himself. Bobby recognized him from all the years the man had been on the news. The first two people on the panel were women—one a housewife born in the USA, and the other an insurance agent for a prominent insurance company. Next was a businessman whose small business employed a hundred and fifty people in the community. Bobby was introduced next as a small business owner whose father had been tragically killed by *Crooked Cop #1.*

Bobby was shocked by the introduction, and he tried to hide his reaction by putting on a smile. He figured that had been why he was invited to the program, but he hadn't expected the introduction to be so blunt. Bobby missed the introductions of the two remaining panelists, a white guy, and the only other black panelist.

"Tonight, we debate as to whether Newport News should erect a statue to honor one of its fallen officers, a man that served his community with distinction for over twenty-five years, dedicating his life to serving others," The moderator said.

Bobby looked at the other black panelist to see his reaction to the introduction, and their eyes met as if they were thinking the same thing. He gave Bobby a pleasant smile and a nod. He was an older man with a significant amount of grey hair on his head and in his mustache. Bobby wondered who the man was.

His attention rejoined the room as the housewife was speaking. "He was such an important figure in our community, serving with distinction for so many years it seems only fitting that we would honor him this way," she said.

"He was not without his critics, and he was involved in more than a few scandals, discharging his weapon in, shall I say, precarious situations. Bobby, what are your thoughts?" The moderator said.

Bobby was taken off guard because he hadn't pressed his button. He quickly organized his thoughts; it was the moment for which he was waiting.

Chapter 53

Bobby sat in his chair, looking at the moderator and the audience at the studio, all of them seeming to be waiting with bated breath. He knew that this was the reason for which he was here, and he cleared his throat and spoke his mind. "I understand that some people may have a different view of this man than I do, but I think it's universally known in the African-American community and to other minority groups in the city that this man was a racist."

There were immediate rumblings from the audience, and at least one of the panelists' microphones caught picked up him saying, "Figures you'd go there."

Bobby continued, unwavering in his position. "I imagine no man who lives is perfect, and I don't expect police officers to be perfect. I do, however, expect them to enforce the law evenly and without bias. This man made a habit of treating minorities as if the law was up to his interpretation and not necessarily to be enforced equally, when you do that, you tell minorities that they mattered less and aren't equal citizens, and that shouldn't be celebrated.

"We have to acknowledge that evil men do good things, oftentimes to cover up or to repent for the bad that they do. We cannot ignore the bad because there is some good and if this officer's record were made public, I think most would be surprised at the number of complaints, questionable arrests, and accusations of police brutality on his record, fortunately for him the police union does not allow that kind of access."

Bobby noticed that the businessman wanted to speak. The moderator asked for his thoughts. "Sometimes, people perceive something to be one way when it actually isn't that way at all," he said as a rebuttal to Bobby's points. "The facts are that this esteemed officer was never convicted of any wrongdoing, so we shouldn't judge this man based on opinion."

Bobby quickly replied before anyone including the moderator could speak, "that's precisely the problem, isn't it? Suppression of information! What harm does it do the public to know statistics on officers paid to protect and serve them? It is the suppression of vital information that has led to this awful man being considered for a statue."

As Bobby spoke, he realized that he might be leading the police to look at his activities more closely, so he softened his words. "I know what it's like to have someone you love tragically killed and I wouldn't wish that on anyone."

The moderator interrupted Bobby. "To be fully transparent, one of the reasons Bobby is on the panel is the fact that *Crooked Cop #1* killed his father during a routine stop that escalated and unfortunately led to the shooting. Which I must also say that Crooked Cop #1 was acquitted of any wrongdoing."

The audience began to chatter at the news, but Bobby still needed to try and clear his name in the eyes of the police.

"That tragedy happened a long time ago and it is why I have a somewhat unique perspective, death doesn't solve anything and this officer's death is a very sad thing, but we cannot ignore the fact that a lot of details have not come out about his career as an officer and until his file is made public it is irresponsible and insulting to the community to erect a statue honoring a man who did not always lead an honorable life."

The other black panelist began to speak without the benefit of an introduction as soon as Bobby paused.

Bobby couldn't believe what had just been said. Apparently, since Crooked Cop #1 had never wronged that panelist, what minorities experienced hadn't really happened? He sat in disbelief for a moment before tuning into what the other black panelist was saying.

"It is unfortunate that many officers involved in wrongdoing are not convicted, and it seems our legal system is set up to protect them. The news shows minorities in the worst possible light and officers in the best possible light. Just as Bobby said, the police union suppresses information and ensures that crooked cops are protected, it's no wonder they're never convicted."

The moderator thanked him for his input and posed a question to the panel. "Should there be more clarity around police statistics, including things like complaints, shootings, inappropriate behavior, and the like?"

It was the question for which Bobby was waiting, but the insurance agent was called on, even though Bobby had pushed his button.

"We have to be sure that the officers' personal information is protected, otherwise no one will want such a job. I feel like more training is needed to help these officers deal with difficult situations. I couldn't imagine having to go through what these officers deal with on the job every day."

Another panelist chimed in, "There are a lot of bad people in the city, unfortunately, and the police need to be on guard when approaching all citizens because they never know what they're going to encounter."

Bobby listened to the panelists share their experiences and support for the statue honoring *Crooked Cop #1* one by one before the moderator brought up a point that seemed to support his and the other black panelist's position, much to Bobby's surprise, "Is it possible that this man did all of these very positive things and at the same time, did all of these bad things? Racism's often hidden, and that's the difficult part in identifying who is racist and who isn't. You don't know until you're confronted with it firsthand, or you've listened to the accounts of others. As I see it, these two members of the panel have some insight that should be considered before we erect a statue to honor someone that seems to be quite a controversial figure."

Just as Bobby was about to smile, another point of view was offered. "It's hard to believe that this man—who, by the way, was a pillar of the community—could have done so many horrible things. What happened to your father," she said, speaking directly to Bobby, "was a tragedy, but it was also an unfortunate accident. As I remember, your father was in the wrong place at the wrong time. I know you were quite young when it happened, so you might not know, but many people felt sad for you and your family."

Bobby felt set-up, he was formulating a response when the moderator turned his chair to the audience. "And that's all the time we have for the evening. We thank our panelists for coming and sharing their thoughts.

"Will there be a monument? We'll have to wait and see, but one thing is for sure, we have a lot to consider in this endeavor."

The panel discussion was over as quickly as it had begun. A young man with headphones and a microphone looking very official looking came over to Bobby to remove his microphone, as he worked to remove the station equipment he spoke softly in Bobby's ear, "You did a good job, that asshole doesn't deserve a statue, he deserves to rot in hell." It was something Bobby hadn't expect to hear from a white person after the panel's comments, but it didn't make him feel any better.

Bobby gave the young man a disingenuous smile thinking to himself that he needed to get the hell out of there. The young man seemed to believe Bobby's smile and went over to the next panelist.

Bobby walked toward the door, past the moderator who thanked him for a job well done, but he continued without comment and quietly left the stage area.

Outside, he noticed that the other black panelist had exited as well. He called out to Bobby, "You did a good job, young man. Your father would've been proud."

"I don't think so. They think we're fucking delusional, that we see things that aren't even there. We're arrested, beaten, or worse, killed, and it's an isolated incident executed by a rogue cop and not a systemic problem that needs to be addressed. The highest-ranking police officials have to be encouraging this; otherwise, it wouldn't be tolerated. If they think we're crazy, nothing will ever change," Bobby responded.

He looked at Bobby with the eyes of a man who'd seen a lot in his years. "You did everything you could, and that's something to be proud of."

Bobby looked into the man's eyes and thought to himself, they have no idea what I'm capable of, and I'm not close to being done. They'll all pay! However, his only response was "thank you." With that, Bobby excused himself and headed for his car.

Bobby pulled into Dr. Chien's driveway to see his two compatriots sitting on the porch, waiting for him with a glass of what he assumed was Glenlivet. He approached them with a look he could tell they didn't expect, one of contentment.

Dr. Chien greeted him with a hug and his glass. "You did a really good job, and we're proud of you. You were thoughtful and kept your cool."

He took a sip from his glass. "Thank you, but it won't make a difference. I'm beginning to think that the only way we'll change the police force in this city is to kill all the ones that have hate in their hearts, but how do you know what's in a man's heart? What's in their hearts is what will be taught to their children, and they will be the next generation of racists. The cycle will never end until we can change how people feel, that's what I was hoping I would do today, but I'm starting to think we can't change the way someone feels if they think the victims of hate are suffering from delusions. Did you hear that guys response to my point? I guess the one thing we *can* do is what we've already started, hold them accountable for their actions and stop them from hurting others."

Officer John responded with a more positive perspective, "I think you did some of that today. You ere articulate and professional discussing a topic that would have sent many men into a fit of rage. I think you did more than you're aware of Bobby."

Bobby climbed up the steps and had a seat on the top one. He stared at his glass as if he'd find all the answers there. "The crooked cops in this city don't have anything to fear. They think they can do whatever they want? Well, we're going to give them something to fear. We will keep doing what no one else will. We have to show them there are consequences for the evil things they do."

Dr. Chien sat down beside him.

Officer John turned to Bobby and said, "They won't know what hit them. Two old fogies like us may not be intimidating to most, but with you, a strong young man by our side, leading the charge, they'd better watch out. That police department and those crooked cops have no idea what we're capable of, but we're going to give them an education. They'd better act right, or they'll pay."

Dr. Chien looked at Officer John. "Who are you calling old?" she asked, and they all laughed a much-needed laugh.

"Let's go eat. I'm hungry," Dr. Chien said, standing up.

As they walked into the house, the headquarters for their work, Officer John confessed that he'd been thinking about his current situation, and he needed to make some changes.

Bobby looked back at him, unsure what he was talking about.

Chapter 54

The next day Officer John walked into the station in his uniform, which he rarely wore when he wasn't at school, but he wanted this to be a formal as possible, he wanted to make a statement. His badge on his hat and left chest, a shiny silver and gold, were polished to a shine. His uniform was crisp and wrinkle-free. His belt and shoes were polished to an almost mirror shine.

He wanted to look the part of the model officer he'd been for most of his life. He gave a nod to the receptionist but said nothing as he passed the desk and went back into the station.

John approached Chief Dolan's door, he ended his call and opened the door to let Officer John in, "what brings you here, John?" he asked.

Officer John went into the office and sat in the chair. He answered Chief Dolan's question, with a question, "Why do you allow racism on the force? Why do you allow racist and dishonorable men in your department? You have the power to ensure the police department is fair, impartial, and supports and protects the community—why do you allow this in the city under your leadership? Do you hate the people of color in this city, too? Black citizens pay taxes, just like the rest of us. They want the same things we do, the opportunity to have families, enjoy what America has to offer, the occasional vacation from work, the pursuit of happiness. Still, you hate them. Why?"

Chief Dolan looked at Officer John, stunned and confused. Officer John had been an important part of their master plan. He was teaching white supremacy and notions of the master race to the kids when they were young. He was tasked with supporting the white students at his school, nurturing and protecting them from the animals allowed at their formerly all-white school. His job had been to covertly show the other kids that the white children were superior. Why was he asking such ridiculous questions?

It was a question Chief Dolan hadn't expected from anyone and certainly not Officer John. He hadn't hired Officer John, but he was told his precinct knew its role when he'd taken the job. He'd also been told that Officer John had excelled at the academy, that he'd taken charge and been the type of leader that ensured everyone stayed in line and were doing what they were told. He was assured that Officer John was a race man which was why he worked the safest but arguably the most important and challenging beat for as long as he could remember.

Chief Dolan looked Officer John in total confusion, was he a coward that was concerned about a few challenges in the department or maybe just a leader that had forgotten his place in the superior race somewhere along the way. Either way Chief Dolan could not deny how well he did his job and could not afford to lose him.

He knew several Chiefs in other departments that had a difficult time finding the right officer to handle elementary and middle schools because it required a delicate balance. The right officer had to restrain himself and not overreact to horseplay, only stepping in when white superiority was questioned and doing so in a manner that didn't threaten.

So many parents complained about the officers at their schools, but no one had ever complained about Officer John. He was an expert at his job, which made the questions he was asking to seem out of place.

Chief Dolan sat for a moment looking at Officer John, was he under pressure from internal affairs or maybe part of some sting operation? Was he wearing a wire?

No, the chief thought. *He's just lost his way.*

Chief Dolan thought about what A.C. Brice had told him about Officer John's relationship with Bobby. He reached out for help, and they had let him down, so he had to go into partnership with that black animal.

Chief Dolan got up, came around the desk, and looked at Officer John, thinking to himself he had let him down.

"John, I understand that things are tough for you right now and you came to A.C. Brice asking for help. I also know that several of the jobs that have been assigned to you didn't work out to your advantage but that sometimes happens."

He asked genuinely, "is it money, is that the problem? I didn't understand that things were that bad for you. There are arrangements that I can make to help you, so you don't have to go into business with that animal Bobby. Is that what this is all about?"

Officer John was a bit shaken, "no, I am ok, just trying to get ahead of things as I approach retirement. That's where the business idea came from. I'm not in any immediate financial trouble."

Chief Dolan gave a frown in disbelief, "are you sure? We can't have you worrying about money in your position, you're too important."

He smiled a wicked smile and winked at Officer John. "You're still our man, John. Don't worry about the news reports of officer arrests and stories of crooked cops, these things come and go, but know that we'll protect you.

Maybe you need to start coming to the meetings again to remind yourself of the real purpose of your work. Why it's so important. When was the last time you came to one of our meetings, we all need to be reminded about out rightful place in this world, you're no exception John?"

Officer John had no intention of going to a White Supremacy meeting, so he said what his chief needed to hear. "I haven't forgotten Chief, maybe I just needed to know that you had my back."

Chief Dolan smiled. "You're doing a great job and service to the cause John. I've not had one complaint about you from parents or teachers. They're blind to your work but know that we're not.

"You have a gift, John. I know seven or eight Chief's that would kill to have someone like you on their force, someone skilled at teaching kids to respect the master race at such an early age is challenging but you do it with ease.

"Supporting our youth and at the same time reminding those animals that we brought them here for a purpose and although we have lost some control, they will never be equal to us.

"Don't lose sight of your purpose. I know you're in business with one of them, and that's okay. Sometimes, we have to make sacrifices to achieve our long-term goals. Are you getting heat about that from some of the men on the force?"

Officer John sat back in his chair and looked up at Chief Dolan, who continued, "Sometimes, our men get upset when these people take our jobs and drain our tax dollars by going on welfare. They get upset when they think about all that we've given them, and yet they want more. They may not understand your purpose for working with them and give you a hard time about it. Is that what this is all about? Tell me who it is, and I'll talk to them."

Officer John listened in disbelief, realizing Chief Dolan thought he, too, believed the Klan's teachings. Why would he of all people think that? Officer John thought about his many years on the force, he hadn't ever done any of the horrible things the crooked cops had done.

The reason hit him like a sledgehammer, he'd done nothing to prevent it either.

He'd looked the other way; made excuses for behaviors he knew were wrong and had done nothing to stop it. He had done this for so long he had gotten a reputation of being one of the crooked cops he hated so much, he just happened to be at the school where in their minds he was manipulating the kids.

He wondered how he'd arrived at that point without realizing his role in all of it.

Officer John looked at Chief Dolan, a man with a family, a good life, and a hatred that blinded him to the reality of the average American. He blamed Black people and immigrants for the country's problems when, in fact, it wasn't their fault at all. Officer John knew it was the fault of lawmakers who allowed corporations and special interest groups to write the laws for their benefit, and not the citizens.

It was the for-profit prison system that pressured cops and judges to arrest and sentence minorities—especially blacks—to harsh, unfair sentences so that rich prison-owners could make money off of them, and the minorities would lose their right to vote.

It was the cuts in education and programs for children to bridge the gaps created by tax breaks for corporations. They were supposed to have used that money to pay workers higher wages, but instead, paid executives millions of dollars a year and the workers the lowest possible wages.

Officer John knew that the out-of-control military spending that didn't actually benefit soldiers or veterans, but the defense contractors who took up too much of the country's G.D.P., that the department of defense spent billions making unnecessary machines of war that gobbled up tax dollars.

He was reminded that it wasn't just his local police force that was to blame, the KKK was a far-reaching network of people, working at the lowest levels of his department to the highest levels of the government. They spoke in code and blamed immigrants and minorities for all the country's problems when, in fact, they were causing the problems with laws they were putting in place which were designed to keep white supremacy alive.

Officer John realized that by not fighting against the racism in his department, he was enabling it, and worst of all, it seemed his complacency over the years had been interpreted as support.

He looked at Chief Dolan and finally saw a man that was apparently too prejudiced to see that the problem with America wasn't its citizens; it was greed, unchecked capitalism, and racism.

Officer John thought long about what to do, looking at the Chief all the while. "There is so much stress that we are under, all of us including me. I think about my typical day having to balance the hate being taught to kids at such a young age and the impact it has, what do we do with it all?"

As Officer John spoke Chief Dolan filled in the blanks assuming all the negative statements were aimed towards Black people not his own racist community.

"Trying to keep a cool head while tending to the needs of so many kids knowing that one wrong word and their parents could and would react in an irrational way, potentially hurting their children, me, or some innocent bystander.

"I think about my stress then compare it to the Officers on patrol, who on a daily basis, encounter situations that they are clearly not prepared for given the outcomes that I see. They, I assume, are reacting to situations based on their training, before joining the force and after. What's missing in the training we receive in the Academy is how to recognize the stress and ask for help.

"We are faced with the worst of humanity and only get support when we discharge a weapon or use excessive force. I think by then it's too late. How do we teach our officers to talk about what they are seeing from day one? I don't know, maybe if support was a requirement as part of the job, every other week or month? Maybe we would unlearn some of the bad and replace it with some of the good."

Officer John was speaking about the racism and sexism, homophobia and self-hate some officers bring to the job that translated into unnecessary shootings and excessive force. He was talking about his own stress dealing with officers that he saw doing awful things to their families. The same families he had to pretend to protect, knowing the problem wasn't at school, it was at home.

He was hoping that his Chief would hear him, recognize the need, and maybe start bridging the gaps in support so that officers didn't act out or harbor the awful feelings they did. He hoped the work He and Bobby had started would one day become unnecessary.

Chief Dolan heard his officer's cry for help and reflected on his confusion with Crooked Cop #3 and why he hadn't gotten help. Reached out to someone instead of jumping off the roof of the abandoned mall. Was Officer John onto something, he wondered? Maybe his officers didn't know how to ask for help. Most were proud men who never asked anyone for anything, how could they be expected to ask for help when faced with these animals and their crap on a daily basis.

Chief Dolan finally replied "John you may be on to something. Let's talk about this more. *Crooked Cop #3* as you know was apparently quite troubled, to an extent I had no idea. Maybe we can prevent any of our other brothers from falling to a similar fate by implementing the kind of support you are recommending?

Officer John was shocked by Chief Dolan's realization. Officer John hadn't even considered what he was proposing would happen, he was mostly just speaking his mind. Looking at the Chief he smiled, "that would be great Chief, I'd love to be involved and help create some sort of structure or program to be a part of the solution."

In Officer John's heart he wanted this more than anything. He was wise enough to know that not everyone would change, some hearts are too hard, and some minds too far gone. The new officers were different, maybe he could help them.

Officer John thought the purpose of his visit had been to confront his chief and potentially quit the force, but he now realized more than ever that he needed to work as an insider to destroy the influence the Klan other White Supremacists had on the department and to help the new officers get past all the hate they came into the department with so they could do the job with honor. Those that wouldn't change would suffer the wrath of He and Bobby, ending up in jail or worse. If he could execute this plan, finding the crooked cops early and help them discover the error of their way of thinking, he could save a lot of people from a lot of unnecessary pain.

He extended a hand to Chief Dolan. "Let's do this Chief, the men deserve it! We won't let them down."

Chief Dolan smiled. "Good man. I will get things in motion. You do not need to carry this burden alone. We are a brotherhood, a family. I'm here to help and thank you for coming in today, John, this could be the start of significant change in the department."

Chapter 55

Officer John entered their office in Dr. Chien's house. She and Bobby were busy doing their individual work in silence. "You will never believe the meeting I just had with Chief Dolan."

Bobby turned towards him. "Was it about what you referenced yesterday, the need for change in your life?"

"Sort of," he responded. "In the Chief's mind I am one of his Klan boys happy to carry out their dirty work at the school teaching white supremacy to elementary school kids. Seems everyone thinks I'm some sort of savant when it comes to it."

"The conversation started like I had planned but ended with him committing to help me start some sort of support group which I think could really have an impact on new officers coming into the force. Talk to them about their prejudices and other demons they are dealing with in the hopes of preventing some of the horrible things they do."

"That would be amazing," Dr. Chien said. "The only way to help people get past the racism, anger, and trauma they've experience growing up is to get them to talk about it, learn how to deal with it and ultimately stop the cycle from repeating itself with their own children.

"Sounds like you had a really productive meeting, where do things go from here?" Bobby asked.

"That remains to be seen but Chief seemed truly interested in the idea, it was as much his idea as mine."

Bobby looked at Officer John with a smile. "The first step to solving a problem is admitting there is one. If you can get the officers to talk, to put in the work, this new support system sounds like exactly what is needed for some real change to occur. Maybe one day our work will no longer be needed."

Officer John smiled a hopeful smile. "One day!"

Bobby looked out the window past the site that would eventually be the location of the statue honoring the man that killed his father, he marveled at the beauty of Southern Virginia with its plentiful trees and flowers. He closed his eyes and felt the slight ocean breeze that managed to make its way 4.5 miles from the ocean through his window, "this won't be a paradise lost. The people here have done nothing wrong, and they deserve to live in peace and safety, and if the police aren't going to provide it," he turned around to face Officer John and Dr. Chien, "then we will until we can change things.

"Well until then, we'll be the defenders of the people against their enemies, not the supposed terrorists thousands of miles away or the neighbor that happens to look different from them, but the crooked cops and the evil rich men they report to.

"They don't know it now, but they made a big mistake thinking that you're one of them, we are just getting started and they are looking right past us because they think we have no power. That'll be their downfall. Which reminds me—where are we putting our next set of cameras? We have some crooked cops to catch."

Made in the USA
Coppell, TX
30 October 2025

62114314R00173